Under the Pong Pong Tree

Under the Pong Pong Tree

HAL LEVEY

UNDER THE PONG PONG TREE

iUniverse books may be ordered through booksellers or by contacting:

iUniverse
1663 Liberty Drive
Bloomington, IN 47403
www.iuniverse.com
1-800-Authors (1-800-288-4677)

ISBN: 978-1-4917-8955-1 (hc)
ISBN: 978-1-4917-7750-3 (sc)
ISBN: 978-1-4917-7751-0 (e)

Library of Congress Control Number: 2015916976

Print information available on the last page.

iUniverse rev. date: 02/03/2016

Contents

Part 1—The Rubber Lady

Part 2—Mike and Maimunah

Part 1

The Rubber Lady

Chapter 1
The House of Tan

Radio Singapura reported news of the invasion without urgency. "The Japanese incursion at Kota Bharu has been thwarted. Their landing craft have gone out to sea, stranding several hundred invaders on the beach. Mop-up operations are under way. Governor Shenton Thomas urges all Singaporeans to carry on in a normal fashion. We are in no immediate danger."

The British command nursed *stengahs* at Raffles, while Captain Hideo Hoda led his troops westward from Kota Bharu, following oxcart furrows that carved a meandering course between dense walls of rank vegetation. Hoda was a seasoned veteran of the Kwantung Army. He carried his malignant hatred of the Chinese in a mind scarred by the bitter memory of his family being wiped out by Chinese bandits on the Manchurian steppes. His standard-issue Showa sword was well tempered with Chinese blood.

A Kempeitai officer, Colonel Kosaka, was assigned to Hoda's platoon as a guide to Mr. Tan's rubber smallholding in the Kelantan rain forest.

———◦———

Mr. Tan's sixtieth birthday was on December 11, 1941. Preoccupied as he was with the rubber business and the more profitable drug trade, he spent little time with his twenty children—except on his birthday, when he viewed them as a group from the comfortable height of the wooden balcony above the veranda.

On that day, the sisters Ah Yeng and Su Yin, both married to Mr. Tan, arranged a special lunch. The master of the house presided at the head of the table, gazing contentedly at his two Chinese wives and four Thai mistresses, seated in the order of their acquisition. The women sat in silence, making no eye contact and moving only to spoon contents from the platters offered by the kitchen amahs.

After the meal, Mr. Tan stood and said, "Summon the children." He left the dining room and slowly climbed the stairs, wheezing and gripping the railing to help hoist his bulk from step to step.

At the top of the staircase, he shouted, "Abdul, bring the bag!" A Tamil attendant appeared from the servants' quarters at the rear of the villa, toting a canvas bag the size of a chicken. He trotted up the stairs and accompanied Mr. Tan to the mullioned door that opened out to the balcony.

Abdul opened the door, and Mr. Tan stepped out. He stood with his palms resting on the wooden balustrade and surveyed the courtyard as his wives and mistresses herded the children into position below the balcony. The women nudged and prodded the children until their reedy, piping voices rose in shouts. "We love you, Papa."

Mr. Tan worked his face into a smile and reached into the bag held open by Abdul. He cast a handful of coins out over the heads of the scrambling children. Two of the youngest, a three-year-old boy and a four-year-old girl, were knocked to the ground, crying and rubbing their heads where they had been struck by large copper coins.

Mr. Tan took no note of the crying children but continued hurling the coins out to different parts of the courtyard, causing the children to move in waves, following the metallic rainstorm.

"Papa loves you, children!" he shouted as he continued to shower largesse on his progeny.

Suddenly, gunshots crackled from the rubber trees. Several of Mr. Tan's bodyguards ran toward the villa, but before they reached the gates, they were cut down by uniformed soldiers dashing through the grove.

Mr. Tan abandoned his family and stumbled downstairs to a gate concealed in the rear wall of the compound. He ran through the gate and found himself surrounded by Japanese soldiers under the command of Captain Hoda, who looked past Mr. Tan to a man in civilian clothes, standing in the shade of a pong pong tree. The civilian nodded crisply. Two soldiers seized Mr. Tan and forced him to his knees. Hoda drew his sword.

Mr. Tan craned his neck to gaze imploringly at the civilian, who looked away. Mr. Tan shouted, "Mr. Kosaka! Help me, please! I am your friend, and—"

Hoda swept his sword in a deadly arc and stepped back, avoiding the crimson spurts.

The women and children huddled in the courtyard as soldiers ran through the villa, chasing the household staff out to join them. Mr. Kosaka approached Hoda and said, "Captain, as an officer of the Kempeitai, I have authority in the operation of this plantation. Sergeant Hayashi's squad will remain here and be responsible for meeting the rubber quota. Make that clear to your men."

Captain Hoda, still brandishing his bloody sword, shouted, "Leave them alone for now. Put them to work to run this place, and if they give you any trouble ..." He drew an index finger across his throat.

Kosaka and Hoda were interrupted by two soldiers dragging a Chinese field worker into the courtyard.

"We found this one hiding in a hut out there. What shall we do with him?"

"Finish him," said Hoda.

Kosaka peered at the cringing Chinese. "Wait! You are Wu Feng, are you not?"

"Yes, sir," said the Chinese man, sagging in the grip of his captors. Then, recognizing the civilian in charge, he asked, "Mr. Kosaka?"

"You have a good memory." Kosaka turned to Hoda and said, "Let us not waste this man. He knows the property and is a capable field manager. He is to continue in that capacity." Then he turned back to Wu Feng and said with a cruel smile, "That is, as long as you are agreeable."

Wu Feng answered promptly, "Yes, sir. Yes, sir, it would be a privilege."

"Very well," said Mr. Kosaka. "You have much work ahead of you ... and now, Captain Hoda, on to Singapore."

Ah Yeng stood defiantly and shrieked at Mr. Kosaka, "So this is how you repay our hospitality."

Chapter 2
Singapore, 1942

The Goh family listened to Radio Singapura while the amah cleared the remains of the evening meal. Sixteen-year-old Li Lian was a beautiful girl with a flawless golden complexion, wide-set dark eyes, and full, unrouged lips. Her ebony hair was coiled in a chignon secured with an ivory comb. She was tall for a Chinese woman, having been genetically spared her mother's short legs and low-slung rump. A faint fragrance enveloped her from the floral scent that she had been permitted to use since her last birthday. Her mother already had started to compile a list of eligible possible suitors—sons of wealthy merchants, tin miners, and plantation owners, who would combine flesh and fortune to carry the Goh lineage into an abundant future.

Mrs. Goh and the children waited for the head of the family to speak.

Goh Kok An owned a small shipping line that carried passengers and freight from Keppel Harbor to Calcutta and returned with any available cargo—occasional consignments of Tamil field workers or rosewood logs from the port of Rangoon. His captains once had enjoyed shore leave in Singapore as merchant seamen. They returned to recapture the intoxicating memories of their days as rootless adventurers and found employment on Mr. Goh's aging steamers. Their fists managed the lascar crews, and they settled into a comfortable routine of discipline at sea and relaxation ashore with Malay mistresses. When a Goh Line vessel was in port, its skipper generally could be found slumped over a sling at a waterfront dive on Collyer Quay.

Mr. Goh sat back in his armchair and said, "Must trust the British to defend us, what? Governor Thomas tells us that no matter what happens up-country, Singapore is in no immediate danger. Of course, guarantee of safety—cannot—so we must prepare for the worst. The Brits could maybe sacrifice all to save their miserable skins. We must look to ourselves for security."

Fourteen-year-old Ronald had a worried expression. "But, Papa, the governor said that we are in no danger."

"I know," said his father. "I don't wish to alarm you, my son, but we must be realistic."

Mrs. Goh spoke. "No more blind faith-*lah*. Now you should know our plans. You agree, Kok An?"

"Yes, Hwai Ping. Soon Singapore goes under, but there is enough time for us to get out. I already made wire transfers to Zurich. The Swiss keep money safe."

Li Lian sat quietly with her hands folded in her lap. "Are we going to Switzerland, Papa?"

"No, no, I think we will be better off in this part of the world. This morning, I heard from Mr. Lorimer of the harbor board. He wants to meet with me next Monday on an urgent matter." Seeing their concerned expressions, he waved his hand and added, "But I don't wish to burden you with business affairs."

"What do you think he wants to discuss with you, Papa?" asked Li Lian.

"I'll find out soon enough, but please, no more worry," said Mr. Goh.

"And meantime," said Mrs. Goh, "we try to live in a normal way. Tomorrow we dress in our Sunday best and go to church-lah. The people in the next pew know that we are faithful Christians, and they will expect to see us tomorrow. We must not disappoint them."

———◇———

At Wesley Methodist Church, Reverend Hobart ended his homily on good and evil with a footnote to calm the congregation. "This is a time that challenges our faith and may raise questions in some of you about God's purposes, but we must not permit ourselves to deny Him, even in our darkest moments. However, even God would not expect you to suffer through what might be a cruel occupation. Therefore, I strongly advise you to leave this island for a safe haven, if such might be available to you. As for me, I shall remain here and accept the fate ordained by the Lord. If I am permitted to do so, I intend to keep this place open as a house of God, and I shall welcome any invaders who might wish to avail themselves of our Christian ministry. Amen."

After the service, Reverend Hobart stood at the church entrance, nodding gravely as the parishioners filed down the long granite stairway to Fort Canning Road, where they lingered in forlorn family groups. The Gohs went to their favorite restaurant for Sunday lunch and picked at platters of Hainanese chicken rice. Mr. Goh, facing an uncertain future, spoke to his dejected family.

"Of course, we are trying to liquidate our business interests, but these things take time. Soon, Singapore will be finished, and who would be foolish enough to buy a small shipping line, even at a bargain price, when he is certain to lose everything to the enemy?"

Mrs. Goh was a recognized expert on antique Chinese porcelain, which she sold from her curio shop on Orchard Road. She said, "I already crated up my most valuable things for a fresh start in a new place. Papa has spoken of India."

Her husband said, "India is best for us. I have business contacts there. The *Malay Star* is due in three days. We can refuel and be away in two or three hours. Let us finish packing so we can leave when the *Star* arrives. I will see Ben Lorimer tomorrow at tea time."

———◄○►———

The next day, Mr. Goh drove to Keppel Harbor and entered the office marked Benjamin Lorimer, Director, Harbour Board.

"Ah, yes, how good to see you, Kok An. Join me for tiffin?" He called to his secretary, "Miss Ng, tea and scones for Mr. Goh, if you please."

Mr. Goh sipped and nibbled, waiting for Lorimer to speak.

Lorimer touched his lips with the linen napkin. "Kok An, as you know, Singapore is in a precarious position, and matters will be much worse before long. Many British civilians and some well-connected Chinese already have secured passage on transport ships headed for Sumatra. I don't know if that will be a safe destination, but at least those who leave now can buy a bit of time to make safer arrangements. I am pleased to tell you that I am able to arrange your evacuation from Singapore. You and your family ... by the way, how is Mrs. Goh and your two lovely children? I remember your beautiful Li Lian—such a sweet child. She must be quite a lovely young lady now. I recommend strongly that you take advantage of the opportunity to get off this doomed island."

"Benjamin, you are a true friend, and I thank you for me and my family. However, the *Malay Star* is due tomorrow. If you wish to help, I would appreciate a rapid turnaround so we can refuel and clear the Outer Roads as soon as possible. We are packed and ready to go. We will head for India and a new life, if the Jap swine keep their bloody hands off that poor country."

Mr. Lorimer removed his spectacles in a weary gesture. "If that's your decision, Kok An, I wish the best for you and your family. I hope you are not making a mistake. At any rate, you can count on my cooperation when the *Star* arrives."

—◦—

East of the Nicobars, Captain George Cooper stood at the helm of the *Malay Star* as the bomber approached. A torpedo dropped from its belly, and a red patch flashed as the *Nakajima* passed overhead. The steamer shuddered from the explosion amidships.

The sturdy Scot put down his binoculars and turned to the first officer. "Bugger the bahstids. Prepare to abandon ship."

The crew launched the lifeboats and clambered aboard. They watched from a distance as the *Star*'s bow rose in a stately salute. The old ship sighed and spiraled slowly to rest in a trench a thousand fathoms below the surface of the Andaman Sea.

—◦—

Malay villagers watched impassively as the Japanese streamed down the peninsula, many riding bicycles and clattering along on steel rims after the tires were shredded. Some sat astride water buffaloes, urging them on with *rotan* whips. Great columns of acrid black smoke rose as British sappers destroyed rubber stores along the line of retreat. Refugees from the North, fleeing from the invaders, crowded into Singapore, adding a half million consumers to the already strained services for food, housing, and hygiene.

Looting of food markets brought severe retaliation by the police under the hastily imposed emergency regulations. As the peril deepened, whiskey stored in waterfront *godowns* was incinerated in the hope of defusing the drunken orgies of rape and slaughter that were inflicted upon the hapless civilian populations of Hong Kong and Shanghai.

The British command suffered a strange paralysis of indecision, unable to muster an effective resistance, despite a huge superiority in manpower and arms. Daily air raids destroyed much of Singapore's infrastructure. Peirce and MacRitchie reservoirs came under attack, and the rupture of water mains threatened the health of the entire island.

Unnerved by the prospect of massive disease and starvation, General Percival surrendered the entire Singapore garrison on February 15, 1942. The agony of the occupation replaced the agony of war.

◄○►

Mrs. Goh wept throughout the day and tried to console her guilt-laden husband. "Kok An, we must not think about it. We may never know what happened to the *Star*. At least we are still alive."

His misery matched hers. "For how long? Who can say? The Japs could kill us all. How can I protect the children? Our Malay servants have abandoned us. We must stay out of the street."

A week after the surrender, three soldiers burst into the living room. A sword-swishing sergeant grabbed Kok An by the shirt front and yanked him to his feet. Another soldier wrapped a fist in Mrs. Goh's hair and hauled her from the sofa. She screamed. Ronald leaped at the tormentor and pounded him on the back, shouting, "Let her go!"

The soldier shoved Mrs. Goh aside and thrust his bayonet into Ronald's rib cage, driving him down onto the thick Tibetan carpet. He planted a muddy boot on Ronald's chest and wrenched the blade free. A strangled cry came from Mrs. Goh as she threw herself on her son's inert body with her hand over the gushing wound, trying to keep the life from draining away.

The sergeant pulled Kok An close and laughed, discharging a burst of foul breath. "Chinky man, your stolen wealth cannot protect you. Now go. Take old lady with you." He snapped the blade at Li Lian. "Pretty daughter, you stay."

11

The other two soldiers prodded Li Lian's parents into a long trail of Chinese civilians, driven at bayonet-point toward Changi Prison. They passed the intersection at Jalan Eunos, where a dozen residents of the Malay settlement watched the wretched parade in silence. Several older Chinese faltered, and one fell. Without hesitation, the soldiers bayoneted all and kicked them to the side of the road.

Kok An saw an old friend wobbling several yards ahead. "Steady, Ling Pow, you are courting death." A Japanese blade put an end to Mr. Goh. Hwai Ping shrieked and ran to his side. The blade descended once again. Heads and torsos lined the roadway as guards dispatched the weak and lagging in mad, mindless slaughter. A sudden downpour washed over the grisly scene, and the monsoon drain carried a crimson stream out to the South China Sea.

———◇———

In the drawing room on Scotts Road, Li Lian stood with eyes shut tight, her mind locked in paralytic fear. She shuddered at the crashing sounds of vases and mirrors being destroyed with rifle butts. The soldiers turned to looting, pocketing Mrs. Goh's ivory figurines and snuff bottles. When they tired of the game, they dragged Li Lian to a bedroom and threw her on a mattress. She flopped helplessly as the victorious warriors of the Rising Sun thrust her one way and another, ripping off her clothing. Hard hands crushed her breasts, as the men penetrated her slender form again and again. She screamed in pain and screamed and screamed. After the brutal assault, she lay mind-numbed and naked, with blood-streaked thighs. The sergeant stuffed his penis back into his pants, retrieved his sword, and announced, "A virgin for the comfort house."

At the front door, she winced as disembodied hands slapped her bare buttocks and shoved her roughly out of her home. She stumbled and fell to the walkway. Jagged bits of limestone gravel dropped from skinned, bleeding knees as the hands yanked her to her feet. A lorry approached, sounding a claxon. The soldiers flagged it down and threw Li Lian over the tailgate into a cargo of weeping women. One of the women threw a jute rice bag over Li Lian's body. Li Lian grasped the rough fabric on both sides and pulled it close to her ravaged torso, her only protection from further torment.

The lorry drove to an imposing stucco villa on Cairn Hill Road.

The driver dropped the tailgate and prodded the women up the concrete stairway. Two dull-eyed Korean women escorted the new residents to a large drawing room containing smashed furniture and bloodstained rugs. Armed soldiers supervised a cleaning crew of barefooted coolies and blue-clad Hakka women. One of the soldiers walked to Li Lian, who stood against the wall, naked and catatonic. He ran his hands over her breasts and buttocks and said, "Ah, pretty Chinky girl. We meet later, maybe."

A Chinese mama-san in a Japanese silk kimono and green slippers entered the room. As she surveyed her bedraggled, sniffling charges, her eyes lingered on Li Lian's blood-spattered ivory form. She addressed her recruits in a firm voice. "Young ladies, welcome to your new residence. All your needs will be supplied by the Imperial Japanese Army. In return, you will give comfort and affection to its brave officers, who will treat you with respect and show you much kindness. I know that this is a difficult time for you, but you will be paid for your services, and those funds can make life easier for your families, if they wish to accept your generosity. Now, remove all your clothing and pile everything in the middle of the floor. You will find a clean dressing gown hanging in your room." The mama-san clapped her hands. "Come, come! Off with your clothing."

The women looked at one another, and some started to undress. The mama-san strode back and forth, encouraging them to shed their garb. Finally, all were naked, holding their hands over breasts and crotch. The Hakka women took the piles of clothing from the room.

"Very well, ladies. Now you are to clean yourselves, and you must remain fresh and dainty day and night. Your Japanese friends are quite fastidious. You will go to the shower room. There are towels in a linen closet in the hallway. After your shower, you will be escorted to your individual rooms. Some of your new friends might wish your company in a private bath. The Japanese are much given to that practice. We will be open for business after a doctor checks your health."

She escorted the women from the room but took Li Lian aside. "Dear child, I see that you have been treated cruelly. I know that this is a terrible ordeal, but you must be strong. One day, the horror will come to an end. Does your family know where you are?"

Li Lian's voice quivered. "They killed my little brother, and they hurt me. Mama and Papa are gone."

"You can rest until the doctor comes for the inspection. But there are things you must learn in order to survive in this life."

—◦—

Li Lian lay on the bed in her small room, suffering relentless pain. She left the bed only to go to her washbasin, trying to scrub away the violation.

The doctor arrived the next day. Each woman mounted a gurney for a pelvic examination, while an assistant took blood samples and vaginal swabs for bacterial culture.

Two pregnant women were taken away, crying hysterically.

The doctor returned in three days and spoke to the mama-san. "Here is a copy of the regulations for operating a military comfort house."

The mama-san said, "I am familiar with the regulations."

"You can open for business." He handed her a large box of yellow condoms. "Clients are required to use condoms."

"I am aware of that."

He ignored her remark. "They are in short supply. If necessary, you must wash them out for reuse. The women are healthy enough for the work, except for the girl named Goh Li Lian. She is infected with gonorrhea. I will arrange for her disposal."

"No, no, she is innocent. She was raped."

"All the women were raped. She was the unlucky one."

He turned to go, but the mama-san took his arm. "Wait, Doctor. You know that she can be cured. I was transferred here from the Geylang comfort house. Several of the women there had gonorrhea, but they were cured with sulfa drugs and went back to work. Please, Li Lian should not be wasted."

The doctor raised an eyebrow and smirked. "You seem to have a special interest in this young lady. Do you want her for your own use?"

The mama-san thought for a moment. "Ah, Doctor, I know you are a man of the world." She stepped closer. "There are many appetites." She turned as though to leave and casually brushed her hand against the front of his trousers. He leaned into the touch, so she added slight pressure with the back of her hand and waited for his reaction. There was none, so she tweaked his trousers, pressing his stiffening penis between thumb and forefinger. "Doctor, do you like that?"

He said nothing, but caressed her breast, seeking a nipple with his own thumb and forefinger.

"I know you are a busy man, but perhaps you would care to join me for tea in my office."

"That could be a pleasant diversion."

Fifteen minutes later, she held a vial of sulfanilamide tablets. With a faint smile, she muttered inwardly, *They're all the same. The power of a hand job.*

Li Lian was cured of the infection in five days.

The mama-san visited her room. "Now you must start to work, or they won't let you stay here. Whoever enters this room must be serviced. Do not dally with idle talk. Help him undress, if that is his wish, and hang his uniform on the wall hooks. Take his hand and lead him to the washbasin. Handle his penis gently. Skin back the foreskin and wash with antiseptic soap and warm water. That will arouse him and reduce the possibility of infection. By this time, he will have a prominent erection." She showed Li Lian how to roll a condom onto a mop handle. "Leave a little space at the tip. You must do this every time, and you must wash yourself thoroughly after each visit."

She started Li Lian with a shy, bespectacled second lieutenant, who ejaculated into her hand during the washup. He dressed and departed hastily.

Her next customer was a mature captain. He kissed her breasts and fondled her for twelve minutes. With three minutes left on his fifteen-minute ticket, he entered her, came lustily, and left the ticket stub on her side table.

As the stack of stubs grew, Li Lian developed a set of maneuvers that promptly terminated the encounters.

At the end of the first month, she traded the stubs for military scrip, to be used on a shopping trip to Arab Street. The women, under armed guard, visited the rows of shop houses that lined both sides of the street but were able to buy only a few trinkets. Nevertheless, they were happy for the respite.

Chapter 3
The Fishermen

The Japanese maintained order in Singapore with savage efficiency. The Kempeitai established their headquarters in the old YMCA building on Orchard Road. Luckless Chinese civilians, taken there for questioning, seldom emerged, other than in a wooden box after dark. Chinese heads were impaled on metal stakes driven into the front lawn, reminding Singaporeans that they existed in a perpetual state of terror.

As an amusing diversion, the Kempeitai trucked groups of Chinese to a banyan tree on the fairway of the third hole of the Royal Island Club golf course. They were ordered to stand under the tree while a Japanese noncom slashed through the leaves overhead. This dislodged thousands of *keringa*, fierce red ants, whose lifestyle involved using their larvae as bobbins to spin out silk threads, molding the banyan leaves into secure nests. Disturbed as they were, the keringa descended and inflicted a fiery torture on the prisoners until machine guns put the prisoners out of their misery. After each episode, the ants formed into construction battalions, some holding torn leaves together with their jaws and hind legs, while others repaired the breach with their babies.

—◦—

Captain Hoda was responsible for herding the vanquished English, Australian, and Gurkha soldiers into concentration camps. He hated this assignment, considering it too passive and bureaucratic. A constant stream of war prisoners from the Dutch East Indies competed for space with the eighty thousand prisoners of the Singapore garrison. As the demand for prison space grew, Hoda ran a barbed wire palisade around the *padang* to serve as a holding pen until permanent facilities could be arranged.

—◇—

Li Lian's house was Hoda's favorite nighttime destination. He bought half-hour tickets from the mama-san as soon as the house opened for business and demanded Japanese women, fresh from the homeland. He preferred the demure ladies of Kyoto, who were rotated through the other comfort houses in Singapore and were not always available.

—◇—

At her first menstrual break, Li Lian joined three women in a small lounge on the upper floor. Two were Japanese. The third greeted Li Lian and said, "I know you, but you do not know me. I am Mei Lin. I covered you with the rice bag in the lorry, when we were forced into this work. I am happy to see that you look much better now than you did then."

"I thank you, Mei Lin. I am Li Lian. When I was a little girl, I heard about the monthly period, and it scared me. Now it is the only thing that gives us relief in this life. How are you surviving?"

"Well enough. I just look at men as mechanical beasts who wish to empty themselves of their secretions. But I must warn you about one of them—Captain Hoda. Avoid him if you can. He's a vicious monster. Look at this." She opened her smock and lifted a breast with one hand, displaying livid patches in the shape of fingerprints. "And this." She turned and lifted the smock to reveal angry bites on her buttocks. "I'll have to explain the scars for the rest of my life. I complained to the mama-san, but she is afraid to report him to the military authorities."

The mama-san was careful to keep Hoda away from Li Lian, but he heard of her through whorehouse gossip. A forty-year-old major described her—"What a beauty. She's exciting, but it's like fucking my sixteen-year-old daughter." Hoda demanded a session with Li Lian.

"Please, Captain Hoda-san, leave her alone. I beg you. A new girl is coming in from Kobe. She will be very popular. I will put you at the head of the line."

"I want Li Lian, and I want her now. Take me to her if you want to see the light of another day."

"Ah, Captain Hoda-san, you make my life difficult. Here is a condom, and please, no rough stuff."

Li Lian sat on the edge of the bed, naked, as required by house rules. She affected the submissive demeanor that inflated the vanity of her clients. Her door opened, and she heard Hoda's gruff voice.

"Good evening, Li Lian. We meet at last. Do you know who I am?"

"Yes, Captain Hoda-san. I have heard of you from the others. You hurt them." She sensed the cruelty behind the tight lips on an unsmiling face. "I am sorry that you came to my room."

He undressed and stood before her. "You must not be sorry, and you cannot choose your customers. I will not hurt you."

"You must use a condom."

"Open your mouth, and there is no use for a condom."

"Please. I don't like that."

"You don't have to like it. Open." He grabbed fistfuls of hair on both sides of her head and pulled her face against his erection. She had no choice but to accept him, and he exploded in her mouth. He sat on the bed next to her. "I have time left on my ticket." She endured the exploration of her body until the time expired. He placed the ticket stub on her table. "I'll be back." He dressed and left.

He returned often, forcing intercourse without a condom. He took her as his preferred comfort woman and was surprised to feel the stabs of jealousy when he thought of her other contacts. He also frequented the Royal Island Club, which had a secret stash of whiskey that escaped official destruction when the Japanese takeover seemed imminent. Hoda defied the ban on alcohol in comfort houses, and his drunken visits to the brothel terrified the mama-san and her charges.

On one such night, a sodden Hoda visited the brothel and demanded Li Lian's services. He brushed past the mama-san and walked unsteadily toward Li Lian's room.

The mama-san trotted after him and took his arm. "Please, Captain

Hoda-san, she is entertaining another client, but she should be available soon."

"What other client? I want her now." Hoda swept his arm hard against the mama-san's bulk, causing her to fall heavily.

From the floor, she wailed, "No, no! Major Ogawa must not be disturbed."

Li Lian's door opened, and Major Ogawa emerged, wearing only his shoes and underwear, with his uniform draped over an arm. A cartridge belt and holstered pistol were fastened at his waist.

"Enjoy yourself, Captain. Sweet little thing."

Hoda contained his anger as Ogawa strode to the common room and joined several other officers in various states of undress, talking and toying with nude women.

Hoda seethed at having been preempted by the senior officer and carried his resentment into Li Lian's room. She stood at the washbasin with legs spread, cleaning herself with a wet cloth. His mood worsened when he saw the envelope containing Li Lian's visitation tickets. He imagined a coupling for each stub. Swaying drunkenly, he dropped his pants and clutched Li Lian's head to his groin.

She worked earnestly for several minutes, sucking and tugging at the spongy member, but it remained limp. Li Lian backed off to rest her aching jaws and whispered, "I tried."

In a rage, Hoda struck her repeatedly, and she fell back on the floor mat, semiconscious and bleeding from the nose and lips. Hoda pulled up his trousers and left.

The mama-san entered the room. "I am deeply sorry for what that beast has done to you. That Hoda-san—a monster like all of them." She washed the blood from Li Lian's face and breasts. "Rest a while. No more business today." She thought for a moment and added, "I think you need more time to recover. Take two more days. Relax with the ladies in the lounge."

Li Lian lay on her mattress, trying to dispel the horror by urging sweet memories of her former life to fill her mind. She thought, *I must not allow myself to be destroyed. They must pay for what they are doing to us.*

The following morning, Li Lian studied her bruised face in the small mirror suspended over the washbasin and touched her swollen lip. She felt stronger in the light of the new day and left her room to visit the menstrual lounge. The two Japanese women sat together, ignoring their Chinese and Korean coworkers. Li Lian approached a familiar face. "Good morning, Mei Lin. What a relief it must be—having your period."

"How nice to see you here, Li Lian. Welcome to the whores of Singapore. We heard about your battle with Hoda." She reached out and smoothed Li Lian's hair and patted her lip lightly. "It looks like you lost the war—and it's not my period. Just a few days off to recover from urethritis—uncomfortable but better than making fuckee with the emperor's nancy boys. How are you feeling today?"

Li Lian looked to Mei Lin as an older sister. "I feel well enough, no matter what they do to us. How long before you must go back to work?"

"Three more days. Extra time from the doctor because I sucked him. He expects the same thing at every monthly examination. He thinks I love him, but if I had the chance, I would cut out his heart and feed it to the dogs. How long do you have to recover?"

"The mama-san says two days is enough, but I must get out of this horrible place or I'll die—also the baby."

"I am not surprised to hear that you are pregnant. Hoda must be the daddy. Why didn't you make him use a condom? No, don't answer. I know how it must have been with that creature. The important thing is to get you out of here."

Li Lian held back tears. "Oh, Mei Lin, is it possible?"

"There is a chance. The laundryman who picks up baskets of sheets and towels twice a week is my uncle, Hong Fat. We exchange messages in the baskets, and maybe we can arrange your escape."

Li Lian felt a flicker of joy. "I know who he is. He left tire sandals and a torn shirt for me to wear last month on a trip to Arab Street. If you can help me, I will be forever grateful, Mei Lin. But if escape is possible for me, why not for you as well?"

"I have thought of that, and I have chosen to stay in this vile place until the war ends, if it ever ends. The Japs have attacked the United States, inviting their own destruction. When that happens, I have scores to settle. Then I will join with those who would liberate us from imperialistic domination. I am a communist, devoted to the welfare of humanity. If all goes well, after you deal with your pregnancy as you wish, you are welcome to join us to continue the fight. You are like my little sister, and I care deeply for you. Since we have no business tonight, I will come to your room."

◦

The door opened, and Mei Lin entered silently. Li Lian lay naked under a light sheet. Mei Lin slipped out of her cotton chemise and entered the bed next to the young girl. They embraced and caressed. Each found the other's erect nipples with gentle fingers and soft lips. Mei Lin whispered, "My sweet, wounded little bird—let me comfort you." She reached for the tube of lubricant that always was present on the bedside table.

The mama-san passed Li Lian's room on her nightly tour and was pleased to hear the feminine murmurs behind the door.

◦

Hong Fat delivered the hampers of soiled sheets and towels to the *dhobi ghat* on the Serangoon River and dumped the contents. A folded piece of paper fell out. His wife retrieved it. "Ah, Hong Fat, another note from your niece. I hope she is holding up well, considering …"

Hong Fat read Mei Lin's message.

His wife asked, "Is she all right?"

"Oh, yes, but there is something I must do. I will explain later. Now I must talk to my cousin at Keppel Harbor."

◦

Hong Fat's cousin was a fisherman named Boon Hok, who worked with his Malay helper, Saleh bin Rafiq, to extract a meager living from the sea. Before the war, their proa was owned by Boon Hok. Under the Occupation, it was registered with the Japanese Marine Police in the name of the Malay, while Boon Hok was recorded as a hired hand. This was a practical arrangement, because a Chinese owner always was persecuted by the Japanese authorities. Saleh agreed that they would split the proceeds of their fishing business evenly.

22

They moored their boat in the protected waters of Keppel Harbor, venturing out daily to a *kelong* owned by Saleh's village on the southeast coast of Johore. They collected fish from the trap, gave some to the *penghulu* of the village, and took the rest to the market site on the banks of the Singapore River.

At low tide, they waded the reefs for *trepang*, relished by the Chinese in a soup or stew. This was an important money crop, but trepang collecting was hazardous because it coexisted with the stonefish, which had a poisonous spine on its dorsal fin. The stonefish, resembling a lump of granite, remained stationary in the shallow tide pools, and waders who stepped on them received painful, although seldom fatal, wounds.

When there was a sparse yield at the kelong, the fishermen headed east, where the Singapore Strait mingled with the South China Sea, to fish with baited hooks. Hong Fat parked the lorry near Collyer Quay and searched the harbor for Boon Hok's proa.

———◄◦►———

Boon Hok and Saleh sat idly over a lunch of cold fried fish and noodles and four bottles of Thai beer. Saleh was an observant Muslim, but he allowed himself the latitude of the occasional bottle of beer when he was on the water. As they ate, they scanned the shimmering surface of the sea. Boon Hok casually pointed to the distant horizon and said, "Look out there. The garfish are agitated."

Saleh also had seen several two-foot-long silvery arrows emerge from the surface without apparent effort and project themselves about twenty feet in a shallow trajectory before reentering the water with scarcely a ripple. He said, "Yes, and there is the reason for their agitation." He swept his hand beyond the garfish to a black fin moving leisurely toward the presumptive prey.

Boon Hok started the outboard motor, leaving the lateen sail lashed to the boom, and Saleh lifted one of the harpoons from the storage hooks. He secured a coil of rope from the harpoon to a log float and stood in the prow as the boat bore down on the shark fin. Boon Hok, well practiced in shark hunting, cut the engine at the correct moment and maneuvered the proa to intercept the shark's course. The boat drifted into the path of the shark.

The shark veered away from the large, silent object, and Saleh hurled the harpoon. The shark moved away, stripping out the coiled rope, and Saleh dumped the attached log over the gunwale.

"It's a great tiger shark," said the Malay. "At least twelve feet long. This will be a profitable day."

They followed the floating log for more than an hour and finally caught up with the exhausted shark. A second harpoon thrust put an end to the huge fish. They lashed it to the outrigger and sped to the market area at the mouth of the Singapore River, where cooks and housewives gathered to wait for the fresh catch.

Nodding and smiling at their audience, the fishermen sliced open the belly of the great fish, and hauled out the entrails. Suddenly they stood and backed away. A leg was visible, enclosed within the thin stomach wall. The onlookers gasped and disappeared. The fishermen hastily abandoned the shark and sailed the proa out to their mooring.

The Japanese Marine Police visited the shark and confirmed that the leg was human. At an official hearing, Saleh told the authorities that a man-eating shark was bad *joss* and could bring disaster to the fishermen and their families if the water *djin* associated them with the shark. That was why they had to leave the shark and rush off as soon as possible.

They were let off with a reprimand after promising not to let it happen again. The leg was cremated, and the shark carcass was ground up for chicken feed. The episode was covered by the local press. The Japanese, with their history of unspeakable cruelty against civilian populations, failed to see the irony in their solicitous concern for a single human leg in the belly of a shark.

———◇———

Li Lian met Mei Lin at the evening meal and asked hopefully, "Have you heard from your uncle yet?"

After five days, Mei Lin said, "It is arranged. The mama-san hates the Japs, and she will help you get away. Take only those items that will fit in your batik bag, and be prepared to leave at a moment's notice."

Li Lian burst into tears and kissed Mei Lin's hand without speaking.

On the next laundry pickup, the mama-san packed Li Lian into a rattan hamper under a load of soiled bed linen. Hong Fat drove to the dhobi ghat and was greeted by his cousin. They unloaded the hamper.

His cousin bent over and talked to the hamper. "I am Boon Hok. You speak Ingrish, okay?"

A muffled voice from the hamper said, "English, okay, also Hokkien, also Malay. Difficult to breathe. Please, can I get out of here?"

Boon Hok lifted Li Lian from the hamper and steadied her as she regained her balance. "I am a fisherman, and I work with a Malay named Saleh bin Rafiq. He just arrived in our proa, and we will take you to a safe place."

Saleh maneuvered the proa to the ghat, and Li Lian stepped aboard, assisted by Boon Hok. Saleh covered her with a spare sail until they cleared Serangoon Harbor and headed into the South China Sea. Saleh gave her a fisherman's broad-brimmed straw hat and spoke to her in Malay. "I think we are in the clear. We will take you to my *kampong*, where you can have your baby in safety. After that, who can say?"

Li Lian, wept with joy. "How can I ever thank you? You have risked your lives to help me. I will do anything you think best."

Boon Hok asked, "Do you know the father? Or perhaps it's best that you don't know—or care."

"Yes, I know him. A Japanese officer—Captain Hoda. My baby never will know its father. You must promise me."

The fishermen nodded in agreement.

The proa hugged the east coast of Johore, sailing northward until noon. A Japanese cutter appeared in the distance, heading south, and Saleh studied it with his binoculars. "They're heading in our direction, so we had better try to reach that kelong ahead. We must act like fishermen. We can't outrun them."

They lowered the sail and ran on the outboard motor. Nearing the kelong, Boon Hok cut the engine and eased the proa to one of the pilings supporting the platform. Saleh tied up to an iron mooring ring. He helped Li Lian to the bamboo ladder and steadied her as she climbed up to the platform. Both fishermen followed her, and Boon Hok said, "You will be safe in the hut as long as the Japs ignore us."

The fishermen left Li Lian in the thatched hut and went out to the narrow plank pier to raise the net at the end of the fish trap. Several grouper and a dozen small silvery fish lay in the net that the men left a foot below the surface.

Suddenly, Li Lian shouted from the hut, "They are coming!"

The fishermen looked up from the net as the cutter glided slowly to the edge of the shallows, about a hundred meters from the kelong. It dropped anchor, and a tender was lowered from the deck. Two sailors clambered aboard the tender and rowed to the kelong.

"Ahoy, fishermen, how's the catch?"

Saleh and Boon Hok said nothing for fear of saying the wrong thing.

The sailor repeated, "Are you deaf? I asked you about your haul. The captain is waiting for lunch. Dip out the best fish, and put them in this basket. Make it fast. Here—catch." He tossed the basket to Saleh, who caught it and placed it on the plank deck.

The fishermen looked quickly at each other, grateful for the sudden reprieve. "Yes, sir," said Boon Hok. "We have some fine grouper that your captain will enjoy, with our good wishes." Saleh untied the long-handled net from the base of the platform and dipped out two of the largest fish. He placed them in the basket, and Saleh handed them over to the sailors. "We are proud to serve the Imperial Navy."

The fishermen watched as the cutter raised anchor and continued south until it was out of sight. Saleh fetched a package of food and a bottle of water from the proa, and the fishermen joined Li Lian in the hut.

Saleh laid out pieces of bread and fried fish. "This is a poor meal, but it will satisfy our hunger."

That evening they arrived at their destination, a Malay village on a spit at the mouth of a sluggish, cocoa-colored river. The village was mired in a mangrove swamp with no access, except by sea.

Saleh lashed the prow line to an iron ring at the pier. He climbed the weathered teak ladder and greeted a villager sitting on the plank floor, with his big toes stretching a fishing net.

"Ahmad, old friend, still mending nets, I see."

"*Salam alaikum*, Saleh. It's good to see you. You have managed to stay out of the clutches of the Jap'nees. What brings you here?"

"I must see the penghulu—to take care of a friend."

Li Lian's head appeared above the plank deck of the pier. Ahmad grinned. "Saleh, you old macaque. Malay girls not enough for you?"

"No, no, no, not my girl. She needs help."

Li Lian climbed onto the deck, followed by Boon Hok.

Ahmad looked admiringly at Li Lian and then greeted the third visitor. "Salam, Boon Hok. I see that you and Saleh are still partners. Business must be good." The penghulu arrived. Ahmad swept his arm toward Li Lian. "Look who's here, Dain. Our fishermen have come back, and they bring us a pretty gift."

Saleh embraced the headman. "I am pleased to be back home, and I have brought a young lady who has escaped from the Japanese. She needs our help." He turned to Li Lian. "Li Lian, I want you to meet our penghulu, Dain Mohammad. We have been friends for many years." He took the penghulu aside to explain Li Lian's predicament.

Saleh and Boon Hok bid farewell to Li Lian, and climbed down to the proa for the return to Keppel Harbor.

Chapter 4
Guadalcanal

Hoda carried on sullenly with his despised job of managing prisoners. He went to Java under orders to arrange sea transport of a large contingent of captives to Singapore and then to a prison camp in Sumatra. Included in the group were several Australian army doctors and nurses who were dragged out of a small military hospital after the dysentery-ridden patients were slaughtered. The medical people, still in their soiled hospital garb, boarded the transport ship, along with the wives and children of Dutch military and diplomatic personnel.

Hoda summoned the most attractive nurse to his cabin after the internees' evening meal of rice and fish. "Ah, Miss Rosetti—such a pretty name," he said, studying her identification tag. "You are an experienced member of the armed forces of your country, are you not? Surely you must understand the penalty for being captured out of uniform by soldiers of the victorious army." His ingratiating smile changed to a fierce grin. "A firing squad is the customary punishment." He noted her terrified expression with satisfaction. "I am not a cruel man. I understand that you were caught up in a situation beyond your control. So was I. That being the case, we can find some comfort together on this tedious trip."

He stood and walked to her side, grasped her upper arm, and drew her toward his bunk. She pulled away and stood silently, with fists clenched at her sides. Hoda exploded in a fury and threw her onto the mattress.

She emerged from the cabin at dawn, her face bruised and tearstained.

———◦———

A week later, Hoda visited the brothel in Singapore and found a Korean mama-san selling the entrance tickets.

"Take me to Li Lian."

"Not here."

"Where?"

"Not know."

<hr/>

Hoda filed weekly reports on the prisoner census. Whenever he entered headquarters for this purpose, he requested a transfer to an active battle zone.

"Captain Hoda, aren't you happy here?" chided Lieutenant Koshino, who handled the paperwork. "All the food, sake, and Chinky girls you could ever want." Koshino also frequented the brothel on Cairn Hill Road, and had sampled Li Lian several times. When he finished, she always told him, "No need to tell Hoda-san."

<hr/>

Koshino delivered Hoda's POW report to the commanding officer of the garrison.

"Captain Hoda is here again, sir, complaining, as usual. Shall I send him away?"

"Ah, no. This time we may have something for him. Send him in."

Koshino smirked and said, "Captain, this might be your lucky day. The old man will see you."

Hoda entered and saluted.

"Take a seat, Captain Hoda. I am aware of your itch to see some action. You have made a pest of yourself, but I appreciate your desire to fight for the emperor. I have something to suit a man of your temperament."

"Yes, sir, I am prepared for anything."

"I am sure you are. Here's the assignment. Colonel Ichiki is on Guam, training a detachment of two thousand men to invade Midway and bring us within striking distance of the Hawaiian Islands. This is all you have to know right now. The time for the attack has not yet been set. I have been informed that the second in command is incapacitated with cholera. You are to be his replacement. Get packed and be ready to fly out in two days. Banzai."

Hoda squared his shoulders, saluted, and left the office. He passed Koshino, swatted him on the shoulder, and said, "Enjoy Singapore, Lieutenant."

Koshino grinned and said, "Good news, eh?"

———◄◦►———

Hoda flew to Guam and took over smoothly as Ichiki's second in command. In August 1942, the detachment boarded two destroyers and headed east. While they were in transit, the American First Marine Division landed on Tulagi and Guadalcanal. Half the Ichiki detachment was redirected to Guadalcanal, ordered to destroy the American invaders.

Ichiki landed unopposed with nine hundred men at Taivu Point, twenty-five miles from the Guadalcanal airstrip. He left part of his force on the beach to guard supplies and led the rest along to coast to capture the airfield.

Ichiki formed his troops in a coconut grove near the Ilu River. A sandbar across the river was an ideal bridge to the other side. It was past midnight when the Japanese started the attack with a mortar barrage. The Americans dug in across the river, waiting for the assault.

The Japanese dashed across the sandbar into withering Browning Automatic Rifle fire. The survivors fled back to the coconut grove to regroup. The next morning at dawn, a reserve marine battalion crossed the Ilu upstream and cut off Ichiki and his men in the grove.

Later that afternoon, the marines went in and finished off the demoralized and disorganized Ichiki detachment. They were methodical in their slaughter but took casualties of their own. Wounded Japanese, begging for help, suddenly launched grenades, killing some of their tormentors.

Hoda gripped his sword and stood amid the carnage with his feet planted in the mud. A marine rushed at him, firing his BAR. Hoda's face contorted in pain and rage, and he fell, twisting and groping for the sword that landed not far away. The marine continued his rush but tripped on an exposed root and sprawled forward, losing his weapon. He landed on the

31

struggling Hoda, who had just managed to grasp the sword. Under the weight of the marine, Hoda freed his arm and slashed weakly.

The marine, Corporal Francis Cagle, threw up his left arm, intercepting the blow. In a fury, Cagle slammed his helmeted head into Hoda's face. He yanked his fighting knife from the scabbard on his right boot and plunged it into Hoda's throat. Only then did he look down to see his blood-soaked left sleeve. He felt a hand on his shoulder and twisted suddenly to stare up at a mud-spattered member of his squad, Fishy Gorton, who said, "I saw the whole thing, Frank. It's over now. Let's get you patched up."

Some wounded Japanese tried to escape, but several light tanks chased them down, running over dead and wounded, filling the treads with flesh. Several of Ichiki's men had taken to the sea, trying to escape by swimming underwater for as long as they could hold their breath. The marines took potshots at their heads as they broke the surface. All the Japanese swimmers were killed but two, who were the only survivors of Ichiki's detachment of 790 men. The marines lost thirty-five.

Throughout the night, crocodiles thrashed on the beach, devouring their grisly feast. Marines sat on the banks of the river, firing at crocs and dead Japanese with the residue of the mad energy of battle, until they were stopped by an artillery captain, who shouted, "You guys made this mess. Who the fuck's supposed to clean it up?"

The next day at dawn, the marines moved among the corpses, scavenging for souvenirs of the battle. Frank Cagle, with his repaired arm in a sling, went into the coconut grove with the rest of the souvenir hunters and found Hoda's body. He went through pockets and pack and came away with a bloodstained leather wallet and Hoda's sword, and then he headed back to the mess tent for a breakfast tray of reconstituted scrambled eggs, bacon, toast, and coffee. He went outside and sat on a blasted palm log next to Fishy Gorton.

"Glad ta see ya, Fishy," he said. "I guess ya came through the punch-up okay."

"Yeah, hi, Frank. How's the arm feel? Say, I saw you out there, scrounging stuff from that Jap that you killed yesterday. The guys have so much shit we'll need a cargo ship to get it all home." Fishy and Frank finished their breakfast in silence.

After breakfast, the Seabees moved abandoned Japanese construction equipment out to the Ilu battle site and heaved dead Japanese and crocodiles onto payloaders for disposal. Seven hundred eighty-eight Japanese soldiers, including Hoda, and twenty-six crocodiles were dumped into a gully, followed by three fifty-five–gallon drums of aviation fuel and an incendiary grenade.

Frank's platoon sergeant, Carl Wilbur, was killed by a sniper in the coconut grove, and Frank was promoted to replace him. Fishy Gorton was promoted to corporal, replacing Frank as squad leader.

———◦———

The Japanese continued their unsuccessful assaults on Guadalcanal, determined to destroy the American garrison. Several thousand fresh troops landed at the Mataniko River, with orders to encircle and capture Henderson Field.

The marines met this threat by sending three battalions to cut off the Japanese troop concentration on the coast. They trapped the Japanese against the riverbank under a torrent of artillery and mortar fire. The marines closed in for the kill but were caught in the cross fire of two machine gun emplacements that had remained silent through much of the battle. For almost ten minutes, the marines were pinned down, unable to complete the destruction of the Japanese troops. Suddenly, the Japanese machine guns were silent, and the marines completed the mop-up.

After the battle, the Japanese machine-gun nests were located, and all their gunners were dead. In one of the nests, Sergeant Frank Cagle was found on a stack of dead Japanese. Frank's BAR clip was empty, and his fighting knife was imbedded in the chest of one of the enemy gunners.

Fishy Gorton had stormed the machine-gun nest at Frank's side and insisted on carrying his friend's body from the battlefield. When the litter-bearers caught up with him, Fishy helped carry the litter for an hour as they walked back to the base along the jungle trail.

"Let go, Corporal," said a medic, when an ambulance drove up to collect bodies. The medic pried Fishy's fingers from the litter grips.

Back at the base, three chaplains conducted services for their respective denominations, and "Taps" echoed from the surrounding hills. Night fell on the lengthening rows of white crosses in the military cemetery on Guadalcanal.

Fishy gathered Frank's belongings, including Hoda's bloodstained souvenirs, and packed them for shipment home.

———◦———

Four-year-old Michael Cagle and his mother, the former Janine Foster, were sitting at the kitchen table in their ground-floor apartment in Standish, Massachusetts. The doorbell rang.

Janine opened the door, and an old man in a Western Union cap said, "Good afternoon, ma'am. Are you Mrs. Francis Cagle?" He held out a black-bordered yellow envelope.

Her hand flew to her mouth when she took the telegram. She kept her composure and said, "Won't you step in?"

The man removed his cap and stood stiffly in the small entry. "I am very sorry, Mrs. Cagle. I offer my deepest condolences."

"Thank you. Wait," she said as the man turned to leave. "Let me get my purse."

"It's really not necessary, ma'am. Again, my sincerest regrets." He walked out to his bicycle, waved good-bye, and rode away.

Janine opened the telegram. "The president of the United States regrets to inform you …" The rest of the message indicated that more complete information would follow.

Soon an official government letter arrived, stating that Sgt. Francis J. Cagle had served in the great tradition of the US Marine Corps and gave his life for his country; that he was given a respectful burial on the field of battle; and that his personal possessions would be forwarded to his family when said possessions arrived from the Pacific theater of operations.

———◦———

Several weeks later, the bundle arrived. Janine unwrapped the package and ran her hands over Frank's uniforms. She touched two First Division Guadalcanal shoulder patches and the battle souvenirs, including Hoda's sword, which had been cleaned. She found her old letters to Frank and a note of condolence addressed to her from one of Frank's buddies, Thaddeus

Gorton. She repacked everything and stored the bundle in a bedroom closet.

In February 1943, Janine received an official letter notifying her that Frank had been awarded the Medal of Honor for his heroic action on Guadalcanal. It would be presented to her by the president at a special ceremony in the White House Rose Garden. Travel arrangements and a night in a Washington hotel would be at government expense. Janine took Mike with her to meet the president.

———◦———

Janine and Mike returned to Standish, and she put a gold star in the window.

Chapter 5
The Kampong

The penghulu took Li Lian's hand. "Come, Li Lian, you must rest after your ordeal. I extend to you the hospitality of our humble village. You may move in with my number-one wife, Zaharah."

Dain had just completed construction of a stilt house for Hani, his young fourth wife. He thought that Zaharah's increasingly subordinate role might be eased by the responsibility of caring for Li Lian through her pregnancy. Li Lian also would have the company of Zaharah's two children, Ramli and Siti, and the children of the village, who streamed through the house for the endless snacks laid out by Zaharah.

◄◦►

Li Lian lay on her sleeping mat, plagued by memories of Singapore. Later that first night, Dain entered the house, socialized with Zaharah and the children for a half hour, and left—to sleep with Hani.

In the morning, Li Lian joined the family for breakfast and was overwhelmed by Zaharah's loving attention.

After the meal, Ramli helped Li Lian to her feet. "Come, Li Lian, I will show you our village. You must learn about your new home." They walked into the morning heat, and Li Lian was startled to see a large pigtailed macaque tethered next to the house.

Ramli laughed at Li Lian's alarm. "That's our *brok*. He collects coconuts for us. Stay away until he gets to know you. The only ones who can handle him are me and Papa. Come. I show you."

He attached a long lead to the macaque and led him to a nearby coconut palm. The beast leaped onto the trunk and effortlessly ran up to the clump of coconuts. Ramli gave a slight tug on the lead. In response, the obedient brok twisted a ripe coconut until it fell to the ground.

◆◇◆

Kampong life was tranquil, and Li Lian settled into the unhurried atmosphere. The Malays were kind to her, and she accepted their kindness with gratitude. She insisted on helping with the household chores and established a routine of doing the laundry at the community well and gossiping with the women who gathered there throughout the day. Li Lian spoke bazaar Malay but rapidly became more fluent in that simple tongue. She noted the raw, pustular skin lesions on many of the children and asked if they were contagious.

"Oh, no," said Zaharah, "the children all have those sores but no bother, unless they get bloody. If a child falls and scrapes a knee, those sores happen. It's part of a child's life. Sometimes a doctor comes from Singapore to treat the children."

Li Lian feared for her unborn child. She intended to leave it at the village but wanted to protect it during childhood. She said, "Maybe if the children wear some foot cover, the skin will stay nice. I would like my baby to wear sandals always. Will you see to that, Zaharah?"

"Okay," said the older woman.

One day, Siti took Li Lian's hand and led her to a narrow path through the lush undergrowth. "Come, Li Lian. I will take you to my magic place."

Li Lian followed the girl along the forest path for a few minutes until Siti stopped, crouched, and pointed. "Li Lian, look at the *kupu-kupu*—see how beautiful."

Ahead of them, a shallow puddle bubbled up through the jungle rot. Iridescent black-and-blue butterflies surrounded the puddle, sucking up the sulfurous water through an uncoiled proboscis functioning as a soda straw. Clear drops slowly accumulated and dropped off at the other end.

Li Lian loved the spectacular Rajah Brooke butterflies and often visited the puddle for moments of quiet amid the bustle of village life.

As the months passed, Li Lian's body swelled, until the life growing in her chose to make an exit. When her labor entered the final stage, a woman brought banana leaves into the house and placed them next to Li Lian.

She turned her head to look at the leaves and asked, "What for?"

The woman said, "This we must do. No matter."

Li Lian was seized with an expulsive contraction, and her daughter was delivered into the hands of Zaharah.

After the delivery, Zaharah wrapped the placenta in the banana leaves and tied the package securely with nipa fiber. She took the bundle to the shore and sent it out to sea on a bamboo raft. Zaharah explained to Li Lian that this was a Malay custom ordinarily reserved for royal afterbirths. According to belief, evil spirits resided in the placenta, which must be sent out as a sacrifice to the sea gods. Otherwise, the bad spirits would remain to plague the village. Although Li Lian was not of royal ancestry, the baby was delivered in the house of the penghulu, and it was best not to take any unnecessary chances.

As the women watched from shore, a black triangle sliced through the oil-calm sea, and the little raft flew skyward, driven by the shark's nose.

Li Lian agreed that the baby would be named Maimunah and would stay with Zaharah and be absorbed into the penghulu's family. She would adopt Islam and the Malay culture, language, and style of dress. Maimunah would have the status of *anak beli*—a bought child, which was a term applied to a non-Malay child adopted into a Malay family. It was understood that such a child never was to meet its biological mother.

Li Lian carried Maimunah everywhere in the kampong and to the seashore for refreshing dips in the warm, salty water. She collected pandanus leaves for weaving mats, and she sat under the *attap* roof at the Indian shop, nursing her baby and chatting with the fishermen who returned to the village pier to escape the afternoon heat. Li Lian and Maimunah became part of the fabric of the little community.

As Maimunah changed from newborn to infant, Li Lian was increasingly troubled by memories of her tortured life in Singapore and the paternity of her baby girl. She handed Maimunah off to the women of the village for longer periods and even sought out new mothers who would be happy to serve as wet nurses. When Maimunah was four months old, Li Lian told the penghulu that it was time for her to leave. Maimunah would stay with her new family, and Li Lian would go into an uncertain future, fighting the Japanese oppressors.

Dain was prepared for this moment. He called for Li Lian's rescuers to come for her.

Chapter 6
The Red Brigade

Boon Hok and Saleh arrived a week later. Zaharah prepared a meal of fried conger eel that Ramli had speared earlier that day. As they sipped sweet café au lait, Saleh briefed Li Lian on the plan for the next day.

"We leave at dawn and sail north. We have arranged for you to be turned over to some of our people, who will take you to one of our forest camps. It is a location that I mapped out a few years ago when I worked on a rubber estate. Now it is being put to good use."

He looked at Li Lian with an expression of tender concern and added, "You understand that you will be in constant danger of discovery, so we must be very careful. In the unlikely event of capture by the Kempeitai, you must leave behind any possessions that might be traceable to you or your former life. We must not endanger others."

"This is all that I own," she said, handing her batik bag to Saleh.

He took the bag and turned it over to the penghulu, saying, "For safekeeping."

Dain handed the bag to Zaharah. "Hide it well."

The next morning at dawn, the fishermen provided a broad-brimmed straw hat, drab trousers, and a black shirt to disguise Li Lian for their sea voyage. She dressed in the fisherman's garb and thanked Dain and Zaharah for their kindness to her and Maimunah, the new member of their family. After a last glance at the sleeping Maimunah, Li Lian walked to the pier and climbed into the proa. Zaharah left a basket of food to sustain them on their journey. They headed out as the rising sun plated the surface of the South China Sea.

Several hours later, they eased into a narrow cove. Saleh leaped ashore and tied up to a mangrove root. They picked their way up a shallow slope, through the jungle debris and leaf mold, flushing colorful birds and a startled tapir. A flatbed truck waited under a leafy overhang. The truck was loaded with long wicker baskets containing live pigs. The baskets constrained the pigs, who quickly learned the futility of struggle. Two Chinese truck drivers sat on a flat, dark basalt rock, drinking beer.

Boon Hok led Li Lian to the truck, while Saleh stayed behind to avoid defiling himself through contact with the pigs.

One of the drivers greeted them with a smile, flashing two gold teeth. "Welcome to this leech-ridden forest. This young lady must be Li Lian. We have been expecting you. Has she been told of our travel arrangements?"

Boon Hok said, "Not precisely. We thought it best to wait for this moment."

The comment startled Li Lian, and she said, "What about the travel arrangements? What must I know?"

"We must think ahead," said Boon Hok. "Take precautions to reduce the risk of discovery."

"What are you trying to say?" said Li Lian. "I understand the danger of discovery, but that is the chance we take."

Boon Hok said, "There are Japanese sentry posts between this place and our destination. We must arouse no suspicion as we travel the road, so we—"

"Why travel along a road where there may be checkpoints?" Li Lian interrupted, "That doesn't seem safe to me. Why can't we just hike through the forest?"

"That would take us a long time," said Boom Hok, "and there are mountain ranges that we must cross. No, we must go by road, but we have made preparations. We have driven that pig truck along the road a few times, delivering the hogs to market. The sentries are accustomed to us by now. The plan is to wrap you in a muslin sheet for protection from the pig filth and store you in a wicker basket, just like the pigs. We will stack the pigs on top and drive through the checkpoints, just as we always have done. I am sure the plan will work. Are you ready?"

"I have been through much worse," said Li Lian. "Let's get started."

"Good! Now, I suggest that you remove your clothing before we wrap you, so that you will have something to wear at the end of the trip. You may go behind the truck while you undress."

"My sense of modesty no longer is an issue in my life," said Li Lian. She quickly stripped off all of her clothing and stood naked before the men.

Averting their eyes to conceal their embarrassment, the men proceeded to wrap her completely in the muslin sheet, covering her face with only a single layer of the thin fabric.

"I feel like an Egyptian mummy," she said, giggling.

"Can you breathe all right?" asked Boon Hok.

"Yes, I am fine. Now what?"

She remained standing as they lifted a pig basket over her head and brought it down carefully, enclosing her entire body.

"Now we will tip you and lift you onto the truck." It was done. For added protection, they covered her with a brown tarpaulin and loaded baskets of squealing pigs on top. Boon Hok and Saleh bade them farewell and headed back to the cove to board the proa for the return trip to Singapore.

The pig truck moved slowly out of the clearing onto the only paved road through the mountains. They approached a column of Japanese soldiers, who taunted them but moved to the side of the road to permit the truck to pass. They came to roadblocks, and the Japanese guards obligingly raised the barriers without demanding identification.

A half hour after passing through the last Japanese checkpoint, the paved road gave way to a dirt road. An hour later, the drivers lifted an exhausted and foul-smelling Li Lian from her basket, next to a remote mountain stream. The drivers unwound the soiled muslin sheet, and Li Lian scrubbed herself in the stream with a cake of brown soap. She dressed in clean peasant trousers and a threadbare cotton shirt, saving her own clothing for later use. She climbed up into the cab, joining the two drivers. They maneuvered the truck for three hours into mountainous terrain, until the dirt road faded into the forest.

Soon several armed Chinese men emerged from the dense greenery and beckoned to Li Lian to join them. The men unloaded six of the pigs, still in their baskets, and carried them through the green jungle curtain. They returned with six empty baskets and loaded them back on the truck above the remaining pigs. The driver started the truck and departed with the surviving pigs to another destination.

One of the men approached Li Lian with a roll of tape and explained, "Before we walk any farther into that green hell, I must tape your trouser bottoms tight around your legs. That will give you some protection from the *lintah*. Those fellas can ooze through the tiniest hole, even a shoelace eyelet."

Li Lian shuddered with disgust at the thought of the leeches, as the man taped her trousers. Then she and her companions walked into the forest, following a rudimentary footpath for a quarter of a mile. The path widened, and they came to an oxcart that held the six pigs, Li Lian's former travel companions, hogtied and lying silent. The tethered ox munched delicately at the weedy undergrowth. One of the armed men untied the ox and invited Li Lian to sit next to him on the plank seat.

Li Lian said, "Thank you, but I would prefer to walk. I'm not yet ready to ride with the pigs."

The driver took the reins and prodded the beast into its deliberate gait, followed by Li Lian and the rest of her escort. The party trudged through uncharted country, along a primitive track lined on both sides with great heaps of brush. The men switched off handling the reins every half hour.

After walking for an hour, Li Lian fainted on the trail. She awoke to find herself propped up on the plank bench next to the driver. Her head was covered with a wet towel. She smiled at the men, who were relieved to see her in control of her senses.

In the darkness, they stopped at a clearing with a stone fireplace and evidence of previous use. One of the men built a fire and filled a rice pot with water from a metal jerry can. As they ate their sparse meal, they were joined by several *orang asli* carrying spears and parangs, who slipped silently from the forest and seated themselves on logs near the fire. They wore sarongs and various items of Japanese military wear, including cartridge belts and gray, split-toed army shoes. One of Li Lian's escorts ladled rice into the coconut shells the visitors held out.

All ate in silence, except for a few muttered words in an unfamiliar language exchanged between the aborigines and Li Lian's companions. When they finished their meal, the aborigines filed into the forest, followed by the oxcart, through an almost invisible opening in the wall of vegetation.

One of the drivers, self-appointed as Li Lian's mentor, said, "The orang asli are on our side against the Japs. They are very helpful in keeping the forest trails open. You saw the brush piles along the path. The aborigines go in there every day and hack out the overgrowth with their parangs. Without them, we would be trapped in the jungle, unable to move with any speed."

Li Lian asked, "Where are we going now?"

"To their village to spend the night. It's just a short way."

They soon entered the village clearing, where the headman and the entire population of about a hundred stood together, waiting to greet them. The huts were not as refined as those of the Malays, but they were tightly thatched against the forest rains. The aborigines welcomed them with a ceremonial meal of their tribal specialties, including a malodorous preparation of what appeared to be semisolid small animals, withdrawn from sealed bamboo joints and offered up on banana leaf platters. Li Lian's mentor whispered, "Taste it, and nod in appreciation. We need these men."

Li Lian plucked a bit from the serving leaf, held her breath, and swallowed. She sat with her eyes closed as she battled a wave of nausea. She later learned that the delicacy was fermented jungle rat, prepared by placing a rat, coated with slaked lime, in a segment of hollow bamboo, sealing the ends with clay, and burying the container in jungle humus for several weeks. The semiliquefied rats were unearthed when it was determined by mysterious factors that they were suitable for consumption.

In the morning, they were under way again, retracing their path to the rest stop of the previous evening. One of the drivers knelt near the fireplace and felt indentations in the soft earth. "*Harimau*," he said, tracing the pug marks of a tiger. The party continued the journey, with the armed guerrillas now walking on either side of the ox to protect it from a hungry predator that might still be lurking in the vicinity, sniffing out a large meal. The rest of their trek was uneventful.

As night fell, they reached their destination, where they were greeted by the main guerrilla contingent. The pigs were unloaded and driven into a fenced mud wallow to await their turn to be butchered. A corral held horses and mules, which were the chief mode of transportation on the jungle trails.

Li Lian was assigned to a lean-to, roofed over with the ubiquitous horizontal bamboo poles with rotan-tied nipa palm fronds, making a water-repellant cover. The camp contained several Malay stilt houses that were luxurious in comparison with her shallow lean-to, but Li Lian was grateful for whatever was provided for her bare existence. She arrived with nothing but the clothes she wore and a dull bait knife that she found at the kelong where she spent the day with the fishermen.

A camp woman gave her a rucksack containing some basics—towel, soap, toothbrush, hairbrush, sandals, antimalarial and water purification tablets, undergarments, feminine items, and a gray cloth cap with a small, red circular device over the bill.

The woman then said in the Hokkien dialect, "Now sit on this big rock. Time for haircut. Otherwise, get tangled up in vines and thorn bushes." She produced iron scissors and went to work.

Li Lian, freshly shorn and wearing her Red Chinese Mao cap, arranged her belongings in the lean-to on a flat rock that she dragged in to serve as a dressing table. Her barber showed her how to prepare a snug bed by tying bamboo poles together with flexible vines and weaving ferns into the framework to form a mattress and quilt-like cover. Although the lean-to was to be her home for the indeterminate future, she wondered how she might graduate to one of the stilt houses.

More recruits filtered into the camp for the next three weeks, bringing total strength to about two hundred.

Li Lian assumed that she would be expected to provide sexual relief to any man who expressed a need, but she was surprised to learn that the communist men were highly disciplined and even prudish in approaching the women.

The commander of the cadre, Lim Chu San, discussed the sexual issue during one of their training sessions. He advised the men that sexual relations were not forbidden, but as there was equality of the sexes, it would be preferable if contacts were initiated by the women. Men were physically stronger, and they must not—under any circumstances—impose themselves upon the women. Rape would not be tolerated, and any man convicted of that crime would be summarily executed by a single bullet behind the ear. It was imperative that high morale be sustained at all times. Living conditions were difficult enough without the complication of sexual tension.

Li Lian attended regular orientation sessions and pledged loyalty to her comrades and the principles for which they would fight—chiefly, to free the nations of Southeast Asia from all foreign domination and to further the goals of world communism. Li Lian swore allegiance to the leaders and became a full-fledged member of the MCP—the Malayan Communist Party—assigned to the Fifth People's Brigade.

As part of the strategy devised by the party leaders, the MCP force was renamed the MPAJA, the Malayan People's Anti-Japanese Army, and units were distributed throughout the deep jungles and mountainous regions of Perak and Kelantan. The guerrilla program was supported by the British, who planted officers of Special Operations Force 136 in most of the communist encampments. These commonwealth officers were valuable in bringing intelligence reports to the guerrillas and in expediting the shipments of arms and supplies from Burma and Thailand.

Shortly after her arrival in the camp, Li Lian met Gordon Wallace of Force 136, who worked side by side with the communist guerrilla leaders in training the new recruits. Wallace was a red-bearded giant who lived in a thatched hut on a bamboo platform. His personal needs were satisfied by young Malay and Chinese women, who rotated in their service on a regular schedule. The rotation of services was required by Wallace, who did not wish to become dependent upon an individual woman. Among their household chores was the removal of leeches and ticks from Wallace's body after his jungle scouting ventures. When he returned from those undertakings, his woman of the moment dropped her domestic chores and hurried to the veranda to greet the large man, who could be heard throughout the camp, bellowing, "Bloody buffalo leeches!" He shed his clothing as he hurried home and stepped up to the veranda naked, presenting himself to the woman with arms extended and leeches decorating his great expanse of skin.

After one such foray, Wallace returned to camp with a Chinese man dressed as a peasant. At the morning muster, he introduced the visitor as Loi Tak, the secretary general of the Malayan Communist Party, who was on an inspection tour of the guerrilla camps.

Loi Tak had organized a meeting of the Communist Central Committee to coordinate anti-Japanese resistance activities. The meeting was to be held in a Chinese squatter settlement a few miles from Kuala Lumpur. After his visit to Li Lian's camp, Loi Tak went to Kuala Lumpur to prepare for the meeting. A week later, word filtered back to the camp that the Japanese had learned of the meeting and had ambushed and wiped out the entire Central Committee, with the exception of Loi Tak, who had been detained in Kuala Lumpur and did not attend the meeting. Gordon Wallace made no reference to the ambush during his regular training exercises, but he became agitated and short-tempered as he continued in his role as the British liaison officer.

—◦—

Farming squadrons of about a dozen men and women tended vegetable gardens, and sacks of rice and tapioca were stored in food dumps located strategically throughout the mountainous back country. The camp cooks supplemented the vegetarian diet with pork for the Chinese cadres and goat for the Malays. Pig squeals shattered the predawn jungle stillness as the butchery was carried out at four in the morning, in keeping with Chinese village custom.

Mule trains visited the food dumps weekly to resupply the camp larder. Li Lian's first assignment after she had adjusted to camp discipline was to go on one of these shopping trips. Two men led the mule train, and Li Lian brought up the rear, armed with a rifle and weighted with a cartridge belt slung diagonally from shoulder to waist.

They threaded their way along a narrow forest path and camped overnight at a rest stop in a small clearing. After the mules were tethered, one of the men cracked a mud seal from a tree hollow and removed a bundle wrapped in banana leaves and secured with nipa ties. He unwrapped the bundle and removed a roasted dried monkey that was to be their evening meal. Li Lian controlled her squeamishness, and the man explained that this was a gift from their aborigine allies. He placed a five-pound burlap sack of rice in the tree hollow in a gesture of thanks.

They resumed their journey at dawn, with their wide-brimmed, straw peasant hats serving as umbrellas against the inevitable heavy downpour. At noon, they arrived at the vegetable garden to collect a welcome load of greens and yams. To their dismay, the garden was a shambles, and several of the workers were sitting on the ground in a daze. When they saw the mule train, they arose and greeted the visitors.

"What happened? Were you attacked by the Japs?" asked one of Li Lian's companions.

"Oh no, much worse," said a gardener. "*Gajah. Gajah tunggal*—rogue elephant. Look up there." He pointed to a nearby tree. A thin Chinese man was lodged in a tree crotch about twenty feet from the ground. He was motionless, and the unnatural angle of his back indicated that he had a broken spine and most likely was dead. "And there." He beckoned to them to follow. In the devastated garden patch, two men were stretched out, covered with blood. "Trampled," said the gardener, "and dead. It's a wonder any of us survived. He burst out of the forest, angry and hungry. We ran, but they"—he swept his arm toward the three victims—"were in his path. You should warn the others. That gajah is running amok."

Li Lian and the mule skinners remained an extra day to help clean up the garden. They gathered what food was available and returned to their base, where they warned of the rampaging rogue.

<hr/>

The brigade had a firing range, and Li Lian became a sharpshooter with a light machine gun as well as a .25-caliber compact Beretta that Chu San gave her for self-protection.

This was an asset in her first raid on a convoy trucking rice and vegetables to the Japanese garrison in Kota Bharu. The communists ambushed the column as the first truck slowly drove onto a rickety wooden bridge over a creek. Sappers dynamited the bridge and fired upon the guards on motorcycles, flanking the trucks. Li Lian fired her Beretta at a guard and was surprised to see him fly off his motorcycle and splash into the water.

The engagement was brief. The Japanese had a machine gun mounted on the last truck. It started its chatter, and the attackers withdrew, leaving several dead comrades in the undergrowth.

Li Lian returned to camp with her unit after a two-day march, and she trembled uncontrollably when she settled into her lean-to. The delayed reaction was repeated on several later raids, until she became a battle-hardened, reliable campaigner.

By the time she was eighteen, she was viewed as an older "auntie" by the young children, who had been recruited and brought into the camp by the party zealots. Most of these children were Chinese orphans whose parents had been exterminated by the Japanese in Malaya and Singapore and whose remaining families, if any, were unable or unwilling to support them.

Twelve-year-old children toted their .25-caliber rifles next to the adults—
and often died next to them. The children frequently went out, unarmed,
on scouting expeditions to determine Japanese strength in their various
garrisons in northern Malaya and the Kra Isthmus. They were inconspicuous
urchins who were masters of minor theft and living off the land.

Chu San had an invasion route map taken from the body of a Japanese
infantryman, and, as the children returned with their intelligence, he marked
the locations and shifting strength of the Japanese troop concentrations.
He noted their armaments, trucks, tanks, and visible food supplies. The
communists were expert sappers, and explosions and conflagrations
illuminated the soft nights.

One of the sites that was under observation was a walled compound of
a rubber estate about fifty miles north of the brigades' encampment. The
estate was occupied by a Japanese garrison known to be supplying rubber
for military use. The groves of rubber trees were cleared periodically of the
lush undergrowth. Brush piles studding the groves were ideal habitats for
pit vipers, which killed two or three tappers a month. The Japanese soldiers
feared the reptiles and almost never ventured into the groves. They also
avoided the surrounding forests, after some of their number were killed and
consumed by tigers in the dense jungle growth.

The forests became the domain of the communist patrols. Li Lian led
a small group that spied on the rubber estate. She took her unit out for
a week at a time, varying their route to avoid discovery. They located the
latex curing sheds, where the white liquid was coagulated with acid and
pressed into sheets. They identified the fire-scarred structure, where the
raw sheets were laid out on wooden racks and smoked over carefully tended
beds of smoldering charcoal. At one end of the smokehouse, the sheets
were baled for storage. The old road into the plantation had deteriorated
under the monsoons and was little more than a muddy sluiceway reclaimed
by the jungle. Li Lian reported the rubber buildup to Chu San, and they
deliberated on the proper timing to attack for maximum destruction.

Li Lian said, "A small amount of rubber has been taken out on mules,
perhaps for quality testing, but the bales are piling up. I think we should
not wait much longer."

Chu San pondered and said, "That might be so, but remember that
we can do this only once. If the attack is successful, the Japs will move in

a battalion to guard the perimeter. Let's give them two more weeks for additional rubber accumulation, and then we go."

Li Lian said, "I accept your judgment, Commander, but if you have further thoughts, I would be pleased to discuss them with you tonight in my hut." Her soft smile stirred Chu San.

"Thank you, Li Lian. I believe there are other things that we might consider. Will nine o'clock be acceptable?"

"Quite acceptable, Commander," answered Li Lian, and they became lovers that night, Chu San flattered by her acceptance, and Li Lian indifferent to the sex act but looking forward to more comfortable accommodations.

A week later, Li Lian and her patrol made another trek to the rubber estate. She returned to the stilt house she now was sharing with Chu San and reported that the rubber stores were much larger, and the bales of smoked sheet now were being stacked in the open, exposed to the perennial bursts of rainfall.

"I think the time is now, Chu San."

"I agree," he said. "Good work."

They left at midnight, pacing themselves to arrive at the rubber estate in three days. With Li Lian in the lead, they picked their way through the forest, and arrived at the estate as scheduled.

"Conditions are ideal," whispered Chu San. "We attack in one hour. Pass the word to the squad leaders."

At two o'clock the guards' throats were cut. The sappers dashed to the fuel tank identified by Li Lian and drained diesel oil into their buckets. They raced to the rubber stores and cast the oil over the bales, placed their charges, and lit the fuses.

The explosion was deafening, and the stench of burning rubber filled the grove. Thick black smoke billowed up, and a great sea of flame cast orange light against the stand of trees.

The entire garrison, armed with guns and grenades, came streaming out—naked or in nightclothes. The guerrillas manned a heavy-duty machine gun on a tripod aimed at the main gate.

The Japanese burst through the gate and were mowed down by the machine gun. Two of the guerrillas ran through the carnage with pistols, finishing off any that moved. While this work was in progress, the fuel dump exploded, illuminating thirty dead Japanese sprawled in the dust.

As Li Lian viewed the scene, two Chinese women in silk kimonos and slippers came running out of the house, screaming, "Save us! Save us!" One of the guerrillas was about to add to the death toll, when Li Lian grabbed the barrel of his gun and raised it to the sky. She said, "Wait—they are Chinese, and they are desperate."

The two women ran to Li Lian, stumbling over the Japanese bodies, and one of them gasped out, "Please help us! We are prisoners of those dogs. Whoever you are, take us with you. Please, please."

Chu San ran up and shouted, "Kill them now!"

Li Lian shielded the women and said, "No, they come with us." Her dark eyes flashed.

Chu San turned away from Li Lian's fierce gaze and chose not to engage in a test of will at the moment of victory. He relented and said, "They are welcome, but they are your responsibility. Let's get out of here."

"No, no, please wait," said one of Li Lian's new charges.

"What now?" said an irritated Chu San.

"Wu Feng. We cannot leave him." The woman ran toward the rubber forest, waving her arms and screaming. "Come! Come quick!" As she neared a shed just inside the rows of rubber trees, a gaunt Chinese man, dressed in coveralls, stepped from the doorway. He ran over Japanese bodies, stooping to pick up a pistol that lay next to one of the corpses. He stooped again and ripped a bandolier from the shoulders of another.

"Wu Feng! Hurry! Hurry! We are leaving!" She grabbed his sleeve and dragged him to the band of guerrillas. "Now we go."

Chu San accepted Wu Feng into the guerrilla force, and they retraced their arduous way back to their encampment.

The younger of the rescued women was near collapse. Li Lian led her to a mattress in an abandoned hut once occupied by a guerrilla slain in battle. The older woman wanted to talk, and Li Lian was prepared to listen.

"Li Lian, I must get the terrible memories out of my mind. I am Mrs. Tan Ah Yeng, and the other woman is my younger sister, Mrs. Tan Su Yin. We both were married to the same man, Mr. Tan Cheng Lock. He owned the rubber estate but made a fortune in the drug business. The Japanese chopped off his head when they stole the estate. They also killed all our guards. That first night, we heard a tiger growling behind the compound, and in the morning our husband's body was gone. We found his head, and the Japanese laughed at us and told us to bury it at the edge of the forest. The men you killed moved in with us. They were soldiers whose job it was to keep the rubber going out to Japan. They spared Wu Feng to manage production. They treated us very badly, but at least they provided food. One by one, our children disappeared. The young girls were taken to the soldiers' rooms. We could hear their screams in the night. In the morning, the girls were gone. Some of the boys ran away. Soon all were gone. I think we never shall see any of them again. Please, let us stay with you. We can cook good. You will see."

The sisters proved themselves at the cooking fires, even with the limited food supplies, and the camp folk were elated when they saw Ah Yeng striding to the commander's stilt house, waving a shopping list. As an added benefit, their initial suspicion of Wu Feng was relieved when he took on many of the hated chores of kitchen cleanup.

Chapter 7
Chu San's War

After the Battle of Midway, the Americans gained control of crucial island strongholds, turning the war in the Pacific against the Japanese. Finally, Little Boy and Fat Man settled the issue.

The Japanese in Singapore were reluctant to accept news of the surrender, and business was brisk at the comfort house on Cairn Hill Road.

———◇———

Mei Lin sat naked on her bed, her head bowed passively, as the lieutenant entered her room. She raised her head and smiled enticingly. He undressed, placed his uniform on the floor next to the bed, and rested his holstered gun and cartridge belt carefully on the neatly folded layers. He handed his brothel ticket to Mei Lin, and she added it to the growing stack in the drawer of her dressing table. The lieutenant straddled Mei Lin and said, "Let's make it fast. I must go to drink sake at *Syonan Ryokan*."

Mei Lin delivered the lieutenant of his secretions. He rolled off the bed and went to the washstand. As he stood urinating into the basin, a gruff English voice commanded, "You buggers are prisoners of war. Pull out your prick, and get out here quick."

The mama-san's voice rose above the clamor. "The Japs surrendered!"

The lieutenant turned in midurination to face his pistol in the hand of Mei Lin. She fired twice and stepped aside to avoid the falling flesh.

———◇———

Mountbatten supervised the capitulation of the Japanese and visited Changi Prison to address the ragged, emaciated residents. The British moved back to Singapore and Malaya and set up a tenuous military government resembling the prewar colonial bureaucracy.

—◦—

Lim Chu San, commander of the Red Brigade, never wavered in his dedication to free the Asian people from Western domination. He met with other party leaders to formulate plans for demoralizing the Brits with surprise attacks on military and civilian infrastructure. His hope was that the people would rise up, perhaps behind his leadership, and strike mighty blows for freedom. He reported that in the final months of the war, his forest brigade was depleted in skirmishes with desperate Japanese units fleeing northward through the jungles. He requested stepped-up recruiting efforts to fill the ranks.

The chairman of the central committee listened attentively and said, "I am sympathetic to your wishes, but the people need a rest after their years of suffering under the Japanese heel."

Chu San waved off the response and said, "We have sacrificed years of our lives in the jungle to bring an end to the Japanese insanity. Now you and others, who have benefited from our efforts, are reluctant to continue the fight to overthrow the Western oppressors."

"The people will come around," said the chairman. "A general strike is being organized throughout the country at the present moment. It is bound to expose the indifference of those in authority to the well-being of the workers." The chairman spoke softly, as though his wisdom and judgment were superior to the hotheaded demands of Chu San, an impetuous man, lacking the gift of sober reflection. He said, "You must remember, Chu San, it was one thing to battle the Japanese to avenge their vicious cruelty. The British are another story."

"Yes, they are rotten in different ways," Chu San interrupted. "Arrogant and self-important."

The chairman continued. "But as colonial imperialists, they did not give themselves over to orgies of rape, pillage, head-chopping, and physical torture. They organized their domains efficiently and brought services to the subjugated people. They built buildings and created parks and provided good drinking water and health care."

"You sound as though you are on their side," said Chu San.

"No, I am not, but I understand their methods. They fostered education, bringing native people to England to be dazzled by their advanced culture, and they even introduced a general sense of civility. The people were lulled, while the English stripped them of valuable resources."

"If you are correct, how can we arouse the people to revolution?" inquired Chu San in a calmer tone.

"We must plan carefully," said the chairman. "The Opium Wars no longer drive the Chinese to anti-British furor. The drug now is supplied routinely from the Golden Triangle, down the Straits of Malacca, to any Chinese who cannot overcome his addiction and can afford a few pellets of *chandu*."

Chu San listened respectfully and then said, "What you say may be true, but nevertheless, we must encourage a drive for freedom and independence in our people. How can men live under the yoke of imperialism?"

"Your idealism is admirable, my friend, but it will take more than a call for freedom to rally people to our cause when they scarcely know that they are not free. We Chinese are pragmatic people. With the defeat of Japan, I am afraid that most of us will fall back into our complacent lives under the supervision of the British overlords."

"We must not allow that to happen!" declared Chu San, speaking with passion. "Get me the men I need, and we will bury the English in a campaign of terror. The survivors will leave this part of the world thankful that they were able to escape with their skins."

The chairman folded his arms and cocked his head to the side as he studied the countenance of Chu San, whose dark eyes gleamed with fervor. After a few moments of quiet thought, the chairman said, "Very well. You shall have your replacements—all experienced guerrilla fighters."

◄○►

Within days, a lorry loaded with armaments led a busload of recruits directly into Chu San's camp on a new laterite road. Among them was Mei Lin, who emerged from the bus wearing a Japanese officer's uniform, with rolled up trousers and sleeves. A cartridge belt was strapped to her waist, and her hand rested lightly on a holstered revolver.

The People's Anti-Japanese Army was renamed the People's Anti-British Army, and hit-and-run attacks were carried out against targets of opportunity. During this time of terror, many European managers of rubber estates were murdered in an effort to disrupt the economy of Malaya.

In 1948, the British authorities declared a state of emergency in order to deal with the random violence of the communist cadres. The emergency regulations authorized curfew, detention, suspension of civil rights, and the death penalty for the guerrillas.

The communists were driven deeper into the forest. They reestablished their earlier contacts with the aborigines, leading them to believe that they still were fighting the Japanese.

In an effort to neutralize this influence, the British-led National Security Forces established platoons of their own fighting aborigines, providing them with arms, uniforms, food, and supplies for their villages.

The aborigines made arrangements among themselves, choosing to be recruited by either the communists or the government forces, and agreeing to consolidate their support for the side that won.

Lim Chu San continued to plot against the British, with Li Lian's tacit, if unenthusiastic, support. She was starting to question the wisdom of anti-British terrorism, with its ruthless killing and destroying and the jungle life of deprivation. She came to realize that her efforts of the past years were motivated less by Chu San's revolutionary rage and more by her hatred of the Japanese.

Much to Li Lian's relief, Mei Lin lost little time replacing her in the commander's bed. Mei Lin also brought fresh energy to the brigade and helped Chu San plan daring attacks on British military installations. They decided to move against the airfield at Alor Star in a night attack on the fuel depot. Chu San, Mei Lin, Li Lian, and two sappers traveled in a lorry with dynamite, blasting caps, and fuses concealed under crates of string beans and leafy Chinese greens. They rested in a field next to a creek, with a water buffalo lying peacefully in the mud.

At night, they crept into the fuel depot, avoiding a Sikh sentry. The sappers set their charges, lit a two-minute delayed fuse, and ran back to the truck. They heard the blast as they were on the run. Looking back, they saw a row of rain trees silhouetted against the flaming sky.

The next morning, a news report from Kuala Lumpur announced that the Sikh sentry was killed in the explosion and fire.

Over breakfast coffee, Li Lian said to Chu San, "How sad it is that we caused the death of that innocent man."

Chu San said, "He was working for the British, so he wasn't entirely innocent. The cause is larger than any single life, innocent or not."

Li Lian felt a surge of anger and knew that she could not continue in what she now saw as mad adventurism. She was twenty-three years old, and most of her life still was ahead of her. She also yearned to see Maimunah, who knew nothing but Malay kampong life. Li Lian had tried to forget her little girl, but the abandoned infant persisted in her memory.

———◇———

Any reservations Li Lian might have had about leaving her jungle comrades were resolved one day when Ah Yeng, speaking as usual for both sisters, said, "Li Lian, I must talk to you about something that has been on our minds for some time."

"Of course. What is it?"

"We are grateful for your hospitality, but the Japanese are gone, and now is the time for us to return to the rubber estate with Wu Feng to reclaim our property. Su Yin and I hope that you might accompany us to help smooth the way. Our husband conducted all the family business, and we have no knowledge of how to proceed."

"You have suffered much, and if you think I can help, I shall be happy to go with you." Li Lian saw this as a convenient excuse for extricating herself from the Red Brigade. Li Lian and the sisters met with Chu San. Li Lian said, "The war is over now, and our lives are changing. Ah Yeng and Su Yin wish to return to their estate, and I wish to go with them. There probably are squatters in the compound, and there could be problems. They need my help, and I no longer am useful here. I request your permission to leave the brigade."

Chu San thought for a moment and said, "Ordinarily, I would not agree to such a request, but I see that you are looking beyond us, Li Lian. Would you plan to return?"

"Will it make any difference?" she asked. "Others have left the camp, feeling that their work was finished with the defeat of the Japanese."

"If you are not a dedicated party member, it would be better that you leave," said the commander.

"I also must find the little daughter that I left behind when I came to join you," said Li Lian.

Chu San raised his eyebrows and said, "I know about your past in Singapore from the friends of Saleh who brought you to our camp so many years ago, but I had no knowledge of a child." His eyes narrowed as he spoke. "You understand the price of betrayal, do you not?"

"Of course."

Ah Yeng said, "You never told us of your daughter."

Chapter 8
Towkay Li Lian

The next day, Li Lian, the sisters, and Wu Feng packed their few belongings and set out on foot to the rubber estate.

This time, with no need for stealth, they used the well-trodden paths through the forest. The first night, they were welcomed in a camp of aborigines, where the headman knew Li Lian well and greeted her cordially. In two days, they arrived at the estate.

There were unmistakable signs that the Japanese had returned after the original garrison was wiped out by Li Lian's raiders. Rubber production had been reestablished and bales of raw rubber were stacked, awaiting transport to Japan. The road to the storage shed was completed, and trees still showed the charred scarring from the brigade's old attack.

Ah Yeng looked disapprovingly at Tamil children playing outside the gates. Several young boys popped a soccer ball from foot to head to foot in the weedy courtyard in front of the villa. It was a relaxed country scene. Three goats chomped on stubbly grass, and two dogs ran out of the compound yapping at them. The gates were open. One was hanging off its iron hinges.

They went up to the front door, found it unlocked, and walked in. "Ai-yo-yo, my damask draperies," moaned Su Yin. The draperies had been torn apart for use as sleeping covers on the floor. It seemed as though four or five families had taken up residence in the large living room.

An Indian woman walked out of an upstairs bedroom to the top of the broad staircase. "Hallo, you," she said. "What you want?" She spoke Tamil.

Ah Yeng spoke simple Tamil from her earlier days when she'd had Tamil servants. "This my house. What you do here?"

The woman said, "This our house now. You have proof? Where your ownership papers?"

Men wandered in from the rubber groves, and Ah Yeng argued with them heatedly. Suddenly, she broke off the argument and said to Li Lian, "Let's go. They understand only one thing."

"Where are we going?" asked Li Lian.

"Just come-lah," said Ah Yeng.

Li Lian and Wu Feng followed the sisters through the rubber trees. They walked three miles along a trodden path and arrived at the village. Many of the villagers ran to the sisters with outstretched arms, welcoming them with warm embraces. Ah Yeng located the penghulu and asked for help. The headman listened gravely. Then he told her to wait in the village, while he visited the compound with some men. Li Lian watched them file into the forest carrying parangs and rifles.

"What are they going to do?" Li Lian asked apprehensively.

"No need to worry. Ibrahim is an old friend. We and our husband always were kind and generous to him and his village. Let us sit under the attap and have a drink."

They rested, and the sisters chatted with the women of the village who gathered around them, offering Malay cakes and cups of *gula melaka*. Wu Feng recognized an old friend and shouted greetings.

The men returned four hours later. The penghulu said in Malay, "Now you can return."

"What did they do?" asked Li Lian.

"They took care of the problem," said Ah Yeng.

Li Lian, the sisters, and Wu Feng walked back to the compound and found it deserted—no people, no goats, no dogs. They entered the villa and stood amid the mess.

Li Lian said, "Shall we clean it up?"

"Oh no, I will hire women tomorrow to do that," said Ah Yeng.

"How will you pay them?" asked Li Lian.

"I'll show you," said Ah Yeng. "Come-lah." She found a candle and a match in the kitchen and led them to a large kitchen closet. She pulled out all the brooms, mops, and buckets and reached down to grip a narrow handhold at the very bottom of the rear wall of the closet. She lifted, and the wall raised a few inches and then came away, exposing a terra cotta brick wall.

The younger sister said, "Ah Yeng, I never knew of this false wall. Why have you kept it from me?"

Ah Yeng said, "You had no need to know, little sister. Now it makes no difference." Then she worked one of the bricks out of the wall, reached in, and pulled out a heavy canvas bag. She reached in again and pulled out another bag, and another, and another. She tipped one of the bags so the others could look in. In the faint candlelight, they saw the glitter of gold coins.

"See? I knew it would be here," said Ah Yeng. "This was our husband's special hiding place. He used the bank for the rubber business, but he made much more money from the other business, and that was how we lived so well. What we didn't spend went into this wall." Ah Yeng sighed with relief. "This was the main reason for our return. As for the estate, we have no use for it. We have had enough of this miserable life in the jungle." She looked at Li Lian and then at Wu Feng, as though including him in her planning. "Well, Li Lian, we never can come back to this place. If you wish, you can move into the compound. We will give you control. If the rubber business becomes profitable, you might wish to buy the estate later. We don't know about the rubber, and neither do you. But you will have Wu Feng as the estate manager, if he is agreeable. The Malays in Ibrahim's kampong were very close to our husband. They are looking after the place now. You are a young woman, and you can take anyone with you—friends, lovers, husband, your daughter. It would be nice for her—maybe lonely, but you could have more children."

Li Lian embraced Ah Yeng. "Most unexpected. I thank you for your generosity, and I accept with gratitude."

The Tan sisters said, almost in unison, "We owe you our lives."

Then Ah Yeng addressed Wu Feng. "I hope you will agree to remain here and see to putting things right. I know you always have dealt fairly with Ibrahim, and he has relied on you to keep the tappers on our payroll. I see that your old shed is still standing. Are you willing to work the rubber again? You can live in the villa until you build a nice stilt house for yourself."

Wu Feng never had thought of a life away from the rubber estate, and he said, "Thank you very much, and if you have no further interest in living up here, I will be happy to serve Li Lian as the new *towkay*."

The next day, a few of the villagers came to the compound to clean up the mess. In three days, the place was presentable, and the gate was back on its hinges.

Ah Yeng said, "Now we must go Singapore-side to see if anything is left of our family."

Li Lian said, "I too must try to put an end to the horror. If I find my old house in Singapore, I could never set foot in it, but I will sell it to help with expenses up here."

Ah Yeng packed the four bags of gold in an ordinary steel trunk for transport to Singapore. Wu Feng loaded the gold trunk into a Japanese truck abandoned at the rubber storage warehouse and drove the women to Kota Bharu. Ah Yeng found a turbaned money changer at the Old Market and traded a gold piece for Straits dollars. Hot and hungry, the travelers stopped at a nearby stall for bowls of Hokkien mee, the specialty of the Kota Bharu food hawkers. They sat at a teak picnic table under an attap sunroof. Suddenly, Su Yin raised her head from the bowl. With noodles dangling from her chopsticks, she burst into gasping sobs. "Cannot be here more," she whimpered. "Home, home."

"Ai-ee, little sister. Calm yourself. We are going home. The bus leaves in the morning."

The women checked into a hotel, and Wu Feng stayed with the truck to guard the gold. He slept in the front seat, holding the 8 mm Nambu pistol that he'd seized from the Japanese corpse at the rubber estate.

In the morning, they went to the bus depot. The bus driver hefted the gold into the luggage compartment and said, "It feels like you have rocks in this trunk."

Wu Feng returned to the compound with instructions to recruit a few men to keep out squatters. Li Lian and the sisters arrived in Singapore twelve hours later, after a hot, dusty trip.

They checked into a hotel near the bus depot. After an uneasy night, Li Lian took a trishaw to Scotts Road. The driver pedaled around bomb craters, shouting imprecations at forlorn groups of tattered Japanese soldiers who labored at bayonet-point in cleanup squads.

Li Lian was not surprised to see a pile of rubble where her old house once stood. She approached a man raking the lawn next door and introduced herself. "I am Goh Li Lian, and I once lived under that wreckage. Do you know how that happened?"

The man leaned on his rake and said, "Yes, I remember you and your family. Your parents are gone, and I offer my condolences. After you all disappeared, some Japanese officers moved in and treated us with great brutality. I am happy to say that they paid with their lives when sappers blew up the house and everything in it. However, the Japs retaliated most vengefully. Many of our neighbors were trucked to Changi Beach to face the machine guns. We mourn them to this day."

Li Lian then ordered the trishaw to Keppel Harbor and asked if any of the fishermen knew Saleh. One of the older Chinese boatmen, operating a motorized sampan, approached Li Lian and asked tentatively, "We have met before, have we not?"

Li Lian peered at him, searching her memory, and said excitedly, "Boon Hok? I never can forget you. I owe you my life." They embraced warmly. "And what of Saleh? I would like to see him again. Do you think I might find him at the kampong?"

"I don't think you will find him there."

"Where is he?"

"Out fishing, maybe."

"When do you think he might return?"

"I do not know. We dropped anchor together a week ago, and I shared my lunch with him. He gave me an extra bottle of beer."

Li Lian said, "I must go to his village to see if he exists and to see my daughter, who is in the care of the penghulu's family. Will you take me there in your sampan?"

Boon Hok agreed without hesitation. "Yes, Li Lian, whenever you are ready to leave."

They satisfied their hunger with bowls of turtle soup at a food stall near the Jardine Steps and departed at noon. Boon Hok guided the boat offshore for five hours and pulled into the estuary early in the evening. They went to the attap shelter and found the penghulu sitting at his customary table with a bottle of beer.

He beamed when he recognized the beautiful woman with Boon Hok. "Li Lian, how good to see you again. What a gift from Allah that you survived the war."

Li Lian embraced Dain and asked about Maimunah.

"She's seven years old now and as beautiful as her mama."

"Where is she now? Can I see her?"

"Yes, she might be asleep for the night. Come—we'll go to the house of Zaharah."

Li Lian allowed her tears to flow as she knelt beside the little girl. Maimunah opened her eyes and stared at the strange woman. Speaking Malay, Zaharah said, "This is Auntie Li Lian. She has come to visit you." Later that night, Li Lian slept next to Maimunah and was overjoyed to awaken in the morning with her daughter nestled next to her.

She was disappointed to learn that Saleh was away, and no one in the village had any idea of his whereabouts or when he might return. Saleh's occasional absences from the kampong were deliberately ignored by the villagers. They knew of his position in the resistance, and the less they knew of his activities, the better they could avoid betrayal under harsh questioning by British authority.

—◁◦▷—

Betrayal of another kind was behind Saleh's current absence. After Saleh's lunch at sea with Boon Hok, a junk appeared in the distance, moving slowly in their direction. Saleh casually finished his bottle of beer and said, "How good it was to see you again, old friend. Presently, I have other business, and it would be better if you left me here at anchor." He looked for a moment at Boon Hok without changing his expression and then turned away.

As an old comrade, Boon Hok knew that questions were out of order. Something was afoot, and it was to be none of his concern. "Very well," said Boon Hok. "I wish you well." He hoisted his anchor and departed, without a second look at the approaching junk.

When Boon Hok was well away, the junk's engine rumbled deeply, melting away the distance to Saleh's boat. The junk pulled alongside, and the skipper nodded to Saleh, who returned the nod. The junk took Saleh's boat under tow and headed north past Kuala Trengganu to an island, Pulau Perhentian, where Saleh moored his boat at a fishing village in the care of the headman. Saleh boarded the junk, and they made their way into the Gulf of Siam, sandwiched between the east coast of the Kra Isthmus and the west coast of Cambodia, with forty fathoms of tropical sea beneath their keel.

They maintained a steady speed of twenty knots for a day and a night. At dawn, they entered the mouth of the Chao Phraya under sail. They approached the Bangkok waterfront and were met by a harbor pilot, known to the crew, who maneuvered the junk to a rotting wharf a half kilometer away from the main piers. Four Chinese in black pajamas and straw peasant hats boarded the junk and squatted on the teak deck to guard the vessel. Saleh and the three junk crewmen climbed onto the blackened timbers of the wharf and disappeared into a jumble of warehouses and ancient shops.

They stopped at a teahouse and reviewed their plan quickly and quietly. The quartet walked through the city until they reached their objective, a walled compound with the gate guarded by a tall, turbaned Sikh. One of the crewmen asked the Sikh for directions to a good local Chinese restaurant; the second pinioned his arms, and the skipper cut his throat. They walked to the front door of the house and knocked. A Siamese servant opened the door, and the four burst in and confronted a handsome Chinese man standing at the foot of a curving staircase.

"What is the meaning of this?" he said, and then he recognized Saleh. "Why, hello, old comrade," he said with a wry smile. "How nice of you to pay me a social visit," he added with aplomb.

"So this is what was bought with my gold," said Saleh. "Your blood is miserable recompense for all who paid for your treachery."

Loi Tak fell, with Saleh's kris planted in his heart, the faint smile still playing about his lips.

Shortly after Saleh's trip to Bangkok, a note arrived at the British governor general's office, informing him that their wartime agent living in Bangkok was no more.

◄◊►

Saleh returned to the kampong and was elated to find Li Lian and Boon Hok sipping Sinalco under the attap at the Indian shop. After warm embraces, he said, "The three of us are together once more. The war created our friendship, and it continues today."

Li Lian said, "What you say is true. The war also led to the creation of my daughter. I agreed to give her up to be adopted by the penghulu, but I did not give up my love for her. I want her to have a good life without knowing how she came to be."

Saleh said, "Our Maimunah is a lovely child, well loved in the village. I have watched over her since her birth and will continue to be her protector."

"I depend on you to see that no harm comes her way," said Li Lian, "and I wish to provide opportunities for her that may go beyond the village."

Saleh took Li Lian's hand and said, "We exist as a family. You may be assured that Maimunah never will be alone in this world. Neither will you. We brought you to the brigade to fight the Japs, and you survived that life. What are your plans for the future?"

Li Lian told the fishermen of her years with Chu San's brigade and of the rescue of the Tan sisters. "To my surprise, Ah Yeng offered me ownership of the rubber estate, and I accepted with gratitude. I intend to make a new life in Kelantan at the house of Tan. I know of your involvement with Mr. Tan, and I hope you can help me learn how to operate the rubber business. If it becomes profitable, I would provide funds for my daughter's education, with something extra to make life easier in the village. If you agree, Saleh, we can open a joint bank account, and I will make deposits for you to use as you see fit."

Saleh said, "I agree to all that you say, and I will tell you what you should know about our activities on the estate. You have much to learn."

Boon Hok touched Saleh's arm and said, "Shall I leave? There may be matters that you wish to remain private."

"No, old friend. We were partners during the war, and my earlier life was of no concern. Stay and listen." Saleh continued his narrative. "I know that Tan married both Kow sisters from Singapore. The older one, Ah Yeng, was like a tiger. Tan Cheng Lock and I met at Keppel Harbor long ago—before the war. We got along well, even though he was something of a capitalist swine. It seems that he was looking for a man he could trust. Eventually, he told me of his involvement in the drug trade and persuaded me to work with him, running opium and other products, mostly heroin, in my fishing boat. I had no wish to be involved in that business, but I was well paid, and most of my earnings went to political activities to free us from British domination. A Japanese agent persuaded Mr. Tan to make opium from raw poppy paste. The factory would be in one of the outbuildings and would not attract attention. I visited the estate, and I know that building—a cinder block structure near the sheet rubber warehouse. Soon my boat sent a flood of *dadah* to the Riau Islands for transshipping to the docks of Jakarta. There, it was sunk in the palm oil tanks of freighters bound for South America. There was a well-bribed chain of customs officials and cargo handlers who ensured that the packets of heroin were retrieved from the tanks and passed on to the wholesalers. The heroin's final destination never was known to Tan. He always took payment in gold and paid me in some of that gold. That is as much as I know."

Li Lian asked, "Are you willing to go to Kelantan with me and help me get started in the rubber business? And can you show me where Tan processed the opium?"

"Yes, I will be happy to help you in any way that I can."

———◄o►———

They returned to Singapore, and Li Lian immediately went to the hotel to see the sisters. The clerk told her that the Tan sisters were given to fits of weeping, and room service food remained untouched. "I think, if you are their friend, you should get them to the hospital. Many local people have been unable to recover from their wartime experience. My sister, for example, never has—"

"What room?" Li Lian demanded.

"One four three."

Li Lian hurried to the room and knocked. There was no answer, but the sobbing in the room could be heard in the hallway. She pounded on the door and shouted, "Ah Yeng! Su Yin! Let me in." She turned the knob, and the door opened. The sisters were sitting on a divan, crying and moaning. "What's the matter? What is happening to you?" Li Lian went to the older sister and shook her by the shoulders. "Quiet. Control yourself."

Ah Yeng regained her composure. "Oh, Li Lian, it's so horrible. It finally caught up with us. Our husband slaughtered; our children violated. Once we were finished with our old life, it seemed as though the whole world fell on us. We've been crying ever since. I can't imagine what the hotel people think is going on here."

Su Yin blubbered, "Yes, we can stand it no longer. Our lives are at an end."

"Please," said Li Lian. "You have much ahead of you. The war is over. You can start over. Don't despair."

Ah Yeng started wailing again. Li Lian slapped her on the cheek and said sternly, "No more, please. Think of what you will do in the days ahead."

Ah Yeng straightened her shoulders and made a further effort to recover. "Ai-ya, Li Lian, you have such strength. Maybe from the hard life in the forest. Before the war, we had the best of everything—servants, beautiful furniture. You saw what those filthy Tamils did to our lovely home—gorgeous silk robes, jewelry …"

Li Lian said, "You also had the strength to share our life in the forest."

Su Yin continued to sniffle and dab at her eyes.

"I know, I know," said Ah Yeng. "We were holding ourselves together. When we checked into this ugly place, we came up to the room and collapsed. We were surviving on your strength, my dear Li Lian. We are older women and set in our ways. It was so false in the forest. Those communists were willing to sacrifice their lives and the lives of others for their cause. We are from the class that they despise—that you despise. You are one of them too." The tears started again.

Li Lian said, "Yes, I was one of them. They nurtured me at a very difficult time in my life, and I felt obligated to them. I respected their hopes for the people, and some were steadfast friends whom I will always treasure." Li Lian paused and thought of Saleh, and Boon Hok, and Mei Lin, and the mama-san in the comfort house who probably was killed for helping her to escape.

Ah Yeng said, "I understand. You are like our daughter. We love you and trust you. After you left to visit your daughter in the village—oh, we were so caught up in our own troubles we never asked if you found her. Please forgive us."

"It's all right. Yes, I found her, and she is a lovely little girl. Her name is Maimunah."

Ah Yeng said, "I see. She was given a Malay name?"

"Yes."

"Well, after you left to see your daughter, Su Yin and I hired a trishaw to take us to our old home. Our cousin Rosi Kow was living there by herself. She was so old and sad—shriveled up and gray. She's not even fifty years old, but she has the look of death. Japanese officers moved into our house, and Rosi became their slave. She cooked, cleaned, did their laundry, and suffered their abuse for three years. She begged us to stay in Singapore and move in with her."

Li Lian said, "You must do that. She needs you. You can live well for many years with those bags of gold you pulled out of the wall."

"Yes, our gold will last for a long time, and you are right. We mustn't just sit and wait for the end. Perhaps I can start a catering business and then maybe a restaurant. The English are back here, and those vile military wives will try to outdo one another with parties and dinners. There should be plenty of business."

Li Lian said, "Now you are thinking more clearly."

"Thank you, Li Lian. What are your plans for the future?"

"My old home is destroyed. I will go north and make your estate my home. Again I thank you for your kindness and generosity. Try to sleep tonight, and tomorrow I will help you move into your old home."

◄○►

The Tans moved in with Rosi, and Su Yin went to her bedroom on the upper floor. She lay on her old bed, pulled a comforter around her, and resumed her weeping.

◄○►

Ah Yeng engaged a lawyer to prepare a document giving Li Lian free access to the estate and full authority over the rubber business. She said to Li Lian, "Let's go back to the house to check on Su Yin. She is unable to come to her senses."

They found Su Yin hugging her pillow, unwilling to leave the bed. Ah Yeng said, "Rest well, little sister. We love you." She led Li Lian to the lower floor, where the gold trunk had been placed on the dining table. She reached into one of the bags with both hands and dumped a pile of coins on the table before Li Lian. "Take this to start the rubber again. Don't count the coins. Just spend as needed. No payback. The rest will keep us for the rest of our lives."

Li Lian was embarrassed and raised a hand to decline the largesse. Ah Yeng swept the coins into Li Lian's batik bag and put a hand gently over her mouth. "Don't speak. Just accept. You can sell off anything in the house for additional funds, if that becomes necessary. Tomorrow, I wish to make you the legal owner of the estate."

The next day, Ah Yeng and Li Lian went to the government center to inquire about transferring ownership of the Tan property. A bureaucrat, recently arrived from England, told them, "You understand that property taxes might be expected, possibly retroactive for the years of the war."

Ah Yeng screeched, "Go collect from the Japanese! They stole everything—our homes, our lives, our rubber. You English let them do it."

The Englishman allowed the storm to settle. Li Lian soothed Ah Yeng and asked the Brit how to get legal help. He suggested, "Wait a few weeks. Government agencies should be in place by then. Since the estate is in Kelantan, you should work through the state capital in Kota Bharu."

Chapter 9
The Rubber Lady of Kelantan

Li Lian and Saleh took the bus north. They made the final leg of their journey by oxcart. At the compound, Li Lian met the Malay guards who had moved into the villa. She invited them to stay until she became familiar with the workings of the plantation. Saleh offered to bankroll the rubber business with his drug-running money from Mr. Tan.

"I appreciate that, Saleh, but the Tan sisters have helped me with gold. I have enough for a while. Let's go to Ibrahim's village. We must start somewhere."

They found Ibrahim at his house. "Ah, you are back. Are the sisters with you?"

"No," said Li Lian. "They intend to live in their old home Singapore-side. The memories of their life up here are too sad, too tragic. But I will live here, maybe for a long time."

"I see. Some of our people are taking care of the villa. Now that we shall be neighbors, can I help you in other ways?"

"I believe so," said Li Lian. "I think you helped Mr. Tan with the rubber business."

"Yes, with the rubber business."

"And the other business as well?"

"Oh?" The penghulu raised his eyebrows.

"She knows about that, Ibrahim," Saleh said. "For now, she must get the rubber business going. We must find a money changer to give currency for gold."

The penghulu said, "You can do what I did. When I needed money to buy things for the village, I went to a jeweler in Pasir Mas. He was a Nepalese and a thieving scoundrel, but he was happy to get the gold that he needed for making jewelry. In that, he was honest and a good craftsman. Indians were his main customers, and you can't fool an Indian with gold, but he fooled everyone else with his Nepalese gems. He sold fake sapphires, rubies, and emeralds to rich Chinese for their mistresses—maybe for a wife, to shut her up. He sold to some Malays, mainly tin miners and a few rubber growers, like Mr. Tan, for his two wives and his beautiful Siamese mistresses—big, shiny rubies, all fake, in fancy gold settings. If you deal with that jeweler, he will try to rob you, but at least you can get currency with no questions asked."

Li Lian handed Ibrahim a bag of gold coins. "I will give you this gold, on trust, and you can bring us Straits dollars. Will you do that immediately? I must be able to pay your people for their services." Ibrahim agreed, and the rubber venture was under way.

When word got around that a new towkay was bringing the rubber back to life, many local people made their way to the compound seeking employment. Li Lian tried to make room for all, and soon she engaged a large staff of servants, gardeners, wash amahs, and carpenters. Li Lian provided the workers with two meals daily, and the gardeners started a truck garden to help cut down on the food bill.

Li Lian and Saleh negotiated the wages with Ibrahim. The workers agreed that he would serve as paymaster, deducting a small amount of the weekly pay for kampong expenses. Ibrahim accepted the decision of a committee of village elders on the amount to be withheld.

Wu Feng recruited the entire village to clear out brush piles and fallen trees. A water buffalo dragged iron chains through the brush piles, dislodging several vipers that they dispatched with parangs. The workers then dumped the debris into a ravine and burned it.

The rubber workers collected tapping pegs and latex-collecting cups from different parts of the plantation, where they had been discarded. They trimmed the rubber trees of dead branches and checked out tapping panels to see if latex still could be coaxed from the old growth.

Li Lian hired mechanics to restore a Mercedes and three Japanese military trucks that would be used for transporting the rubber sheet to the wholesaler's godown. The mechanics also trucked diesel fuel to an aboveground storage tank near the rubber storage shed.

In two weeks, latex was dripping into the collecting cups. The latex was coagulated with dilute acetic acid in the old factory building, rolled into sheets, cured in the smokehouse, and compressed into bales for storage until shipping could be arranged. The tappers were paid for the volume of latex collected, and the sheet-rubber factory workers received a salary and bonus based on the amount and quality of their production.

Li Lian realized that she had to acquire knowledge of the business and an understanding of the economics of the rubber trade that was beyond the range of Wu Feng's field management. She decided to leave the estate to investigate the intricacies of the rubber market. She packed a small suitcase and cosmetic bag and placed her Beretta on the car seat next to her, under a handbag. She had carried the little pistol ever since her years in the forest with the Red Brigade and was expert in its use. It was a valuable companion on her walking tours of the rubber groves, and six vipers already had fallen victim to the weapon.

She drove the Mercedes to Kota Bharu and rented a room at a small hotel. She ate sparingly in the hotel dining room and slept fitfully under a mosquito netting as the overhead fan beat against the oppressive heat. In the morning, she consulted the hotel manager for directions to a private club that she understood was frequented by estate owners and rubber dealers.

She located the club and talked her way into the company of a group of men who were relaxing over their *pahits*. They were enchanted by her beauty and vied for her attention. She found them easy targets for her charm and gained much useful information. In particular, she learned that she would be obliged to obtain a rubber shipping license to expedite the sale of her product.

She also made casual mention of the opium traffic. The rubber growers laughed at that and told her that opium was readily available in Kota Bharu. They assumed that she was interested in opium for her personal use and told her that her needs might be satisfied by a Chinese opium trader, Kun Hua, who frequented a noodle shop in the Old Market.

Li Lian found the shop, entered, and saw its only customer, a paunchy man with wispy graying hair, sagging jowls, and pouches below his eyes.

He sat before a platter of fish head noodles. She approached him and said, "Good morning, sir. Are you the one named Kun Hua?"

He looked up, chopsticks in hand, and nodded slightly. "Who might you be, and what brings you to this humble place? Do you wish to share my simple meal?"

"I am from Kelantan. My name is of no importance. I wish to know if you are in a position to provide poppy paste—ten kilos, if that is possible. I can pay in gold, if you wish, or in Straits dollars, if that is your preference."

He laughed at the request and said, "Do you plan to lose yourself in the dreams for a hundred years?"

Li Lian said, "If you can provide the paste, I can provide payment. If not, can you direct me to someone who can deal with me without comment?"

Kun Hua sensed a strange menace in the manner of this beautiful woman. He held up his hands in a gesture of conciliation and said, "Please, I meant no offense. If you want ten kilos, I can sell you ten kilos. It's none of my business what you do with it. Stay here and have a plate of mee. Have you had lunch? I'll be back in fifteen minutes."

Li Lian sipped tea as she waited for the opium dealer. He returned with a shopping bag, and they completed the transaction.

She asked, "Is more available?"

"I can provide more, if you wish. Are you planning to process it further?"

"I may do that."

"Do you have the buyers?"

"We are seeking them out now, but we are not yet in full production. Are you interested in making a buy?"

"When you can provide product, we can make a deal."

"On what terms?"

"Ten kilos of paste for one unit of number-three heroin. The paste has little value, but there is a ready market for number three. The number four is more valuable. Fifteen kilos of paste for a unit of number four."

Chapter 10
The Other Business

Saleh and Wu Feng met with Li Lian to discuss estate operations. Saleh asked, "Li Lian, how is your gold supply? Do we need additional funds? What did you learn about market conditions while you were away?"

"I realize that we must have money, Saleh. I met dealers and rubber shippers in Kota Bharu and learned that the world market is very bad. With the end of the war, I thought that the demand for car tires would be strong. Automobile sales are predicted to soar, but synthetic rubber is taking over." She laughed bitterly. "What is natural rubber good for now? Rubber gloves and condoms."

"What are we to do?" Saleh asked anxiously. "How about the other business?"

"I have given that much thought. Rubber does not look promising, but we can do well in the opium trade. Wherever there are Chinese, there is opium. The Malays are not caught up in that. Their main vice is chewing betel. Ugh! A vile habit, and there is no money to be made in betel. I also met an opium dealer in Kota Bharu. He is connected with poppy growers in Burma and Siam. The farmers are simple people, like our rubber tappers, but the middlemen are a dangerous lot. We must be very careful. Saleh, your experience with Mr. Tan will be important in this activity."

Wu Feng said, "Don't forget that I also have some knowledge of the opium business."

Li Lian said, "I picked up a letter from Ah Yeng last week at the post office in Kota Bharu. She wrote that Su Yin has more work than she can handle with her sewing. She bought a new electric sewing machine, and

Ah Yeng has opened a small restaurant. But the main thing for us is that one day an Indian man came into her restaurant, and they recognized each other. He was Dr. Virinder Sunteram, who used to work for Mr. Tan. Ah Yeng said he could be very helpful to us and he would bring a letter of introduction from her. He should arrive soon."

"Ah, he must be the Indian chemist I met at Mr. Tan's estate long ago," said Saleh. "The Tamil cook made curry dishes for him."

—◦—

Dr. Sunteram arrived the next day. He had rented a car and driver. A cautious man by nature, he told the driver to stop before reaching the compound. He walked the last mile on the gravel road, carrying an overnight bag.

Saleh greeted him. "Welcome, old friend. I am happy to see that you survived the bad times."

"How good to see you, Saleh. Yes, we have come through the difficult days and are still on our feet," said Dr. Sunteram, a man given to understatement. "Can you take me to the towkay? I wish to present my letter of introduction from Mrs. Tan Ah Yeng."

Saleh took Virinder's bag and led him into the villa, where he introduced him to Li Lian.

"I am pleased to meet you, Miss Goh. Here is the letter from Mrs. Tan. I worked for her husband before the time of the Japanese, and she thinks that I might be of service to you."

Li Lian extended her hand. "We welcome you to the Tan estate. Ah Yeng wrote to me about your work for Mr. Tan, and you may call me Li Lian."

"Thank you, Miss Goh, but I respect you as the towkay, and I understand my position if you choose to take me on."

"As you wish. Perhaps you can tell us how you managed during the war."

"Yes, of course. Those were hard times. I was trapped in Malaya and interned by the Japanese as a foreign national. After the war, I applied for a teaching position at the University of Singapore Faculty of Medicine, but I was turned down because of the absence of documentation and the lack of research publications."

"Mrs. Tan said you might be helpful to us. What did she mean by that?" asked Li Lian.

"I can speak freely?"

"Yes, of course."

"Were you aware of Mr. Tan's other business ... other than the rubber?"

"We know about that."

"Mrs. Tan thought that you might be interested in the other business. Was she correct?"

"I have given it some thought."

"But you would require a chemist to produce the product. I did that for Tan, and I can do it for you, if you wish. My funds from that work are long gone. I never lived extravagantly, but I had to protect myself, and that took much money. Without money, you have no control—over yourself or anything else. The men in this business are ruthless killers, with no concern for human life. That is how it is with such people. The Italian Mafia, the triads—all of them. I faced a crossroad years ago and decided to go the way of Mr. Tan. It was easy, and I was accountable to no one but myself—and Mr. Tan. I closed off other options. As much as I admired him for his industry, I knew that if I ever tried to leave, he would have made my life difficult. So now I am back. You know, once we start on this track, there is no turning back. I am almost sixty now. I have malaria and heart trouble. I don't know how much longer I will last, but if you want me in your business, I will provide service. I would like a small part of the profits—I leave that up to you—and a place to live. Before, I stayed in a room at the back of the laboratory. Is that building still standing?"

"Yes, it still is where you left it, overgrown with strangler figs. Wu Feng will have the gardeners cut away the vines in the morning."

In the building the next day, Dr. Sunteram was saddened by the destruction. "The big stainless-steel reaction vessels are intact—fortunately. But there is nothing else that can be used. I will make a list of what I need, and I would ask if the cook can send me in a sandwich and a cup of tea. We can discuss the terms of employment later."

———◦———

Li Lian hired an English lawyer, Roger Adams, for the rubber business. He accepted a small retainer and agreed to wait for additional payment until the business generated income. He obtained a modest letter of credit from a bank in Singapore and arranged the first sale of raw rubber at the world market price.

Li Lian provided funds for Dr. Sunteram's visits to various chemical companies to purchase the necessary materials—"to set up new teaching labs in colleges," or whatever he judged would be acceptable explanations if he were questioned. Usually, the company salesmen were not only satisfied but expressed hope that they might look forward to future purchases. "You can depend on it" was Virinder's customary response.

A week after he returned with his supplies, the lab was operational. He said to Li Lian, "We are ready to go. All we need is the raw opium."

Li Lian said, "I have ten kilos of paste. Wait here, and I will get it." She left and returned in a few minutes with the glass jars containing the raw material. "Can you get started with this?" She handed the shopping bag to the chemist, who received it with a bemused smile.

"I see you are prepared for the venture," he said.

By the end of the week, Dr. Sunteram had completed the synthesis. He brought it to Li Lian. "Here are two units of the best number-four heroin that I can produce. It's known as *China White*. There was a decent yield from that batch of paste," he said. "A unit is called a kilo block in the business, but it really is only about seven hundred grams." He handed her a small vial. "This is a sample of the final product—for testing."

She uncapped the vial and asked, "How do you know it is heroin?"

"Taste," he said. He showed her how to dip a slightly moistened little finger into the white powder and touch it to her tongue.

She did so and said, "I don't taste anything."

He said, "Wait."

Soon a warm sensual feeling flowed over her body, and she said, "I feel it now."

He said, "It also can be sniffed like cocaine. Don't do that. You may like it too much."

She said, "But you do it for testing, don't you?"

He said, "Yes, but only after purifying an industrial batch of at least twenty kilos. If I let myself taste it too often, I would be lost. I never have taken it by needle and never will. Do you have customers yet?"

"The supplier of the gum will take back this batch, for gold or more raw opium, but he said he could not keep doing it. He has heard rumors of a crackdown by the British. Some of the political people are even recommending a death sentence for dope dealing or even for possession of any amount of heroin or an ounce or two of hashish. It will be very risky from now on. We must be careful. I will deliver this to the dealer in return for more raw material so you can keep working."

Li Lian chose an inconspicuous old Vauxhall sedan for the first heroin run. She drove to Kota Bharu and met Kun Hua at the Old Market. He directed her to a run-down garage on Jalan Temenggong. She drove the car into the garage, where three glowering Chinese were hunched over plates of pork and greens at a table made of rough-cut teak planks.

Li Lian offered the heroin blocks and said, "This is the beginning. Our agreement was triple the amount of the last batch of paste for these blocks. That is thirty kilos."

Kun Hua weighed the blocks. Then he unwrapped a corner, touched the white substance with a moistened finger, and tasted. He smiled and pointed to a wooden crate. "There it is. Thirty kilos. Should yield plenty of number-four heroin. You can do business with that." After a pause, he said, "I should tell you that this might not continue much longer. I have been selling paste for several years, but I can't hold off the authorities much longer. The English have become suspicious of the local Malay politicians that I kept well greased. If things get too hot, I might lie low for a few months. I have made much money but not as much as I could have made with an operation for manufacturing heroin."

Kun Hua loaded the crate in the trunk of the Vauxhall. As Li Lian watched, she felt an arm around her waist and a hand cupping her breast. She twisted out of the man's grasp and spewed a stream of Hokkien invective, which he found exciting, issuing from such beautiful lips. He smirked and came at her again.

She screamed at him, "Stay away! I'm warning you."

Aroused by her anger, he growled, "Warning me? How warning me? You need some of this." He grabbed at his crotch, laughing roughly, and lunged at her once more. As he did, she reached under her jacket, and her hand came out, spitting fire.

"Ai-ai-ai!" he screamed, grabbing at his crotch again as a bloodstain spread over the front of his trousers.

She leveled the gun at the others. Guns bulged at their hips, but they remained frozen in their seats. She snarled, "Don't move, or the next one goes into his head."

Kun Hua gazed at her in admiration. "What a woman," he murmured.

An idea was taking root. She said to him, "If you get these trained monkeys out of here, I would have a word with you."

He waved them out of the garage. "Give us a few minutes."

They helped the wounded man out, and the dealer said, "Yes? What do you want to say."

Li Lian knew that this was a dangerous notion, but she said, "You are cutting down, and I am building up. You have a source of opium. I have some leads but no source of paste. Perhaps we could join forces. It could be extremely profitable for both of us, if you can overcome your fear of the authorities."

He considered her offer. "There is the question of trust, and there is the question of my cut of the profits. What do you propose?"

She laughed scornfully. "Do you want a written contract? You provide the raw material. I am responsible for processing, packaging, and shipping the final product. I have all the expenses of supplies and professional services. You will receive eight percent of the gross sales. Done?"

He had a downcast expression. "I would think more like twenty percent. Done?"

"You buy the paste from the mule trains for practically nothing. Twelve percent, or I will look elsewhere. Done?"

Smiling broadly, he held out his hand and said, "I accept, Boss."

Li Lian said, "I need your three gunmen for protection, even the fool I shot. When he is well enough, I want all of you to come to my compound. They are your people, and you pay them from your end of the profits. I will send a truck and driver for you. Not too much luggage. Attract no attention. I give you credit for knowing how to keep your mouth shut." Then she drove the Vauxhall out of the garage and was back at the compound by nightfall.

Saleh and Dr. Sunteram were unhappy to hear of her adventure. "We are spreading ourselves too thin. The more people in on this, the greater the danger to us. There is the fear of exposure or blackmail by those criminals."

Li Lian said, "He has the source. At the first hint of blackmail or betrayal, they all die. Our friends at the kampong will see to that."

Wu Feng drove Kun Hua and his three accomplices to the estate and installed them in an abandoned stilt house. The target of Li Lian's Beretta, minus one testicle, sought out Li Lian and apologized profusely. He asked if he could be her personal bodyguard.

Li Lian said, "First, prove yourself." She spoke to Kun Hua, saying, "We can process all the paste you can supply. Make the arrangements."

Kun Hua went to the poppy fields in Burma and arranged for monthly shipments of five hundred kilos of exudate to be sent by mule train down to the Kra Isthmus. Saleh would pick it up in his fishing boat at an isolated cove north of Katani and bring it up the Golok River on favorable tides.

With Li Lian's approval, Dr. Sunteram brought in two bespectacled first cousins from Madras as assistants. They had master's degrees in chemistry and looked forward to putting their theoretical knowledge to practical use. Some of the field workers also were trained in the laboratory work. Soon there was regular production of at least forty units of heroin weekly. Saleh ran the final product, sealed in waterproof kilo blocks, down to his old connections in the Riaus. The triads moved the heroin out of Asia into the world market.

◄○►

In two years, Li Lian's drug dealings generated an enormous hoard of gold. She also accumulated a giant stack of United States thousand-dollar banknotes.

Other suppliers offered competition, and the triads sent word to Saleh that there had to be improved speed of delivery, or the business would be terminated. The old boat was too slow, even with a new engine, and the trip to the Riaus took him a week. Now, times had changed, and speed was essential.

When Li Lian heard this, she acted fast. She told Saleh to take charge. He designed a boat with a false bottom and had it constructed in Sumatra. It was forty-two feet long and was powered by one of the four supercharged gasoline engines from an American PT boat left behind in the Philippines at war's end. He would have preferred to use the PT boat itself, but, at seventy-eight feet, it would have drawn attention from the coast guard. Machine guns from the PT boat were mounted fore and aft, concealed in hatches. The new boat was registered in Sumatra as a recreational vessel, with Saleh listed as the owner. The boat had a head, flying bridge, and small galley and slept six comfortably. Dummy fishing rods were placed in rod sockets to disguise the boat as a deep-sea fisher. Access to the false bottom was by way of a small hatch hidden below the live-bait tank.

Saleh took pride in the new boat. He took it out on trial runs, checking speed, maneuverability, and fuel consumption. At full throttle, the planing hull had a top speed of forty-five knots and could outrun any coast guard vessel in local waters.

On the first business run, Saleh and Kun Hua and one of his armed thugs delivered sixty units of heroin to the Riaus and returned with the customary payment in bullion.

—◇—

Li Lian relied on Wu Feng to keep the latex flowing, and he, in turn, was dependent upon Penghulu Ibrahim for a constant supply of tappers. Laxity in clearing the underbrush had led to occasional deaths among the tappers from viper bites, and replacements were needed to maintain production. Many of the tappers were women, who were more dependable in keeping to the work schedule.

The tappers went out before dawn, when the flow of latex was greatest. They made a diagonal eighth-inch slash in the bark below the previous day's cut and hung a cup below to collect the dripping latex. After finishing their allotment of trees, they made their rounds again to empty the cups into a pail. By noon, the latex stopped flowing in the heat of the day, and the work stopped.

Li Lian had little interest in the rubber. It was a front for the other business, but she appreciated the skill and dedication of Wu Feng and deferred to him in all matters pertaining to rubber production. As world rubber prices continued to slip, Wu Feng and lawyer Adams became alarmed at the growing deficits in the operation.

Adams always was welcome at the estate, and legal business was conducted during extended social visits. He learned of the heroin factory from Wu Feng and faced a decision—either give up his lucrative account or put himself at Li Lian's disposal in all of her commercial interests. Brushing aside his own ethical reservations, he cast his lot with Li Lian.

Sitting at lunch in the villa, Li Lian and Adams planned a strategy to guarantee immunity from interference by government authorities.

Li Lian said, "I know in a general way that those in power have certain expectations. I must know how much they expect and how often they expect it. I depend on you to see to it that they remain blind and deaf. Now, what do you advise?"

The lawyer said, "You must have a free hand for the enterprise. That will take continuous payoffs. The Siamese have it built into their system of government. The Malays are learning from the Siamese."

"I have plenty of gold," said Li Lian. "I have given freely to the locals for their silence, but I fear that the bigger fish may come around to satisfy their greed. Give me your opinion on how we should handle them."

Adams said, "It would be advisable that we preserve the appearance of openhandedness as a gesture of friendship, rather than as obvious bribery. I recommend that the gold be fashioned into wrist and ankle bangles and decorative chains that could be passed on as expensive gifts to the wives and mistresses of assorted functionaries who could make trouble. Tasteless, of course, but they can serve our purpose. If this is satisfactory to you, all we need is a gold worker who can fabricate these things."

"Yes, I think that would be a good way to proceed. For the making of these baubles, I have just the man."

Li Lian commissioned the Nepalese jeweler to convert gold coins into an assortment of heavy pieces of jewelry. Li Lian presented the showy items at a series of small dinner parties. Adams discreetly suggested to the recipients that Li Lian would have no objection if the gifts were melted down and recast into ingots—for safekeeping, he made clear.

He made another contribution in recommending that the rubber be phased out over a five-year period, replacing a fifth of the acreage annually with oil palm. The oil was easily pressed from the fruit of these palms and was prized as a versatile, high-caloric cooking oil throughout Southeast Asia. It also was used in soapmaking and in many other value-added manufacturing processes. There was a ready market in India and Pakistan and little fluctuation in the spot price. The Malay rubber tappers could easily be retrained to harvest the great clusters of nuts from the low-growing oil palms.

Li Lian considered this advice and told Wu Feng of the lawyer's recommendation. "Get started immediately," she said. She was curious to see how this venture would turn out, and she had nothing to lose, as she had been tolerating the rubber losses for at least three years.

With the amount of gold that Li Lian had smeared over any officials who might have presented the slightest threat, she became a guest in constant demand at dinner parties and all manner of social gatherings. She was fawned over and praised for her generosity in supporting schools and hospitals. Swains of all colors and class pursued her. She was the mystery woman, the femme fatale, the dragon lady of their fantasies, beautiful and unattainable.

Li Lian also arranged her own grand soirees. The guests were told to bring their opium pipes for a convivial smoking session at the conclusion of the evening, with opium supplied by the hostess.

———◦———

Gradually, the plantation was converted to oil palm, and the rubber tappers were retrained to harvest the palm nuts. Li Lian was surprised at the profitability of the palm oil venture, a legitimate operation without the danger of heroin.

The villa was completely renovated and refurnished. Dr. Sunteram, almost seventy years old, married a young kampong woman to comfort him in his late years. They were raising two children in their new house on ten acres, given to them by Li Lian as a wedding present. She said, "You need the security of ownership if anything should happen to me."

The Sunterams were invited to all Li Lian's social events, but Virinder warned her that the exposure was very risky, especially when she invited foreign dignitaries.

Once she invited an actor who was a culture hero to the local population. He appeared with a gorgeous Siamese girl and occasionally lapsed into the mannerisms of the king of Siam, to the delight of the guests, who kept their eyes on him all evening. He took it all in good humor, and the party was the talk of the Kra Isthmus for weeks.

Chapter 11
Maimunah

The years passed, and Li Lian again was seized with a desire to visit Maimunah in the kampong, but first, she wanted to go to Singapore to see the Tan sisters and sign the documents giving her full ownership of the rubber estate. The Tans left the price up to Li Lian. She made a generous offer that the sisters accepted without question. Roger Adams placed the funds in escrow in the Tans' Singapore bank and met with their lawyer to complete the sale. He registered the new deed in Kota Bharu.

◄○►

Maimunah was ten years old and had attended the village school for four years. Li Lian wished to extend her education beyond the limitations of the kampong school. Adams suggested a boarding school in Switzerland, where she would associate with children of privilege and become accustomed to European society. Li Lian wanted Maimunah to have that opportunity, and money was not an issue. Language, however, *was* an issue. Saleh spoke to the penghulu about moving Maimunah to Singapore so she could attend an English-language school. There were both English and Chinese language-stream schools in Singapore. The Chinese stream fed into Ngee Ann College. The English speakers aimed for the University of Singapore.

Li Lian wanted Maimunah to know the Chinese language as well, especially Hokkien, her family dialect, and Mandarin, the language of culture and diplomacy. The Chinese schools, however, were breeding grounds for communism, or, as its adherents called it, a "progressive" form of government. Li Lian had had her fill of that and would not expose Maimunah to that thinking in her impressionable years.

Maimunah moved in with the Tan sisters and enrolled in an English-language school. Su Yin sat at her sewing machine and turned out school uniforms and a social wardrobe for Maimunah, who had adopted Western dress, in keeping with the custom in Singapore. Maimunah also enjoyed wearing the ornate silk pajamas and cheongsams created in the classical style by Su Yin. Maimunah volunteered to help Ah Yeng in the restaurant, waiting on tables and helping in the kitchen.

She remained with the Tans for five years, growing up tall and beautiful like "Auntie" Li Lian, who visited her frequently and had her own bedroom in the Tans' house.

On a prearranged day in 1957, Maimunah departed for Switzerland, with a tearful send-off by the Tans, Li Lian, Saleh, and Roger Adams, who had arranged for her acceptance by the school in Lausanne.

Maimunah had agreed to return to the University of Singapore to study medicine, but she made it clear that her career decision would be hers alone. In Switzerland, she excelled in her studies and added French to her linguistic repertoire.

Her roommate was Valerie Barlow, the daughter of an English government official. They both were war babies, and they discussed the state of the world as it existed when they were born.

"You mean you don't know your parents?" asked Valerie.

Maimunah said, "I was born in a Malay village. That's all I know. I don't know who my parents were. You might say that I was an orphan, although I am part of a Malay family now."

Valerie looked puzzled. "But where does the money come from? This is a very expensive school."

Maimunah tried to shut down further questioning by saying, "Oh, some of my mother's relatives are quite wealthy, and they wanted to give me a good start in life."

Valerie persisted. "If they are your mother's family, why didn't they tell you about her and your father? What happened to her, and why did they leave you in a primitive village?"

Maimunah flared. "It wasn't primitive, and it's none of your business."

Valerie said, "Oh, Maimunah, I meant no harm. I want us to be friends, and I won't ask you about those personal things. War does strange things to people. My daddy told me a little about the wartime. He has a very important job in England now, but in the war, he was not well liked. He told me that he thinks England might have fought on the wrong side. Maybe Hitler would have been all right, if people gave him a chance. My daddy said that he was a better organizer than Churchill or the Jew Roosevelt. Daddy hated that horrible Stalin. Communists are like poison to him. I've done a little reading on the war in a history course I took last year, and it was so confusing."

Maimunah also had read history in her Singapore school and accepted the interpretations of her teachers. She resolved to do independent reading and find her own way to the truth. One of the main problems she had in understanding the background of the Second World War was her awareness of an ingrained sense of the Asian people that they were united as fellow victims of the white man. If the whites were the common enemy, how could it have happened that early victims of Japanese savagery were the Chinese and Koreans? She decided that the Japanese call for combined action to overthrow white domination was a fraud—propaganda designed to diminish resistance and create a compliant Asian population who would come under the domination of the Japanese Empire.

As she pondered these matters, she thought that her prospective medical studies might be too rigid and confining. She might serve her own curiosity about the human state better by broader academic pursuits in political science and psychology. She believed that there were qualities common to all people, regardless of the trappings of race and culture that influenced human behavior and attitudes.

She dropped her Islamic identity, replacing it with no faith in particular. If anything, she considered herself a humanist, taking people as she found them and doing harm to nobody.

Valerie invited Maimunah to England for the Christmas break. Indifferent to the Christian ceremony, Maimunah sat uncomfortably with the Barlows in their Anglican church in the Cotswold Hills. At dinner later that evening, the insupportably stuffy Mr. Barlow proudly and minutely detailed the laborious rethatching of the roof of their two-centuries-old pink limestone cottage.

Back at the boarding school, Valerie fine-tuned her appetite for brandy and boys. By graduation day, at the age of seventeen, she had a well-earned reputation as an irresponsible drinker and a young woman of easy virtue, resulting in two abortions.

Maimunah went along on a few weekend trips to alpine ski resorts but seldom sipped more than half a glass of red wine as she sat before the logs blazing in the great stone fireplace. She was hardly prudish; she had relinquished her virginity one night to a despondent young Swiss, Eric Jost, who had just flunked out of the University of Bern. He declared his eternal love and wanted to take Maimunah to meet his family and make immediate arrangements for a spring wedding. Maimunah let him down gently, unable to visualize a life of eating cheese fondue and trudging, muffler-clad, through snow-coated Swiss winters.

She returned to Singapore and entered the university, winning honors degrees in psychology and social science. Recognizing the racial divide in Malaya, with Malays pitted unsuccessfully against the high-achieving Chinese minority, she decided to accept a teaching post in Kuala Lumpur. Her goal was to try to impart a sense of self-esteem in her Malay students.

She was respected by the British authorities, who considered her a strange fish in a school of minnows. The minnows, in their view, were the Malay masses, who could be kneaded, they feared, into an antigovernment Islamic resistance by their traditional political and religious leaders.

Once the Federation of Malaysia achieved independence, a parliamentary initiative limited access of the ethnic Chinese to places in the university, including the medical school and in appointed government positions.

Chapter 12
Poppy-Stricken

Li Lian walked through the neat rows of oil palm, greeting the workers and receiving their deferential nods. She visited the remaining acres of rubber trees still yielding latex for the benefit of the older tappers, who refused to give up their mastery of the tapping panel.

She invited her associates to join her to discuss business plans. Saleh, Dr. Sunteram, Kun Hua, and Wu Feng gathered at tea time in the drawing room, now opulently furnished with rosewood cabinets, wall panels studded with jade and carnelian, and silk-upholstered teak settees and armchairs. The men arranged themselves gingerly on the rich silk brocade as they were being served.

Li Lian waved the maids back to the kitchen and poured the tea. "We have operated successfully for many years, but now I wish to explain the expanded operation that I have in mind. Virinder, can you process more paste if it can be provided?"

He said, "Yes, we could certainly double the output if we had more raw material."

Li Lian next asked, "Kun Hua, how soon can you increase the allotment of paste from your contacts in Burma?"

Kun Hua shook his head and said, "That is not possible, Boss. They have made it clear to me that they will not increase the paste."

Li Lian then said, "I will not be controlled by others. We will have to take matters into our own hands and grow the poppies right here."

The four men shifted uneasily in their seats, and Kun Hua said, "That would not be advisable, Boss. They are ruthless people and would not allow competition from us. We are at our permissible limit right now."

Li Lian said, "I have heard your warnings before, Kun Hua. Where is your courage? We can increase our profits, and all of you can benefit beyond your dreams. You can be as rich as rajahs. We are across the Golok River from Siamese territory, and the poppies are abundant there. They are much more understanding in Bangkok."

Kun Hua sat in silence but shook his head slowly.

Li Lian ignored him and said, "Wu Feng, I want you to clear a hundred hectares of the old rubber growth, and plant with seed that I already have obtained. Can you handle this for me?"

"Yes, Li Lian, it should not be a problem, but I will have to promote one of my assistants to take over for me on the palm oil side."

"Do whatever is necessary," said Li Lian. She turned to Saleh, who remained silent and glum. Li Lian was aware of his contempt for Kun Hua. "Saleh, you will be of greatest service to the business if you return to your village and overhaul our boat. We will contact you when the next shipment is ready."

Saleh's expression darkened. "As you wish, Li Lian. We have been friends for many years, and that will not change." He rose from his seat and walked to the door.

———◇———

Wu Feng engaged farmers from the Kra Isthmus to operate the poppy plantation, and in three months, a pink-and-white blanket coated the field.

Li Lian was consumed with the new activity. She had learned that a hundred hectares of poppies should yield about fifteen hundred kilos of raw opium, which could be converted to a hundred and fifty kilos of heroin.

She walked slowly through the courtyard, smiling at the servants' children and stooping to pet one of the scavenger dogs that lurked about, waiting for table scraps. Her steps quickened as she entered the oil palm grove. She nodded to the Malay workers and made her way to the manager's field office in a small clearing edged by oleander. Wu Feng was seated at a teak desk, reviewing a stack of business records.

"Good day, Wu Feng. I see you are busy. We must talk."

"Hello, Boss. Of course. I'm just checking oil-delivery receipts against our production records. It looks like a very good month."

"Is there anything unusual in the shortfall?"

"Still holding at about two percent. I told our tanker drivers to turn their backs while the dock workers drain off a few barrels from each load. It keeps them happy, and the pilfered oil goes back to their villages. By the way, have you thought any more about cultivating more land for oil palm? That four-hundred–hectare strip between us and the kampong is still lying unused. We could easily absorb it into our operation with only a small increase in the work force."

Li Lian stared at her manager and said icily, "Wu Feng, you are the estate manager. I am the owner. Let us not confuse our roles. You are responsible for production of the opium as well as the oil. It is the opium that I wish to discuss with you."

Wu Feng was surprised at her tone and said meekly, "Just as you wish, Boss. I didn't realize that I offended you … but I thought—"

She cut him off abruptly. "Never mind. There may be trouble ahead."

Wu Feng said, "Yes, I know. Kun Hua came to see me. He thinks we should plow up the poppies. Have you decided what to do?"

"Is our crop ready to yield?"

"The capsules are coming along very well. I slashed a few this morning, and the latex flow was good. The harvest period is very short. I had hoped to wait a few more days for the petals to wilt. Then the yield should be greatest."

"Please start in three days," Li Lian interjected impatiently. "I have impatient buyers, and I promised delivery soon. I can't disappoint them. The triads won't tolerate delay."

In three days, more than a hundred workers swarmed through the rows of poppies, slashing bulging seedpods. The white exudate oozed all day and oxidized overnight to the red-brown opium paste that was scraped from the pods the following morning. The slashing and scraping went on for several days. Almost a ton of paste was delivered to Dr. Sunteram and his cousins. They, along with four Malay assistants, worked around the clock to convert the opium to morphine, and a week later, a pungent, vinegary reek permeated the factory area—a sign that heroin was being produced.

Dr. Sunteram supervised the packaging of 150 kilo blocks and told Li Lian that the material was ready for delivery.

"What quality?" asked Li Lian.

"Excellent. The new poppies have a high yield. I brought you an opium sample to try out if you wish. You have become quite adept at judging quality. See what you think of this." He offered her a glass vial containing about two grams of pink-brown pebbles. "I cleaned this up for you."

Li Lian went to a teak cabinet and removed one of her opium pipes and an alcohol lamp. She lit the lamp and lifted an opium bead with ivory forceps. She heated the tiny nugget until fumes rose, and it started to melt. Then she wound the opium onto a bamboo splint and forced it into the pipe bowl. Inhaling deeply, she closed her eyes and sank back into the silk pillows on her divan, holding the vapors in her lungs as she awaited the sweet lassitude.

"Virinder, fetch your pipe and join me, if you wish—and bring Yasmin. This is a good batch."

He left and soon returned with his wife, who was wearing her best batik sarong. Yasmin smiled shyly, revealing betel-stained teeth. Soon they were lost in drugged reverie, eyelids drooping loosely over pinpoint pupils.

Virinder broke the silence. "These beads will yield a very high content of morphine."

"Ah, Virinder, the analytical mind penetrates the opium fog. Well, that's what I pay you for. Now, just relax and enjoy the pipe dreams."

"Yes, Miss Goh. Kun Hua saw us walking to the villa, and he asked if he could join us. He is waiting in the courtyard."

"Let him wait a bit longer, while we do a few more pebbles."

They gave themselves over to their torpor in silence for several minutes. They looked up when Kun Hua entered the drawing room and asked hesitantly, "May I join you?"

Li Lian turned her unfocused eyes to Kun Hua and said, "I have not invited you to join us. This time, I shall make an exception. Yes, you may join us. Do you have your pipe?"

"Yes, Boss, I hoped to try some of the new batch. I also wish to know your thoughts on ending the poppy garden. I am worried that our Burmese suppliers will take matters into their own hands if you wait any longer."

"I have given it some thought," said Li Lian. "Virinder has produced 150 units of heroin from our fields. The finest China White, he tells me. Isn't that so, Virinder?"

"Yes, Miss Goh," said the chemist. "The blocks are already on their way to Batam under a load of cabbage. Wu Feng called me an hour ago from the Esso station in Kuantan. He should arrive at Saleh's village at noon tomorrow. I have saved samples of the product for testing by any other customers that come our way."

Kun Hua said, "Li Lian, I warn you again that our business activities might no longer be tolerated." He turned to Virinder and asked casually, "Have you secured the samples well? They must be kept away from the children."

Virinder said, "They are in the closet in my study. Yasmin and the children never enter. Now, it is time to leave. It will be dark soon, and we must feed the children and put them to bed. With your permission?"

"Yes, of course. Good-night, Yasmin ... Virinder."

"Good-night," said Kun Hua, exerting a slight pressure on Virinder's back, urging him to the exit.

After they left, Li Lian handed the opium vial to Kun Hua and indicated by gesture that he was to help himself to a pellet. Soon, they were in the warm embrace of the drug. They continued feeding molten beads to the pipe.

"Unfortunately, the vial is empty," said Li Lian. "Kun Hua, run to the Sunterams' house and renew our supply."

"Ah, I see that you have a love of the poppy," said Kun Hua. "Perhaps you would prefer this." He removed a vial from the breast pocket of his shirt and handed it to Li Lian. "The fruit of our chemist's labor. The highest purity and worth a fortune in the United States. Those fools—willing to sell their souls for this vial, and this is less than a quarter of an ounce. Care for a taste?"

She caressed the vial, uncapped it, and dipped a little finger into the harmless-looking white powder. She touched the finger to her tongue and waited for the rosy flood. It soon arrived but produced fear and anxiety that she had not experienced before. Her fear became terror as her constricted pupils caused near-blindness in the darkened room.

Kun Hua saw her stricken expression and said, "It's all right, Li Lian. The heroin after the opium sometimes has that effect. It will soon pass." He pushed her back onto the pillow and reclined beside her. They were motionless for a few minutes. "Are you feeling better?"

"Yes," she whispered. Her shoulders sagged, and her hands made little fluttering movements in her lap.

Kun Hua moved closer and lifted her head slightly, adjusting the pillow to make her more comfortable. He lowered his hand to her shoulder, caressing lightly, and then to her breast, waiting for her reaction. There was none. He moved his hand under her kimono and cupped the warm swelling. Neither spoke. Her body remained limp and passive.

Kun Hua fumbled at the kimono sash and slipped the garment from her shoulders. He lowered his head and snuffled like a piglet at the tiny nipple.

Li Lian stirred, turned her head to him, and said mockingly, "Kun Hua, the great lover. You wish to empty your glands, no doubt. Well, be quick about it. The servants know never to enter the room unless summoned."

Kun Hua maneuvered her unresisting body and removed her clothing. He gazed at his prize and dropped his trousers, displaying a bulging belly overhanging his tumescence. He lay above her, gripped her buttocks with both hands, and plunged in violently—before she could change her mind. He pumped furiously, but the opiate hindered ejaculation. Li Lian, beyond arousal, waited listlessly as Kun Hua failed in his effort.

Suddenly, his exertions were punctuated by machine-gun fire. Li Lian pushed both hands against Kun Hua's chest and sat up abruptly, rolling him onto the floor. She stepped on him and raced, naked, into the courtyard. The gunfire continued, and screams were heard from the poppy field. An explosion sounded, and the heroin factory was engulfed in a conflagration fueled by the extraction solvents. A maid ran out with a robe and tried to cover Li Lian's body. She angrily thrust it away. A helicopter rested in the expanse of poppy stalks, its fan slowly revolving. Two men sprayed machine-gun bullets at field workers and rubber tappers.

Kun Hua's three confederates ran from the field office, firing hand guns at the helicopter. The machine guns cut them down. The gunners clambered aboard the chopper. It rose and flew low over the field in a crop-dusting pattern, with white spray jetting from its belly. Then it rose and disappeared across the Golok River.

Kun Hua stumbled into the courtyard, holding up his trousers with one hand. He fastened his belt and waddled to the poppy field, searching for Li

Lian. He came up to her and said, "I warned you—the Burmese. Where are my men?"

Li Lian pointed to the inert bodies. "I think they are dead." Li Lian's adrenaline rush had partially counteracted the opiate, and she resumed control. "We must gather the workers and start the cleanup. At least we collected the opium before they killed the field."

Kun Hua removed his shirt and held it out for Li Lian. She slipped into it, and they walked to the burning ruin of the factory. As they approached it, Dr. Sunteram's two cousins staggered from the wreckage, badly burned and in shock. Virinder wandered aimlessly, wringing his hands and lamenting, "You were warned. Your greed will destroy us all."

"Quiet, Virinder. How is Yasmin?"

"Terrified. She is running back to her village with the children. I don't think she will return to this place. Will my cousins die? What bad joss."

A field foreman came trotting up to Li Lian and said, "We have recovered seven bodies. Shall we call the police?"

"No, no, let us keep this among us. We can have a private funeral on the grounds and bury them behind the villa. Please notify their relatives, and let them know that their silence will be well rewarded."

Ibrahim sent his village *bomoh* to treat the cousins with plant extracts and wet poultices. Virinder stood by helplessly but relieved their agonizing pain with some of the morphine that they themselves had prepared. The bomoh said, "I can do no more. The burns will fester in two or three days, and they will require emergency treatment. You must be prepared to drive them to the General Hospital in Penang."

Virinder said, "Better sooner than later. I will tell the admitting physician that they were caught in a wind shift while burning brush in a woodland."

—◦—

In a panic, Kun Hua loaded a suitcase and his canvas bag of gold into the trunk of the estate Citroen and fled to Kota Bharu. He checked into a hotel and slept fitfully, embracing the canvas bag.

In the morning, he called his uncle in Rangoon and begged forgiveness for failing to curb Li Lian's cultivation of poppies. "Was the helicopter attack necessary?" He described the carnage. "We could have settled the matter in a more civilized way. I might have been killed."

His uncle said, "What helicopter attack? We do not use such crude methods. You must understand that we are not the only ones in this business. You must have an unknown competitor. Unknown to you and unknown to us."

Kun Hua wandered through the night market, visiting familiar food stalls. Back in his hotel room, he pressed the *ah ku* button next to the house phone and ordered a Chinese prostitute from room service. Kun Hua indulged himself for a few days and then drove back to the estate.

He lurked about the villa, ignored by all. One night, he waited until the maids left Li Lian's room. He entered and tried to climb into her bed. She shattered a porcelain teapot against the side of his head. "Leave at once, you ugly toad."

He left sheepishly and retired to his stilt house.

———◦———

Wu Feng and Saleh loaded the kilo blocks into the hidden compartment and topped off the fuel tank. Saleh guided the boat across the Singapore Strait to Pulau Batam and eased it to a village pier in Tering Bay. Wu Feng tossed the bow hawser to a familiar figure standing on the weathered platform. "Chu San, we meet again."

Lim Chu San caught the rope and secured the boat. A Chinese man wearing a gray fedora and a scowl ordered three Indonesian villagers to unload the cargo. "Kalam, be quick and be careful. Fifty blocks on each cart." He counted the blocks as they were stacked on the carts. When the transfer was completed, he handed Saleh a metal attaché case. "The customary rate, in American thousand-dollar bills. No need to count." Gray Fedora followed the handcart procession into the village.

Saleh and Wu Feng headed to the noodle shop next to the ferry slip. Saleh called out, "Chu San, come join us for a glass of beer."

The three men relaxed, sipping beer and slurping mee. Chu San passed a blue pack of Chinese cigarettes to the others. All lit up and coughed.

Wu Feng suddenly stood and shouted, "They have our boat!" The others looked out and saw an Indonesian coast guard cutter pulled up next to their boat. Uniformed men were lashing Li Lian's boat to the cutter.

Chu San said, "No time for sightseeing. Let's get off this filthy little island. Follow me." He led them to a rear exit and down a wooden ladder to the muddy shore. They followed the shore until Chu San disappeared into a clump of mangroves. He reappeared, dragging an aluminum skiff at the end of a towline.

The three men climbed into the little boat. Chu San yanked on the starter rope. On the third pull, the Seagull sputtered to life. Chu San throttled the skiff out of the bay to the moonlit strait. Singapore City glowed faintly on the horizon. With the tension lifted, Chu San said, "It's always a good idea to plan ahead."

The sturdy little Seagull kept the skiff moving on the South China Sea, pausing only for refueling from a one-gallon can stored under a seat. They arrived at Saleh's village, and Chu San remained in the skiff for the return trip to Singapore. Saleh and Wu Feng drove the truck back to the estate and found Li Lian in an opium fog—haggard and malnourished.

They delivered the attaché case to her, along with an account of the events at Batam. She forced a weak smile as she riffled through the stacks of currency. "It's all here. We lost the boat, but it no longer serves a purpose. Wu Feng, you know you have a place here for as long as you wish. The estate still is growing oil palm."

—◇—

Li Lian spent most of the day in her bedroom in the care of her maids. They accepted Saleh's directions without objection but glared with hatred at Kun Hua.

Under constant prodding, Li Lian took meager meals of tea and lotus-seed cakes. She permitted the maids to help her down to the veranda. The northeast monsoon had started, refreshing her with pounding rains. For brief moments, she imagined some of her misery being washed away into the monsoon drains that surrounded the walls of the villa. In unguarded moments, her addiction crushed her spirit. She stoked her pipe with the brownish pellets throughout the day and remained narcotized and constipated.

Meanwhile, Saleh and Wu Feng supervised the clearing away of what had been the heroin factory. The Malay field hands, unaccustomed to such work, suffered cuts from the laboratory glassware. Wu Feng said, "The heroin business is finished. Now we can rest."

Saleh said, "Ah, Wu Feng, It never had to be, and we are well rid of the accursed trade. We must care for Li Lian. She cannot see beyond the glow of her opium pipe. I have ordered Virinder to supply her no longer, but he is a weak man who might be unable to resist her demands."

Wu Feng looked to Saleh as his interim supervisor until Li Lian might find it possible to resume leadership.

Ibrahim stayed in his kampong, terrified that there might be another air attack, but he still assigned field workers to assist with the cleanup.

◦

Li Lian exhausted her opium supply and summoned Dr. Sunteram. He walked through the open gate into the courtyard, where two Tamil gardeners were cutting back the grasses and shrubs that had leaped up under the seasonal rains. The gardeners ignored the chemist, and he looked past them. This mutual nonrecognition was a traditional aspect of the rigid class hierarchy of India, with Tamils occupying the lower ranks and Bengalis the higher. The former carried their subordinate, laboring-class mentality wherever they went in the world, while the latter viewed themselves as a privileged class, with access to higher education and positions of importance in government and the professions.

Virinder approached Li Lian on the veranda and was distressed by her appearance. She wore a beautiful blue-and-gold silk kimono and white satin sandals, but her hair was untended, and she had ceased using cosmetics. Her slender frame appeared shrunken, and bluish veins were prominent on her bony wrists. He averted his eyes from the decaying beauty and pretended to study the little greenhouse lizards clinging to the masonry wall behind her.

"So, Virinder, you have decided to leave us. We have been through much together, but I am not sorry to have our business come to an end. You have been a faithful friend, and I will miss you." She handed him a polished teak box and said, "Please accept this to remember the good fortune we once shared."

Virinder lifted the lid and saw a magnificent jade carving that he recognized as one of Li Lian's rarest possessions. "Oh, Miss Goh, this is a priceless treasure. I am honored to have such a gift. Yes, we have done well together. I have all I need for the rest of my life, and I owe it all to you. Of course, there are those who did not particularly approve of our enterprise, but who is to blame them? It is said that the new government plans to take the strongest measures to end this commerce. At my age, I do not fancy dancing on a hangman's rope. I wish you well in the long life that lies ahead of you. Perhaps one day you might marry. Try not to wait as long as I did. You have much to offer. Now, my dear Li Lian, I must soon bid you good-bye."

He started to rise, but Li Lian touched his arm and said, "There is one more thing. You have supplied me with opium samples over the years—for quality testing. Inevitably, I developed a need that I cannot conquer. You warned me against that, but I became careless. It was always available, and it was the source of our wealth. Oh, I thought I could control its use at one time, but now I know that it has enslaved me. You have given me no opium for some time, but I acquired a few liters of laudanum from Kun Hua's Burma connection. That satisfied my cravings, but now that supply is exhausted, and I don't know how I can face the days without it. I am asking you, dear friend, to resupply me. You must still have opium paste in your possession. Please provide me with all you have left. After all, it belongs to me. I never have questioned you on your production figures, but now you have no further use for the raw material, and I have a desperate need."

He said, "I understand, Li Lian. I regret my involvement in your problem, and I wish I could be helpful. Unfortunately, the attack on the factory destroyed all the remaining opium paste. There is nothing left." He lowered his eyes, avoiding her anguished expression.

"Virinder, I am in great distress. Surely, with all our years of production, there must be something somewhere. Perhaps in your house or in some private place that only you know about."

He kept his head lowered. "I'm sorry, Li Lian. There is nothing left. Now I must go. I told Yasmin that I would join her to help pack for our trip. We are leaving in the morning." He stood, kissed her tenderly, and left. As he walked to the gate, he heard Li Lian's wretched sobs, marking the end of their long association.

The chemist hurried to his house and greeted Yasmin and the children. "Just pack what is necessary. We can buy new things at our new home."

Yasmin said, "The children also are looking forward to their new school. By the way, Kun Hua came and asked for you. When I told him that you were bidding farewell to Li Lian, he said that you wanted him to fetch something from the study. Did he find you?"

Virinder was startled. "Did you let him into the study?"

"Yes. Was that wrong?"

The chemist hurried past her and entered the study. He closed the door and took a metal document file down from a closet shelf and placed it on the desk. He opened it, and his shoulders sagged when he saw that it was empty. His sample vials of opium beads and heroin powder were gone. He instantly recognized the folly of sharing information of his sample collection with Kun Hua. He decided to leave without telling anyone about the theft of the drugs. He could not face Saleh with this information. The Sunteram family vanished in the morning.

Li Lian's maids were distraught at her descent into the agony of withdrawal. They ran to Saleh, begging that he call a doctor to the villa or take Li Lian to the Kota Bharu General Hospital. Responding to the maids' lamentations, Saleh visited Li Lian in her bedroom and found her soaked with perspiration and seized by the stomach cramps of opiate withdrawal. Her suffering was pitiful.

He touched her shoulder and said, "Li Lian, can I do anything for you? Shall I call a doctor?"

"Leave me. Leave me. I must have something for the pain. Where is Virinder?" She tried to suppress a scream, but it escaped her throat as a high-pitched, strangulated shriek.

Saleh shook his head slowly, helplessly, and finally said, "I don't know how to help you." He poured from the teapot and held the cup to Li Lian's lips. She brushed the cup away. He said, "Maybe the bomoh can help. I will return as soon as possible." He left the room and told the maids to try to keep her comfortable until he returned with the bomoh. Saleh mounted a bicycle belonging to one of the Tamil gardeners and pedaled through the plantation to the kampong.

As he disappeared under the palms, a gardener ran to the rear wall of the villa and beckoned to the figure hidden in the undergrowth.

Kun Hua emerged and entered the front door of the villa. As he started up the stairway, the maids tried to block his way. He shoved past them and entered Li Lian's room. He was shocked to witness her hideous suffering.

"My dear Li Lian, we have not been together for a long time. I see that you are in great pain. I am here to help you."

She turned to face him. "Oh," she croaked, "it's you, Kun Hua. I am in such suffering. I can't live like this. Can you do anything for the pain?"

He smoothed her hair and said, "You know you can depend on me." He withdrew a small bottle filled with clear, brownish liquid from his pocket and poured a few drops into the tea left by Saleh. "Here—drink this slowly. You will find it bitter. Let me help you." He raised her head from the pillow and held the cup to her lips. She drank, and he let her head fall back onto the pillow. "You will feel much better very soon."

In less than a minute, she relaxed, and her body assumed a natural posture. She looked at him with gratitude, as her trembling stopped. He sat next to her on the bed, holding her hand and caressing the fragile forearm.

He said, "It's the magic of morphia. The finest morphine sulfate, from your very own garden. It relieves the suffering of humanity. You will be fine. The effect will last for two or three hours, and I will be here when you need me. Now you must try to sleep."

Her eyes were closed already. Kun Hua left the room and confronted Li Lian's maids.

One of them said, "You are not allowed here. You had better leave before Saleh returns."

Kun Hua said, "Look in her room. She is sleeping like a lamb. Isn't it better that way?"

The maids stared in surprise at the sleeping figure.

Kun Hua said, "I shall be in Dr. Sunteram's house for a while. There is no need to tell Saleh where I am. When your mistress awakes, she may ask for me. Then you can come for me." He departed and walked quickly to the vacant house.

—◦—

Saleh soon returned with the bomoh, both riding bicycles. The bomoh brought his medicine bag. They entered the villa, and Saleh asked one of the maids, "How is your mistress?"

"Oh, very well. She is much improved. Don't disturb her. She is sleeping peacefully."

Saleh was perplexed by this news. "But how is that possible? She was in such an agitated state when I left." He paused as the maids remained silent, with downcast eyes. "Just a minute," he said. "Did she have any visitors while I was gone? Tell me—who was here?" They said nothing. He shook one of the maids by the shoulder and repeated, "Was someone here? Was it Kun Hua?"

The maid pulled from his grasp and said, "He helped her. She was so miserable, and he helped her. Please don't disturb her. Let her rest."

"Where is he? Tell me."

The maids said nothing. Saleh went in to see Li Lian and stood by her bed, watching her drugged slumber. In a few moments, he left and joined the bomoh on the veranda. He asked the maids to bring them some refreshments.

"I fear that I have wasted your time, Bomoh. She already has been treated. At least have tea with me before you return to your village." They sat in silence, sipping their tea and nibbling at scones.

The bomoh left, and Saleh went to his room to rest under the overhead fan. He slept for two hours and was awakened by one of the maids, who told him that Li Lian had a visitor.

"Would that visitor be Kun Hua?" asked Saleh.

"Yes," said the maid, "but I was told not to tell you. I don't care for that man. I don't think any good can come of his presence in this house."

Saleh went up to Li Lian's room and found her sitting up in bed, with soup and sandwiches before her on a bed tray. She was eating with appetite, with Kun Hua seated comfortably in a teak lady's chair upholstered in silk damask.

Li Lian smiled at him and said, "Hello, Saleh, thank you for trying to help me in my illness. Now that I am feeling better, you might wish to return to Singapore and resume your life there. Come and visit whenever you wish. My door always will be open to you."

"But Li Lian, do you think this is the right thing for you?"

Kun Hua interjected, "She knows her own mind, Saleh. She built her business on her own. Now she can lie back and enjoy the fruits of her labor."

Saleh's eyes flashed in anger, and he said, "And if her reward is the life of a drug addict? Is that what you worked for, Li Lian?"

Kun Hua smirked and said, "You don't own her. She owes you nothing. Where was your fatherly guidance when she got involved in this business? I was the one who helped her build up her great wealth." He hesitated and then said, "And without receiving a full share of the pot." He glanced at Li Lian, noting her surprised expression. "What I mean is, I have been treated fairly as an employee, but—"

"But what, Kun Hua?" Li Lian joined the discussion. "You have been well paid for your efforts. Do you disagree?"

"I have given years to the business. Never married. Never raised a family. At least Virinder was able to do that." Kun Hua couldn't stop talking, but he looked as though he wished that he had kept his mouth shut. Then he added slyly, "Li Lian, which of us do you need more? I think we know the answer to that."

Saleh said, "Li Lian, no need to answer. I understand your predicament. I hope I shall be welcome here again." He left the room and went downstairs to pack his belongings.

——◄◦►——

Upstairs, Kun Hua moved his chair closer to the bed and said, "Have no regrets, my lovely flower. He is unable to satisfy your needs, but I can." He took a black cardboard box from his pocket and withdrew a syringe and injection vial. He held up the vial and said, "Virinder's final product. I have enough for both of us for a long time. With your approval, it would be convenient if I moved into the villa—to better satisfy your needs."

Li Lian raised no objection, and Kun Hua became a member of the household. He took to bullying the staff, and the cook threatened to leave. Li Lian, with her deepening dependency, marked her days in drug doses and lost interest in the management of the estate. She permitted Kun Hua to introduce her to heroin by injection, accepting the erroneous belief that the intramuscular route was far less addictive than mainlining. Soon their shoulders, thighs, and buttocks were decorated with needle scars.

She offered no resistance when Kun Hua slipped into her bed, but the drugs had left him impotent. On several occasions, he audaciously brought a Tamil gardener to Li Lian's bed to perform for his entertainment. She was indifferent to her degradation.

The staff chose to remain silent, collecting their modest wages from a household fund managed by the cook. In the absence of the high social life once enjoyed at the villa, the work was undemanding.

The situation changed dramatically. The taciturn Wu Feng witnessed Li Lian's deterioration with deep sadness. He drove his motor scooter to the kampong and related the unhappy story to Ibrahim. "We must help her in some way," he said. "I am afraid to seek outside medical help. The new drug laws are in place."

Ibrahim's face darkened. He said, "We must bring Saleh back to help us deal with this terrible situation."

A week later, Saleh appeared and met with Wu Feng and Ibrahim. They agreed upon a course of action. The next day, a gardener appeared at the villa and told Kun Hua that he had a visitor in the courtyard. "Who is it?" asked Kun Hua.

"He said it was very important."

Kun Hua put on a shirt and went out to the courtyard. He saw Saleh walking toward him along the gravel path. "What are you doing here, old man?"

Those were Kun Hua's last words. Saleh stepped in quickly, and the kris flashed.

Later that afternoon, two Malays from the kampong stood quietly, deep in the forest, leaning on shovels next to a freshly dug pit. Ibrahim sat on a rock, solemnly smoking a cigarette. Soon, Saleh and Wu Feng appeared, followed by a wooden wheelbarrow covered with garden debris. A gardener pushed the barrow to the pit, removed the debris, and heaved Kun Hua into his final resting place. The Malays filled in the grave and covered it with leaves and dead branches. The funeral party departed through the leafy undergrowth.

Saleh went directly to the villa. He climbed the stairs and spoke to Li Lian's maid. "How is she?"

"Very sick. She fell under his spell. Maybe she wants to die."

He entered the room and was alarmed at Li Lian's inert form and shallow breathing. "Is she asleep?"

"Don't know. She just lies there. Sometimes we hear her crying."

Saleh saw the vials and syringes and clothing strewn carelessly on chairs and floor. He touched Li Lian's shoulder. "Li Lian, it's Saleh. Can you hear me?" He looked at the ruined face and recalled the Li Lian he once knew—beautiful, wealthy, and in total command of a thriving business, such as it was.

She opened her eyes and whispered, "Saleh? Where is Kun Hua? I need him."

"He had to leave."

"When will he return?"

"I don't believe that he will return."

"But he must. Kun Hua can help me. No other." She looked about frantically and glimpsed the syringe on the side table. "Saleh, get me that syringe and the vial and an alcohol swab. That will help me."

Saleh knew that she would be deaf to his counseling and did as she asked. She coaxed a tiny bit of the heroin solution into the syringe and plunged the tiny needle into her thigh. She lay back, waiting for the drug to bring its relief. "There is very little left," she said. "I must have another supply. Look around the room, Saleh. Kun Hua must have some in a drawer or up in the cupboard."

Saleh searched but found only empty vials. He was uncomfortable, thinking of himself as her confederate, but he had been a drug runner for years—first for Mr. Tan and then for Li Lian. But as long as he dealt with the wholesalers, he was just a link in the supply chain and felt no direct connection to the street addicts. Besides, he saw the drug users as weaklings embarked on a course of self-destruction. He wasted no sympathy on their inability to control their appetites.

"Will you be all right for a while?" he asked.

"Just for a while. Why do you ask?"

Saleh said, "Ibrahim told me about the attack. I want to talk to Wu Feng and decide what must be done to put things right. I will be back in about an hour."

"No later, please. I need your help."

Saleh went out to the field office and found Wu Feng reviewing neglected business documents. "She cannot continue this way. I will bring her daughter back into her life. Maimunah might be able to do what none of us can do. Now let us go to Kun Hua's room and find what remains of his drug supply. Unfortunately, we must support her habit until other arrangements can be made. We both love her and cannot allow her to wither away and die."

The two men entered Kun Hua's room and quickly located what remained of Virinder's old drug samples. They also found the bag of gold that Kun Hua accepted as his share of the drug business. Saleh said, "This is a fortune in gold. Ibrahim can put it to good use to improve life in the kampong. We must also share it with Dain Mohammad. Li Lian must be allowed to think that Kun Hua left without notice because of the termination of the drug business."

Saleh and Wu Feng went to the villa and joined the household staff for the evening meal. An hour later, Saleh heard movement on the upper landing. He looked up.

Gaunt, haggard Li Lian came to the stairhead, her yellow dressing gown lying open and drifting behind her. She peered down and called hoarsely, "Come up, Saleh. Come up."

He mounted the stairs and embraced her, feeling the unfleshed ribs and bony shoulders beneath his fingers. He forced a smile and said, "I am happy to see you walking about. How are you feeling?"

"I am still alive. More than that, I cannot say."

"Perhaps you might wish to go out on the veranda to feel the rain and the evening breeze."

She laughed hollowly and said, "Saleh, you are like a mother hen with one ailing chick. Yes, I would like to go out and taste the evening. Give me your arm, and help me down the stairs."

When they were seated on the veranda, Saleh said, "I wish to speak of Maimunah. Can you openly accept her as your daughter? She has made much of her life, and you should have the joy and satisfaction of a proud parent."

"Perhaps you are right. But the circumstances of her origin must die with me—and with you. Promise me that."

"I made that promise long ago. That will never change. There is another matter that concerns you. Wu Feng and I have located forgotten drug samples that will satisfy your needs until a cure might be discovered." He handed her a small screw-capped glass container. "Here is a supply of opium beads. Try to control your smoking."

She accepted the opium gratefully. "You are such a good friend, Saleh. I knew I could depend on you. Will you stay with me now? Help me run the estate?" She paused. "I wonder how the two Mrs. Tans are getting along. I haven't seen them for such a long time. Well, Saleh, what do you think? Do you want to stop being a fisherman? You should retire from that hard life and live easy up here with me. You can be such a great help on the estate. We are still growing the oil palms, and there is even some rubber." Li Lian babbled on and on, and Saleh listened patiently.

"Li Lian, the opium in your hand is enough for a while. I don't know how much is enough for you, but it is possible to reduce the amount. I have heard of some smokers curing themselves of the habit. Perhaps you should try that. You have made a fortune from the misery of others. Unfortunately, you fell into your own trap."

"Saleh, please don't preach to me."

"I didn't think I was preaching. I have seen the old opium smokers in the death houses in Singapore, lying on their wooden slabs. Lost in their dreams. Waiting to die. Their families bring them little gifts of fruit and cakes now and then, but they would rather smoke than eat. Is that what you see for yourself? Let me help you."

"I am beyond your help, old friend. I shall live out my days right here, doing what I am doing. Thank you for caring about my welfare, but I exist for the moment."

◄○►

Saleh called Dain from Wu Feng's office. "Hello, Penghulu, do you know where I can find Maimunah? I think it is time for her to be reunited with Li Lian. She is your adopted daughter, and our custom prevents anak beli from being claimed by the birth mother. However, Maimunah is a grown woman and may be the only person who can rescue Li Lian from the disastrous course her life has taken."

Dain said, "If you think Maimunah can help her mother, I will speak to the elders about releasing her from the obligations of anak beli. Maimunah is with the Tan sisters in Singapore. She and her Barisan brigade are planning some mischief against the Americans."

Part 2

Mike and Maimunah

Chapter 13
Mike Cagle, 1966

"**G**otcha, you fucker," muttered the racing figure as he cricket-pitched into the tropical night.

The grenade clanked on the tarmac and rolled into a pothole, blasting out a geyser of dirt and pebbles that rained down on Capt. Mike Cagle, of the Twelfth Tactical Fighter Wing at Cam Ranh Bay.

Cagle snapped off a shot from the S&W Special, and the runner sprawled facedown, with a .38 slug buried in his butt. Cagle ran up to him, flipped him onto his back with one foot, and looked down at his ex–crew chief, Dale Collins.

Collins croaked through scraped, bloody lips, "Sorry, sir. Ya gonna finish me off?"

"Not yet."

The MP on night duty in the ready room trotted up with gun drawn.

Cagle said, "Fragger."

The MP held out his hand. "The gun, sir, and the holster and the extra rounds."

Collins had washed out of flight training after a primary instructor commented in the logbook that he was nervous and erratic at the controls. He became a bitter chock-puller on the flight line but eventually worked his way up to crew chief. Collins was a pothead, along with everyone else drawn to the weed that grew everywhere, including the air bases. The cooks even had a special patch of "Jungle Fever" that they cultivated behind the mess hall. Any grunt who tried to nip a few buds would face kitchen justice.

Cagle was an occasional toker himself, especially when coming off the line after flying air cover up north. However, when he learned that Collins had switched to smack, Cagle busted him from E5 to E2 and made it stick at the Board of Inquiry.

Now, only a week later, he sat before another board, with his hands folded like an obedient third grader, while his military lawyer, Jeff Dawson, tried to bend the defense in his direction.

"Gentlemen, when Captain Cagle heard the explosion, he instantly thought of the Vietcong assault on Bien Hoa last year and assumed that a Cong infiltrator had crept up on him as he walked out to the flight line to check his F-4 before taking off at dawn. He immediately shot the invader— or who he thought was the invader—in an effort to save this air base from further attack. In that, he exhibited the highest sense of duty and is to be commended for his courageous action. He had no idea that he was, in fact, the victim of a cowardly act by a drug-addled enlisted man within his own group."

The presiding officer, Major Corbett, rolled his eyes. "Very nice story, Mr. Dawson. You might have a future as a fiction writer. As for you, Captain Cagle, you cannot take potentially lethal action against one of your own air crew, doped up or not. Do you have anything to say in your defense?"

Dawson started to answer, but Cagle grabbed his arm and said, "Sir, there isn't much to say. I busted Collins because he was becoming a menace, and he took exception by trying to kill me. I just drilled him in the ass. He should thank me for not aiming higher."

"Captain, your sarcasm is not appreciated. We are troubled by any fragging incident, especially one that occurs on our own base. Since you were not injured, it's unnecessary for this to go public. Washington is worried about losing support for the war, and we're worried about having you on the premises. There's a target on your back, and the next grenade might not roll into a pothole." He paused and then added, "Captain Cagle, we have already consulted with the general staff, and they agreed with our recommendation that you be grounded and shipped to Singapore for open-ended R&R. If you want to do something about the drug problem in the ranks, you can try to get a lead on the source of heroin sucked up by our people on leave. It's a touchy situation. Singapore has a hard line on drugs. You'll have diplomatic cover as press secretary to a bogus 'Director of Economic Aid' at the US embassy—a CIA guy."

Corbett barely suppressed a sneer. "He's out there on his own and can use a little help. You'll travel 'in mufti' with a diplomatic pouch that should get you through customs. Your hardware will be in the pouch, and you can pick up rounds at the embassy. They're skittish about guns down there, so watch it. If you have a run-in with the local authorities, we'll declare you AWOL. Remember—you're still in the air force and can be recalled at our discretion."

Collins was patched up by the flight surgeon and sent to the stockade to sit on a pillow for a month on an Article 15.

Two days later, Cagle flew from Danang and arrived at Paya Lebar Airport in blistering August heat. The customs officer glanced at the diplomatic pouch and waved him past the desk. He walked through the terminal building, where a sign warned travelers: Dadah Means Death.

At the exit, a Chinese man held up a sheet of corrugated cardboard marked "Mr. Michael Cagle."

"I'm Cagle."

The man smiled broadly, displaying a mouthful of Fort Knox.

"I'm pleased to meet you, sir. I am Henry Wing from the embassy. The ambassador himself asked me to help you settle in after your long trip. Let me take your suitcase."

Cagle followed him to a Buick sedan displaying the Great Seal of the United States on both front doors. A dozen men, looking silly in Hawaiian shirts decorated with palm trees and pineapples, stood in line, waiting to board a bus with *Serenity House* lit up on a glass plate above the windshield.

"Henry, what's Serenity House?"

Henry said, "Oh, yah, that bus makes regular trips from the airport. Serenity House is like a hotel. That's where the soldiers go to relax from the war. They have hamburgers, and pinball machines, and loud music, and maybe girls. The place is off limits to Singapore men—girls are welcome." He twisted his mouth into a smirk.

Henry drove out of the parking lot onto Airport Road, passing through flat, marshy countryside punctuated by stands of wild bamboo and solitary rain trees with great, leafy canopies. An assortment of storage sheds and half-built factory buildings disrupted the rustic tranquility of the landscape.

A sudden downpour sent sheets of water sluicing across the roadway and running off into broad deep ditches. Unperturbed, Henry turned on the wipers and drove on, with rain pounding on the roof and windshield. He turned to Mike. "Southeast monsoon." Henry paused briefly at an intersection and then lurched the car onto Serangoon Road. They entered Singapore City, passing trishaws and the local mixture of Chinese, Malays, and Indians. Most carried attaché cases, and some had three or four gold watches adorning an arm from wrist to elbow. The streets were lined with British-style colonial buildings, Indian temples, and Chinese markets, described by Henry in a tour guide's patter. "More sightseeing, *tuan?* What is your pleasure?"

"Take me to the embassy, Henry. I want to check in and see what the place is like. Okay?"

"Can do. The embassy is a new building on Hill Street—four levels and all glass. Not such a good idea."

"Why not?"

"Sometimes there could be trouble—what with the war in Vietnam and our local people not so happy about that."

Henry turned from Serangoon onto Stamford Road, running beside a busy canal. At Hill Street, they were blocked by a mass of marchers—young boys and girls dressed alike in short blue pants and red neckerchiefs. Grown men marched alongside, burdened with heavy knapsacks.

"What's this all about?"

Henry, unruffled, said, "Oh, *Barisan Sosialis* demonstration. They do this all the time. Communists, I suppose, but they say no, just Singapore nationalists. Anyway, they make much trouble."

The demonstrators sang and chanted as they marched. When they reached the embassy, the men took rocks from their knapsacks and handed them to the young marchers. They broke ranks and rushed to the embassy, hurling the rocks and smashing every window on the lower floor. The marine guards at the main entrance took refuge in the inner hallway but continued to stand stiffly at their new posts, viewing the milling rock-throwers.

Henry drove carefully onto the five-foot way across the road from the embassy. One of the knapsacked adults screamed, "'Merican dogs! Out of Vietnam!" He threw a rock that bounced off the bulletproof windshield.

Suddenly, a beautiful woman dressed in a batik sarong and red kerchief shoved through the mob and ran to the angry rock-thrower. She shouted at him in a Chinese dialect and dragged him away backward, with a fist gripping his collar. He did not resist.

"She seems to be the boss. Do you know her?"

"Oh, yah, that's Maimunah, from somewhere up-country—I think Kuala Lumpur. Comes Singapore-side for demonstrations."

"She looks Chinese, but she has a Malay name. Any reason for that?"

Before Henry could respond, an open-bed truck drove up with khaki-clad policemen facing each other on rows of wooden benches. The truck rolled to a stop. The cops jumped out and ran roughly through the mob, avoiding the youngsters and beating the men with their batons. Many fell to the roadway, bleeding from scalp wounds.

One of the cops tapped on Henry's window and yelled, "Go, go, go!"

Henry edged the car off the five-foot way and slowly made his way into the embassy garage. He led Cagle up a narrow stairway to the reception area at the front of the building, where a tear-streaked receptionist sat at the front desk.

Henry waited for her to recover. "Good afternoon, Edith. I wish to present Mr. Michael Cagle. The ambassador is expecting him. Mr. Cagle, this is Miss Edith Loh, our receptionist."

She looked up, dabbing her eyes with a tissue. "How do you do, Mr. Cagle. It's terrible that Singapore welcomes you like that." She waved a thin arm weakly toward the entrance, just as a cleaning crew trotted up from the basement, carrying brooms and dustpans.

Cagle took her hand, careful to exert no pressure on the fragile fingers. "It's a pleasure to meet you, Miss Loh, and I have been treated very well in Singapore, thanks to Henry. Now that I'm here, is there a space for me?"

"Of course, Mr. Cagle, and please call me Edith. We have a nice office ready for you upstairs, next to Mr. Caruso, Director of Economic Aid. He's a wonderful man and always making jokes. You should get along well." She handed Cagle a small manila envelope. "Here are your official documents, showing that you are an embassy employee. Carry the ID badge with you, and you will have diplomatic immunity—for traffic problems and things like that. We advise all our people to try not to take advantage of their privileged position. Oh, here is the ambassador now."

"Mike Cagle, right?" Ambassador Francis J. Duncan extended his hand. An easy smile softened his air of authority.

"That's right, sir. Pleased to meet you."

"You weathered the rock storm okay, eh?" The ambassador chuckled. "This is getting to be old news here. We have a supply of replacement glass in the workshop—and you can call me Frank. We don't stand on formalities here."

"Happy to hear that, Frank. That was my dad's name."

"I know. Medal of Honor."

Cagle was surprised at the comment but let it pass. It figured—a background search was part of embassy protocol.

The ambassador said, "Now, Henry, I think you should take Mr. Cagle to his flat. Mike, if you are hungry, we have our own little cafeteria in the new wing, or, if you would prefer, your flat is just three or four blocks from the Koek Road market. You'll find some of the best street food there. Try the *gu ba* soup. Get a good night's sleep, and I'll see you in the morning. Things get started here at about ten."

The ambassador returned to his office, and Henry drove Mike to a high-rise building called the Skyscraper, on Clemenceau Avenue. Next to the Skyscraper, people and goats lived in squalid masonry ruins patched with tin and Masonite and roofed over with corrugated patio sheeting.

Henry explained, "Squatters have common-law protection in Singapore. We inherited that from the Brits. If the squatters can sneak onto the land, public or private, and build a structure with a permanent roof overnight—no canvas—they can remain in legal occupancy. I heard that the owner of that lot offered to pay the squatters to leave. So far no success."

They took the elevator to the tenth floor and entered a furnished flat, provided by the embassy for visitors. The flat was spacious, with a large living room, two bedrooms, two bathrooms, a small terrace, and a kitchen entered by a door opening to an outside walkway. The rooms were occupied by many *chee-chaks*, ubiquitous little house geckoes, that crawled up the walls, their tiny toes finding easy purchase in the rough plaster.

Henry invited Mike onto the terrace. "From here, you look out over Cavanaugh Road to the Istana. That's the presidential palace. You might see the president out there playing on his little golf course on weekends."

"What's the president's job?" Mike asked. "I thought the prime minister ran the show."

Henry laughed. "That's our system. The PM's in charge, and he's

Chinese. To balance things, we have a Malay president, Yusof bin Ishak, who has just a ceremonial role. He shows up at new constructions, school graduations—things like that."

◄○►

The next morning, Henry drove Cagle to the embassy.

"Good morning, Edith."

"Good morning, Mr. Cagle. The ambassador is waiting for you. His office is the last one on the right. The door is always open."

Ambassador Duncan was at his desk, talking to two men relaxing in bamboo armchairs.

"Mike, meet Lieutenant Wendell Frost and Ralph Caruso. They know why you're here." There were the customary handshakes and muttered pleasantries. "Wendell is the deputy naval attaché. He likes to know what the Royal Navy is up to at Sembawang. Ralph is our local man of mystery. You'll be working with him on what we hope will be a successful project."

They spoke amiably for a few minutes, avoiding details of why Cagle was run out of Vietnam. Then the ambassador indicated that the meeting was at an end. "Ralph, tell Mike what he has to know and remind him that Singapore cannot officially approve of his activities in Vietnam."

Caruso was a balding, heavyset man with the powerful, sloping shoulders and thick neck of a football player, which he had been eighteen years earlier as an All-Conference center at Iowa. Caruso left after graduation to join the air corps, following the example of campus hero Nile Kinnick, the Heisman-winning halfback who was killed in World War II. Caruso was recruited by the CIA to fly remnants of the old Flying Tiger commercial airline on trouble-shooting missions in Southeast Asia. With the war in Vietnam stumbling to a stalemate, he was assigned to the US embassy in Singapore to try to interrupt the flow of heroin to American soldiers on R&R leave.

"Okay, Mike, I know that you're a fighter pilot who'd rather not be here, and you know that I'm the agency guy in Singapore. A few of us were sent to this part of the world to fight the drug war. I stayed here in the embassy, and the others ended up in Bangkok, trying to chop up one of the main distribution centers. Here in Singapore, we don't chase

119

after marijuana, but the local cops are less tolerant. Anyone caught with a couple of ounces of weed can look forward to a date with the gallows. Hard drugs are where we're concerned. We know that heroin is shipped from up-country out to the islands—the Riaus are a hotbed of smuggling—and then back to Singapore to some remote site in the mangrove mud for a pickup by someone with connections to the soldiers' rest home."

"What happens if we find the supplier?" Mike asked. "We're just a two-man army. Do we call in the Seventh Fleet?"

"We'll figure out something. I've got the middle of the pipe line. We just have to trace it back to the starting point."

"What can you tell me about the middle? Where is it, and how did you make the connection?"

"We have a free hand in this part of the world," Ralph said. "In Indonesia, Sukarno's still the president, but Suharto cut off his balls, and the army calls the shots. Our embassy in Jakarta feeds lists of comsymps to the military, and they do the purging."

"Are they also involved in the dope trade? It's no secret that the Vietnamese military pumps heroin into our troops."

"The triads run the dope business, but everyone's on the take. One of my agency buddies set me up with an anticommunist villager on Pulau Batam—a Muslim named Kalam. I talked him onto our payroll, and he tips me on deliveries. The last one happened a couple of days ago. A hundred fifty units, according to Kalam. I ratted them out to the Indonesian Marine Police, and they made the bust. Grabbed the boat but missed the dope. Kalam told me that the triad guy left a taste for the Indonesians—five units in a shopping bag. The stuff came in on a boat run by a Malay named Saleh bin Rafiq. We wanted to grab him on the delivery and squeeze him for the source, but he made a getaway. We'll find him. There's also an old communist jungle fighter that we have under surveillance. He's a waiter at Serenity House. We think he's at the end of the supply line, feeding the dope to the soldiers on R&R. Our guys are stoned out of their skulls much of the time. When we question them on their source, all we get are sappy smiles. When this rotten war ends, we'll be sending a regiment of junkies home to Mommy."

Chapter 14
South of Singapore

Under the blazing equatorial sun, a sea-going canoe, powered by a battered Chrysler engine, churned northward on the Singapore Strait. Fishermen ignored the boat, knowing that this was a smugglers' corridor, plied by the illicit barter traders of Indonesia and Singapore. South of Singapore City, with the offshore island of Blakang Mati visible in the distance, the stern man cut the engine. Six canoers in batik sarongs lifted paddles from the bilge and shoveled rearward with an easy rhythm, propelling the vessel silently toward the Singapore shore.

A half hour later, the bow-paddler held his wooden blade upright, flexing an arm as though to work out a cramp.

Meanwhile, a patrol boat of the Singapore Marine Police idled at the entrance to Keppel Harbor. A Chinese crewman, clad in a crisp white uniform, swept the sea with binoculars. Suddenly, his body stiffened. He pointed seaward and shouted to the English skipper, "There's the signal!"

"Right! Let's see what the beggars are up to today." With a low rumble, the cutter sliced through the still water and headed for the canoe.

Unnoticed by the lookout on the gunboat, an aluminum skiff, urged along by a spindly British Seagull, suddenly reversed course and moved its occupants to cover among the mangrove roots of a muddy estuary.

The canoe paddlers spotted the cutter bearing down on them and dumped ten brick-shaped packets into the sea. The weighted blocks sank quickly amid a vanishing welter of bubbles and ripples.

The cutter pulled up, and the first mate removed a canvas cover from a deck-mounted machine gun and swiveled it toward the canoe.

The captain shouted in *Bahasa Indonesia*, "You are in Singapore waters without permission! You will be detained pending an official investigation! *Mengerti?*"

The paddlers, slumped and sullen, ignored their captors as a crewman fastened a towrope to an iron ring in the bow of the canoe. The gunboat started slowly, taking slack from the towrope until it rose, dripping, from the water, snapping back the heads of the canoe crew. Then it headed toward the Singapore shore, with the canoe wallowing in its wake.

Aboard the canoe, the bowman sat stiffly, grasping the gunwales on either side. The man behind him furtively drew a British commando knife with a seven-inch blade from a narrow leather scabbard. He plunged it downward, penetrating the soft hollow behind the right clavicle of the man in front of him. The victim collapsed as the executioner jerked out the blade and dropped it overboard, followed by the scabbard.

The marine police lookout, casually observing from the afterdeck, called to the captain, "Sir, there's a bit of a scuffle back there."

The captain turned and squinted at the canoe. "They seem to have settled down now. The blighters never think about being caught. They're probably just yammering about how to get out of this mess." He turned back to the wheel and continued the cruise, picking his way through the clutter of junks, sampans, and bumboats moored in Keppel Harbor. The cutter's bow wave, even at the safe harbor speed of five knots, rocked the small boats at their moorings, bringing forth shrieked imprecations from their occupants.

The gray gunboat, comprising most of the Singaporean navy, was trailed not only by the canoe but also by a choking plume of brown-black diesel exhaust that mingled with the stench of rotting bait fish and greasy cooking odors carried seaward on a sluggish breeze.

The captain guided the cutter to Clifford Pier and shouted orders to two wharfmen in green coveralls. "You two, there! Haul in this canoe, and secure it!" A crowd gathered, watching the spectacle. On the captain's further orders, crewmen leaped from the cutter and restrained the spectators with batons. The wharfmen hauled in the canoe and threw a pair of hitches around a fat iron bollard fixed at the edge of the concrete walkway.

Something, however, clearly was wrong. The onlookers silently stared in horror at the man in the bow, doubled over, head between his knees, and covered with blood.

"Sir, this one seems to be dead." A crewman knelt on the pier, studying the man lying in the bow.

The captain agreed with that assessment and addressed the radiophone. "I believe we have a job for the coroner. Send an ambulance directly and a police lorry for the other blokes in the canoe—five of them. Right. Be quick about it. We can handle the crowd."

Six minutes later, an ambulance careered onto the pier, announcing its arrival with a screeching two-toned alarm—high-low, high-low, high-low. The dead man was dragged from the canoe, strapped into a body bag, and delivered to the morgue. His five live companions were chained together and taken to police headquarters on New Bridge Road.

Chapter 15
The Embassy Group

A taxi stopped in front of the American embassy, and its passenger stepped out and walked to the main entrance. He carried himself with jaw-jutting military authority, reinforced by an aggressive brown mustache. The man nodded to the marine guards, and they nodded in return.

At the reception desk, Edith Loh smiled and said, "Good morning, Major."

"Good morning, Edith."

He entered an office marked Deputy Naval Attaché, where Lieutenant Frost, cool in his short-sleeved tropical uniform, sat at a heavy teak desk, sipping an iced drink. Framed photographs of Butch Halsey and President Johnson hung on the wall behind him.

Frost greeted the visitor. "Right on time, Clark. Take a seat, and I'll call Ralph." He spoke briefly into a desk telephone. "He'll be right in."

The office door opened, and Ralph Caruso entered, followed by Mike Cagle. Caruso introduced Cagle to Billadow. "Mike's new on the job."

Major Clark Billadow, of Australian Military Intelligence, also was investigating the increased heroin addiction of the Aussies fighting alongside the Americans in the jungles and paddy fields of Vietnam. He and Caruso had an abrasive relationship but shared information and resources.

"Well, gentlemen," began Lieutenant Frost, "have you come up with anything since our last meeting."

Billadow spoke first. "You blokes know that I'm at a real disadvantage in this operation. The troops in the field can buy heroin at roadside stands out there. The locals are like kids selling lemonade on a hot summer day. The

125

dope traffic is controlled by the South Vietnamese big shots, whom you don't want to lean on because they're part of the great crusade against communism. My hands are tied. I can't protect my own troops without blowing the whistle on the corrupt government that we are fighting to preserve. Half the soldiers are hopeless addicts, and they got that way on number-three heroin. It's pouring out of the jungle factories, and you are doing nothing to stop it." He paused, visibly angered, and looked directly at Caruso.

"I'm one guy," said Caruso. "I'm not the army, and I'm not the candy-asses in Washington. I know you have a touchy situation, but you've had it for years. What did your people in Canberra do to cut back on the flood of opium to Australia?"

"Hold it. You know what that was about. Where there are Chinese, there is opium. Your Chinese railroad workers used it for the long hard nights without women, and so did ours. It was a trade-off. We both turned a blind eye. A little hypocrisy for a lot of cheap labor. But you know what my problem is. It isn't the opium traffic. It's the heroin addiction in the ranks. Your boys on leave in Sydney bring in tons of heroin and spread it all over the city, turning it into a bloody whorehouse. We can try to put a stop to it with strong-arm tactics, but our own politicians and your military leaders don't want to rock the boat. What the hell are we supposed to do?"

Caruso rested his forearms on the table. "Cool down, Clark. You know our job description. It's not to take on the entire dope empire of the Vietnamese military along with the Shan and Kachin warlords in the Golden Triangle. Our assignment is to clip a loose thread of the distribution network—the one that ships a dozen kilo blocks from the Riaus to some mudhole on the Singapore coast. The stuff gets to our soldiers—Americans and Australians—on leave for a bit of a rest cure in the Lion City. Of course, it's like shoveling shit against the tide, trying to get the soldier boys to give up their dadah in favor of a few snappy games of ping-pong, but that's what the ambassador wants—and here, he's the boss. What we can hope to do is cut off the supply line. But first, we have to find it."

"We may be closing in," said Frost. "That canoe that was towed in by the marine police last Sunday came from Batam, as you both know. I don't know how long they managed to elude the patrols, but we have them now—except for the dead man. We have a cover story for that. I think it will fly. The Singapore people are still investigating, but so far the guys in the canoe have clammed up. They dumped the stuff overboard when the patrol boat showed up, so they think they can't be tried for dope-running. We want the suppliers' suppliers. Anything more at your end, Ralph?"

Caruso sat back in his chair and gave his report. "We know that the canoe was the last leg of the delivery to our guys resting up in Singapore. The blocks that were dumped overboard were peeled off a big shipment that was on its way into the international dope market. The triads control the village where the units were delivered. A motor launch ran the stuff down from a jungle factory up-country. You know that the dead man, Kalam, was our asset. He told me that the last delivery was 150 units of number four that he helped unload at Pulau Batam. I tipped off the Indonesian Coast Patrol, and they grabbed the boat but missed the dope. Kalam said that they were on the take for five units. He also tipped me on the canoe delivery of ten units. He was worried about his safety when he was ordered to lead the canoe paddlers. I assured him that we would protect him. Well, we didn't, and he's dead, and I'm responsible. The Singapore Marine Police told the canoe crew that they had recovered one of the blocks, and if they didn't want their necks stretched, they had better name their supplier. The local cops transferred them to Changi Prison and sent a message by marching them past the gallows. That's probably pointless. The paddlers are simple villagers who would have no idea where the stuff came from."

<hr>

After lunch, the meeting resumed in the ambassador's office. He said, "We do what we can, gentlemen. Ralph, what's the status of the Benevolent Fund?"

"Still solvent. It's in my desk drawer."

"How far can we stretch it? Enough for his wife and—how many children?"

"Four kids—and Kalam's father. He lives with them. I'll deliver it myself when we return the body."

"That's fine. The body will stay in the morgue until after the coroner's inquest. The Indian High Commissioner will make the official arrangements. He's had his finger in everything since Confrontation. Things get clumsy with no diplomatic contact between Singapore and Indonesia."

The ambassador turned his attention to Cagle. "Now you know as much about this sad story as the rest of us. We'll work with the Singapore Marine Police, but they're less cooperative than we would have liked. They're jealous of their authority—afraid that we'll take over and run the show. Any questions?"

"Not yet. Just tell me how I can help."

"Ralph can fill you in."

Caruso said, "Mike, I'd like you to get started on Sunday at Serenity House. That's where our guys spend most of their time on R&R. They're only there for five days, but that's where they find a connection. They disappear when I show up, so I can't penetrate the supply line. You're fresh meat, so you might have better luck. Go in with your credentials as press secretary, and try to interview as many as possible. Check out one of our loaners in the garage. There's an old Ford Consul that's in pretty good shape."

Chapter 16
Serenity House

The following Sunday, Cagle drove to Serenity House. The main entrance was framed with winking green and red neon tubes that clashed with the stodgy British colonial architecture. A sandwich board announced, "Sunday Tea Dance Featuring Jimmy Hung and the Whirlwinds."

Cagle entered a large reception area and felt the stab of air conditioning through his sweaty shirt. The atmosphere was heavy with a familiar weedy aroma, and four banks of ceiling lights cast hard fluorescence on the rattan sofa and easy chairs that held a few vacationers, slouching and smoking. One of them was studying a roach clip. A hyperamped rock beat filled the space with a note-perfect copy of a Rolling Stones tune. The source of the sound was at the far end of the hall, behind swinging double doors outlined with neon lights that matched those outside.

"Can I help you?" asked a woman seated at a small desk next to the entrance. "Are you registered with us?"

Cagle turned to the voice and saw a Chinese woman with cropped black hair, streaked with gray, and bright red lips splashed on a worn face that once might have been considered attractive.

"No, I'm from the American embassy to see if I can be of any help to our servicemen—make sure that they stay in touch with their families back home, that sort of thing."

"You have identification?"

"Yes, of course," he said, flashing the embassy ID.

A man in a Hawaiian shirt entered from the street and walked to the front desk. "Mei Lin, do you have something for me?"

"No, no, another time," said the receptionist. "Go now." She waved a hand to send him away as he started to protest.

Cagle walked into the smoky club room. Jimmy Hung and the Whirlwinds performed on an elevated stage, and Hawaiian-shirted men sat at a dozen tables and several settees. Many embraced young Malay girls in batik sarongs. A few couples danced mechanically, weaving among the tables. Two of the tables were occupied by black men clutching skinny Chinese women dressed in glittering cheongsams.

Cagle stood inconspicuously in a shaded corner, looking over the head-bobbing assemblage. A Chinese waiter with a creased ochre face moved from table to table, jotting orders in a spiral notebook. Suddenly, angry voices rose above the music. Chairs scraped the floor as two vacationers leaped up, shouting obscenities at the waiter.

"Thievin' Chink!"

The waiter stood calmly as one of the shouters lunged at him. The waiter coiled, whirled, and kicked out in an effortless maneuver. The kickee smashed glasses beneath him as he slid across the table onto the floor, screaming. His blood varnished the teak parquet.

Mei Lin burst through the swinging doors and ran to the waiter, shouting, "Chu San, you fool," followed by a stream of Chinese invective. She gripped Chu San by his shirt front and dragged him to the reception area.

The victim of Chu San's attack lay supine, quivering and struggling for breath. His table companion turned him over, revealing glass shards impaling bloody palm trees and pineapples.

Cagle ran to the wounded man and shouted, using his officer's voice, "Don't touch him! You, there—tell the front desk to call an ambulance."

The fallen man was trying to push himself to a sitting position.

Mei Lin ran up and said, "Lie quiet. We help you." She turned to Cagle and said, "You embassy fella, ambulance take too long. You got a car? We take him to the hospital."

Mei Lin wrapped the man in a tablecloth, and Cagle eased him out of the building and into the Consul. Mei Lin shouted directions to the general hospital. "Go, go. New Bridge, all the way to Hospital Road. No need to tell police."

Cagle and Mei Lin maneuvered the moaning victim into the emergency room of the Singapore General Hospital. A Hakka woman, topped by the traditional red headdress, followed them, mopping up blood drips. The physician on duty in the ER glanced at the staggering patient and said, "Ah, bleeding like a stuck pig, as you English say." He gestured to two attendants, who loaded the victim onto a gurney. "Quick—into OR 3." He turned to Cagle. "I'm Dr. Chow Teow Seng, and I assume you are his friend."

"Not exactly; we just met. I'm Mike Cagle from the US embassy. We try to take care of our people on leave here. His dogtag says he's Floyd Tuttle. I'll drop by tomorrow to see how he's doing."

Dr. Chow said, "Please excuse me. I go to work."

Back at the embassy, Cagle described the incident. "The woman seemed to be in charge, but that Chinese waiter was dangerous. Our guy never had a chance."

Caruso nodded and said, "Oh yeah, I know the waiter. They answered our ad and came in recommended by a former member of the Singapore parliament, who was part of the Barisan Sosialis minority. Mei Lin and Lim Chu San were jungle fighters against the Japanese and communist guerrillas after the war. We took them on to keep them under surveillance. What was the beef between our guy and Chu San?"

"Not sure, but Tuttle probably thought he was cheated by the waiter. Overcharged for a beer, maybe?"

Caruso lifted an eyebrow and said, "Not so sure about that. We think Chu San is involved in the heroin pipeline in Singapore. He's on a list that the Brits turned over to us. They're leaving, and we're staying. They traced the guy's history. He's descended from the Teochows in the Riaus, who ran the opium trade in Southeast Asia."

Chapter 17
Dr. Chow

Dr. Chow spent the morning on clinical rounds with a group of third-year medical students. He returned to his office and stopped at the reception desk. "Miss Lu, if there are any calls, I'll be at lunch in the Alumni Center."

"One moment, Doctor. A gentleman from the American embassy just arrived. He has no appointment."

"Ah yes, I was expecting him. Please show him into my office."

Cagle greeted Dr. Chow and asked, "What can you tell me about Corporal Tuttle?"

"He had a pneumothorax—collapsed lung. I patched him up with about forty stitches, and he should be okay—just lost a pint of blood. But he's disruptive, demanding more painkillers than we think is necessary. We notified your embassy that they will receive an invoice from our billing department. Now I'm on my way to lunch at the Alumni Center. Care to join me? You might meet some interesting people."

"Thanks, but first I want to see him for a minute."

Cagle found Tuttle sitting in his room, wrapped in a hospital robe and twisting a towel. "Hello, Corporal. I'm from the embassy. I brought you in yesterday. Any way I can help you?"

"Get me some painkillers, or get the hell out."

"Take it easy. What was the problem with Chu San?"

"That sonovabitch. I'm gonna kill him. I got nothing to say."

———◦———

Dr. Chow escorted Cagle from the air-conditioned iciness of the hospital lobby into the fierce midday heat and into the air-conditioned iciness of the Alumni Center, where they were greeted by the clicking of mah-jongg tiles from a side room. Many of the diners were chopsticking bowls of noodles and prawns sambal, carefully avoiding dangling stethoscopes.

Teow Seng introduced Cagle to his regular lunch companions, who greeted him cordially and competed to add to his knowledge of Singapore. There was, however, a caustic edge to some of the conversation.

Dr. Keng, a professor of pediatrics, was especially pointed in commenting on the American involvement in Vietnam. He said, "Mike, are you enjoying your stay in our country?"

"Yes, very much."

"Well, tell me," said Dr. Keng, "are you at all bothered by the knowledge that five hundred miles north of here, your armies are slaughtering thousands of innocent men, women, and children for no reason other than to swell the profits of your war factories?"

The others at the table concentrated on their mee bowls, concealing their embarrassment at Dr. Keng's remarks. Keng ignored his table companions and pressed on. "I wonder how you happen to be here. You are a young man. Why aren't you up there in the killing fields?"

Cagle controlled his anger and said, "If they want me, they know where to find me. I understand how you feel, Dr. Keng, and I don't know why we got in so deep in Vietnam. I regret all the killing, but I'm not ready to turn on my country just to satisfy critics in this part of the world."

The tension was broken by Dr. Borgos, an internist of Portuguese Malayan ancestry, who was president of the Singapore Medical Society.

Dr. Borgos peered at Dr. Keng and said, "Are you asking this young man to defend US policy? Or to condemn it? His government is satisfied with his work at the embassy. Let it go. Save some of your criticism for your own country. You are aware, as are all of us, that American soldiers are sent from Vietnam to Singapore for a few days of R&R. They are pretty much confined to Serenity House or to a remote villa out of sight of us Singaporeans. When they go on shopping tours, they are 'in mufti,' so we are spared the sight of American soldiers in uniform. It preserves our illusion of neutrality. There also is covert delivery of fuel for the American military forces from tankers moored in the outer roads, well offshore and beyond the view of the local citizenry. It's no secret that lighters transfer the fuel to the Shell tanks on *Pulau Bukum* for later delivery to the combat zone. That operation is even coordinated by our deputy PM. We all know that, but we choose to look the other way. Our hands are dirty in this dirty war as well."

Dr. Keng rose and excused himself from the table.

As they walked back to the hospital, Teow Seng offered some background on the exchange at lunch. "Dr. Keng can't help himself. He was a guerrilla fighter during the Japanese occupation and fought the British after the war. He was a committed communist and still harbors a slight hope for a takeover of the Singapore government by the Barisan Sosialis."

"Well, at least he's consistent in his beliefs, but what about Dr. Borgos?"

Teow Seng laughed and said, "Borgos—a good doctor and a successful businessman. He practices medicine on the private side. He also lived through the occupation. When drugs became scarce under Japanese rule, Borgos set up a pots-and-pans drug factory in the back room of his medical suite. He made simple drugs that relieved pain—most likely crude morphine from some private source of opium paste. The small income from this activity eased his existence. Of course, if the Japanese had found him out, he would have paid with his life. Now he's taking advantage of his pharmaceutical background. He both prescribes and dispenses drugs, putting him in direct conflict with the apothecaries. They're an unhappy lot."

Chapter 18
The Coroner's Court

The first coroner, Dr. Wilfred Pickles, slouched into the courtroom trailed by a faint whiff of formalin and wearing a frown that suggested he would rather have been elsewhere. Pickles was a tall, round-shouldered Oxonian, who settled for a postwar appointment as HM Coroner after being trapped in Singapore under Japanese occupation. He sat at the bench, peering over his spectacles at the man shuffling notes at a side table. Caruso and Cagle sat in the rear row of the sparsely attended proceedings. A press representative sat near them, scribbling in a spiral-bound notebook, as the first coroner described the case before the court.

"This inquiry concerns the death of an Indonesian subject, removed by the marine police from a long-tail canoe illegally traversing Singapore waters. The man bled to death from a wound that punctured the aortic arch. There appears to be some uncertainty on the cause of the wound, but it might have occurred through an accident—an unusual accident, to be sure, but an accident." He nodded in the direction of the man at the table and said, "Dr. Sugai, kindly proceed with your postmortem findings."

Dr. Sugai rose and addressed the first coroner. "Sir, this is a fact-finding inquiry on the cause of death. I hope you haven't drawn conclusions before I have presented the results of my postmortem examination."

The first coroner peered at the speaker and said, "Dr. Sugai, I am aware of proper procedure. Please identify yourself for the record and present your findings."

"Thank you. I am Dr. Takumi Sugai, professor of pathology at the University of Singapore Medical Faculty, and Deputy Medical Examiner in the offices of the first coroner. I performed a postmortem examination on an Indonesian national named Slamat Kalam. He was the lead paddler in a six-man canoe intercepted by the marine police and towed to Clifford Pier. However, Kalam was dead on arrival, with a deep stab wound just behind the right clavicle, coursing downward to penetrate the aortic loop. I probed the wound, and it was seven inches deep, without much taper. I dissected down to the bottom of the wound and found a splinter of fresh bone about an inch long that matches a groove on the inner surface of the right clavicle. The wound was consistent with a forceful downstroke by a pointed weapon—perhaps a stiletto. It is my opinion that the man's death was a homicide, most likely committed by the man seated behind the victim." After further postmortem details, he handed a manila folder to the first coroner. "Here is my report. Will there be anything else?"

The first coroner said, "Since no weapon was found, it might be prudent to leave this case open. The man died of exsanguination, but we cannot say how the wound might have occurred. For example, we might consider the possibility that the deceased might have been impaled by a garfish, commonly seen hurtling through the air at great speed. If that occurred, the bone chip might actually have been a section of the jaw of the garfish. Dr. Sugai, have you fixed and mounted sections of the splinter to determine if it actually was human bone?"

Dr. Sugai said, "With due respect, Dr. Pickles, are you actually proposing a scenario in which a garfish might have flown through the air and hit the man in the neck? Anyone who has spent any time in a boat probably has witnessed garfish leaping from the water in a flat trajectory, but it is highly unlikely that such a fish, even with its long, bony jaw, could have driven itself vertically down into the man's thoracic cavity. The wound was so deep that the fish would have had to have penetrated past its gills and would have remained in the man until the canoe was towed to port. The entry wound also would have been very wide, and that was not the case. No, I don't see this as a fish projectile. I think the man was murdered. Why he was murdered is for the police to determine. As to the histology, I have ultrathin sections of the bone fragment, decalcified and stained. You may see for yourself." He lifted a microscope onto the table and removed a slide box from his attaché case.

The first coroner paused briefly and said, "That won't be necessary.

The cause of the injury cannot be determined with certainty. If additional information comes forth, however, I shall be prepared to reconsider my opinion. This inquiry is concluded."

After the first coroner left the bench, Cagle said, "That was weird. What's it all about?"

Caruso smiled and said, "That's our cover story. We want the story to fade away. The first coroner agreed to go along with it, but he was not a happy coroner. Let's drop by Bugis Street tonight and see who's getting ripped off."

Chapter 19
Bugis Street

At midnight, Cagle and Caruso walked into the sights, sounds, and smells of Bugis Street, a neon-flooded magnet for tourists and their predators. The street was a narrow pedestrian walkway, lined on both sides by food vendors. A single row of bistro tables ran down the center line. The tables were occupied, for the most part, by Europeans, who were constantly harassed by individuals of uncertain gender, clad as women of uncertain virtue. Ralph and Mike ordered chicken rice at a *makan* stall and sat at a vacant table, surveying the scene. A beautiful, torpedo-breasted young person, with purple eyelids and a garish red smile, stopped in front of Cagle and shouted, "Hey, Johnny, buy me a drink!"

Caruso said, "There you go, Mike. You made it with the *kai tai*. Don't be surprised at what you find between its legs. Oh, Christ, the fleet's in. The Kiwis are at it again. The Dance of the Flaming Arseholes."

On the roof of the notorious toilet block of Bugis Street, two naked young men, with trousers at their ankles, shuffled about with fiery tails, cheered on by an enthusiastic audience. The tails were rolled pages of the *Eastern Sun*, ablaze, and held between buttocks cheeks. This was a contest, fueled by an evening at a matelot's pub, in which the one who held out longest with second-degree burns collected a hatful of Straits dollars.

Suddenly, Cagle said, "Ralph, there he is—Chu San, heading for the toilet. I'm going in."

"Hold it, Mike," Caruso said, but Cagle already was moving into the stench of the toilet block. A Tamil attendant sat at a small wooden table near the entrance, guarding a tip jar that held a few coins. The toilet stalls were occupied, and Chu San could not be seen. At the far end, a kai tai was in a heated discussion with a plump Englishman wearing plaid shorts. The plump one took offense and slapped the kai tai, who instantly delivered a knee to the groin, followed by a swift karate chop to the side of the neck, sending the victim sprawling into a puddle of urine on the cement floor. The kai tai walked past Cagle, growled, "Fuck you, Johnny," and went out into the night.

Chu San emerged from a stall, carrying an attaché case. A Chinese man in a black tunic and gray fedora followed him out.

Cagle said, "Chu San, I want to talk to you about that man you attacked at Serenity House."

Chu San said, "I attacked no one. Nothing to talk about. Out of my way." He shoved Cagle and turned to the exit.

In a flash of anger, Cagle grabbed Chu San's free wrist and reached for the attaché case. "What's the big secret here?" The world exploded in a burst of jagged white light, and Cagle's scream died in his throat as he sank to his knees.

Caruso saw two men run from the toilet block and disappear into the festive mob. He raced into the foul space, past the Tamil, and saw Cagle on hands and knees, head low over the steady drip from a gashed scalp.

The terrified Tamil stared at the terminal joint of Mike's pinkie finger resting on a blood smear next to the tip jar.

———◦———

The night nurse called Dr. Chow and said, "He asks for you—head wound and chopped finger."

Dr. Chow entered the ER, still not fully awake, and asked, "What happened?"

Caruso said, "Strange doings on Bugis Street. I found Mike in the toilet block. An English guy was in there and saw the whole thing. Bashed with a bludgeon and finger chopped with a small hatchet."

"Sounds like the work of the triads. Souvenir shops sell the hatchets for two or three Straits dollars, and the tourists who buy them have no idea how lethal they can be. This is a criminal assault. Have you reported it to the police?"

"No, we prefer to handle it ourselves." Caruso handed Teow Seng a small plastic cup containing the joint. "Can you do anything with this?"

Mike, still in a daze, sat on a gurney, as Teow Seng wrapped the shortened digit in a protective dressing and sutured the split scalp with six EZ wound clips.

"Try to think clearly, Mike. I can sew the skin over the open wound, and you will have a short pinkie for the rest of your life. That's the easy way. The hard way requires an expert surgeon to attach the joint. We happen to have one of the best on our surgical staff. Dr. Irene Fong trained in microsurgery at the Cleveland Clinic. She stays busy repairing the damage caused by fishermen's filleting knives. We're keeping the finger joint chilled, but it will be usable only for a few more hours, so it's best to decide as soon as possible."

"The sooner, the better," said Cagle. "I'll go with Dr. Fong, if she thinks she can do the job."

Teow Seng brought Dr. Fong into the ER to determine if the piece was a candidate for surgical reattachment. She approved, and Mike was wheeled into a surgical suite.

Four hours later, Caruso sat next to Mike in the recovery room and helped bring him back into focus. "We have work to do as soon as you're on your feet."

———◦———

Cagle left the hospital with his arm in a sling and took a taxi to Serenity House.

He found Floyd Tuttle, with drooping eyes, stretched out on a wicker lounge in the lobby. "Corporal, let's talk."

"Whaddaya want?"

"Are you ready to tell me about the argument with Chu San?"

"I got no argument with that guy. He's a pal of mine. Just a slight misunderstanding. Coulda happened to anyone."

"How about Mei Lin? Is she still around? Another woman is out at the desk."

"Oh yeah, she took good care of me when I came back from the hospital. Offered a payoff for the little problem."

"Really? How did she do that?"

Tuttle said through a broad smile, "Free pussy, out at her joint at 33 Lavender Street, a coupla blocks past the fuckin' Ay-rab slaughterhouse. Best little whorehouse in Singapore. What's wrong with your arm?"

Cagle returned to the embassy and met Caruso for lunch in the employees' dining room.

"Where do we go from here? Tuttle is addicted and stupid. We can squeeze him. His five days are up, but I just asked the ambassador to get him an extension for medical reasons. He's in no shape to go back on the line. I think we ought to pick him up now."

Caruso said, "That's okay with me, but we don't bring the ambassador in on this. He plays by the rules."

"How about Frost?"

"Wendell's a straight-shooter too. He's called the deputy naval attaché, but I'm not clear about how he fits into the chain of command here at the embassy. Give me the Special. Let's leave the hardware at home."

—◇—

At Serenity House, Floyd Tuttle sniveled, "I ain't goin' with you guys. Leave me alone."

Mike admired the menacing authority of Caruso as he grasped Tuttle's upper arm in a steel fist and walked him through the basement door and into the backseat of the Consul. Mike drove back to the embassy, and Caruso repeated his control over the hapless Tuttle, maneuvering him up the iron stairway from garage to office.

Caruso changed from bad cop to good cop. "Look, Floyd, we're all friends here. We got nothing against you, but you help us; we help you. We know you do a little dope, like a lot of the other guys, but it's no good when you're out on the line." Caruso studied Tuttle's running nose and teary eyes and pressed on. "We're looking for Chu San's supplier."

Tuttle sat with his arms tightly folded across his abdomen. He blurted out, "I need a toilet—please."

Caruso was not surprised and calmly opened the door to his private bathroom. "Help yourself."

Tuttle hurried in, and Caruso said, "Diarrhea. He's in withdrawal." There were vomiting sounds, and Caruso said, "Both ends."

Tuttle emerged, wiping sweat from his forehead with a handful of toilet paper. Caruso handed him a box of Kleenex. Tuttle accepted with trembling hands.

"Now tell us what you know about Chu San's supplier."

"Nothin'. I gotta lie down."

Caruso played the wild card. "We understand, and you can rest in a few minutes after you help us." He opened the drawer on the library table and removed a small vial, uncapped it, and held it out to Tuttle. "We bought this from a street dealer, and we think it might be heroin, but we're not sure. We would like you to taste it, and tell us what you think—just a fingertip."

Tuttle's face brightened, and he complied without hesitation. "Oh yeah, it's the real stuff." The taut expression loosened.

Caruso asked, "Has your memory improved?"

Tuttle sighed and said, "Maybe. Whaddaya wanna know?"

Caruso said, "Let's start from the beginning. What was the argument with Chu San all about?"

"He stiffed me. I paid him half my pay for dope, and he never came through. Mei Lin told me to calm down—the shipment was on that canoe that was grabbed by the marine cops. Mei Lin and Chu San went out in a skiff to meet the canoe, but they hauled ass when the navy showed up. We all read about it in the *Straits Times*. The story about the fish killing the guy was bullshit."

"Did he ever come through with the dope?"

"He sure did. A day later, he gave me what I paid for, but it's all gone now. Same as what's in your bottle. Can I try it again, just to be sure?" He looked hopefully at the little vial that Caruso casually tapped on the table top.

"Do you know where the new stuff came from?"

"No idea. He told me that he found another supplier."

"Okay, Floyd, that's about it." He handed him the vial and said, "This is just between us. Should keep you happy for a few days, but you'd better get into a detox program up in Nam."

"Yes, sir. Yes, sir. Thank you, sir."

145

Chapter 20
Lavender Street

A week later, Cagle pocketed the Special and drove to Lavender Street, a favorite destination of merchant seamen for more than a century. He located number 33, just as two Chinese men wearing shiny blue suits stumbled out of the heavy front door and onto the five-foot way. The taller one leaped across the monsoon drain to the roadway. The other man jumped and slipped down into the runoff of an early downpour, slamming his wrist against the sidewall as he fell. In the angry stream of Hokkien rising from the drain, Mike heard, "Busted pukken Rolex."

The men left, and Mike pressed a button below the beckoning red light, triggering a pentatonal response from the interior. The door opened to a roseate glow that suffused the foyer. Mei Lin appeared, draped in a dragonized black silk kimono.

Mike smiled and said, "Good day, madam. I see I have come to the right place."

Mei Lin tried to swing the door shut, but Mike wedged a shoe between door and jamb and shouldered his way in, carefully favoring the repaired pinkie, which was splinted and taped to its neighbor. A sparsely clad Malay girl, affecting a seductive pose, appeared from beyond a beaded doorway. Mei Lin waved her away.

The girl was replaced by Chu San, who said, "What are you doing here?"

Mike leveled the Smith and Wesson at Chu San's belly and said, "I owe you something."

Chu San ran into a small office, followed by Mike, with Mei Lin tottering behind on spiked heels. A Luger lay on an attaché case on the desk.

"Touch it, and you die."

Chu San backed away. Mike picked up the Luger and stuffed it into his belt. Mei Lin threw herself at Mike and raked his cheeks with crimson claws. Mike swung his right arm and smashed the Special against her head. Chu San grabbed the attaché case and dashed to the front door, with Mike close behind.

Chu San ran along Lavender Street and ducked into a low building bearing a sign that read Ali Kasem Halal Abbatoir. Mike followed him into the gloom, through a long line of slaughtered lambs suspended upside down from a slow-moving overhead trolley. Chu San slipped on the slimy floor and fell heavily, dropping the attaché case. He reached for it and screamed as the slug shattered a metacarpal and continued through the case, followed by a cloud of white powder. Mike kicked Chu San out of the way and grasped the handle of the case with the thumb and two working fingers of his left hand. "Now, we're even." He turned to leave, and collided with a fat, hairy belly above a filthy, flowery batik sarong.

The butcher held a bloody knife in a huge fist and said, "Halal-side. Ingriss not allowed here."

———◦———

Chu San staggered out to Lavender Street, clutching his damaged hand against his chest. Mei Lin ran to him in bare feet, and he fell into her arms, gasping, "He shot me. I need a doctor. Hurry."

She said, "Cannot take you to the hospital with a bullet hole. Too many questions. We go to Wing Fat, close to us on Jellicoe Street."

"You mean that eyes-and-piles doctor that you visit?"

"That's the one. He will keep his mouth shut."

They walked three short blocks to a storefront that displayed a sign featuring a huge pair of eyes staring through giant spectacles. The lettering read Dr. Wing Fat Makes Eyeglasses and Treats Piles.

"Ah, Mrs. Lim, you are early. Your next treatment is a week from now."

"No, no, my husband is hurt. Bullet hole in hand. Can you fix him?"

Dr. Wing Fat examined the hand, and Chu San cringed with pain. "Broken bone. I can clean and bandage, but I cannot fix. You must go to General Hospital." He handed Chu San a small porcelain teacup. "Drink this—laudanum for the pain. Best I can do. Don't come back, and don't say you were here. The health minister is looking for any reason to shut us down."

Comforted by the laudanum, Chu San said, "We cannot go to General Hospital, but I need a real doctor. Maybe Ah Yeng can help. She knows a doctor."

———◄○►———

Ah Yeng stepped out of the trishaw, carrying a bag of groceries. She walked to her villa and saw Su Yin on the veranda. Su Yin stood clutching her housecoat tightly around her girth.

Ah Yeng was alarmed at her sister's unhappy expression. "What is it, Su Yin? Is anything wrong?"

"I am glad that you are here. We have visitors. I think there could be trouble."

Ah Yeng hurried into the villa and confronted the Lims. "Oh, I told you long ago that I would prefer that we keep our distance. Why are you here?"

Mei Lin said, "We need help. Someone shot my husband. We cannot go to the hospital. Call your doctor to come here. I beg you. We helped you during the war. Now you must help us."

Ah Yeng was not sympathetic. "Don't talk to me about the old days. We helped you as much as you helped us. We cooked and cleaned and made life easier for the brigade. If you cannot go to the hospital, you must be in trouble with the police."

Chu San grimaced with pain, and blood leaked through Dr. Wing Fat's dressing.

Ah Yeng's sharp tone softened. "Is there much pain, Chu San?"

He tried to suppress a soft groan.

"Please be careful. Try not to drip blood on the rug. Wait here while I call." She went to the telephone in the foyer and called Dr. Chow.

"I'm sorry, Mrs. Tan. I still have patients in the waiting room. I understand. Please don't shout. No, I can't come to your house. Send them to the emergency room, and I'll see what I can do. No, I won't call the police. I must go."

———◄○►———

Miss Lu said, "Dr. Chow will see you now. Exam room number four."

Teow Seng recognized Mei Lin. "You're here again? You were with the soldier from Felicity House and the man from the embassy."

"Yes, look what he did to me." She pulled back her hair and exposed an angry bruise with bloody streaks coagulated on her cheek. "He also shot my husband for no reason. I want him arrested and put in prison. He's a vicious American dog."

Teow Seng looked at Chu San's wound and called Dr. Fong.

"Another job for me, Dr. Chow? What is it this time?"

"Gunshot. Fractured metacarpal."

"Last time a hatchet chop, and now a gunshot. What's next?"

———◇———

Mike and Ralph sat at the library table in Caruso's office. Between them lay the open attaché case containing ten kilo blocks of China White. One had lost some of its contents from the small jagged hole in the wrapper.

"Good shot, Mike, but now we have to sweat out the halal butcher. We had better cook up a story if he calls the local cops."

Mike shoved the Luger across the table. "Add this to your collection. What do we do with the dope?"

"Let's play it straight. The locals are serious about drug possession, and we are possessing drugs. It's a hanging offense."

"Yeah, I saw the Dadah Means Death sign at the airport. Will we have diplomatic immunity?"

"I doubt if that's ever been decided. Let's hang on to the attaché case for a while. We can pin it on Chu San when we decide to get rid of him."

Chapter 21
Ah Yeng

M iss Lu pressed the button on the intercom. "Dr. Chow, Mrs. Tan Ah Yeng is here for her follow-up."

Ah Yeng ignored Miss Lu and walked directly into Teow Seng's office. "Hello, Doctor. I see you are waiting for me. Good—I have a busy day, and I am sorry for making a problem for you."

Dr. Chow looked up from his desk and said, "Let's forget about it. You look well. How do you feel?"

"Tired all the time, and I'm running out of pills. Su Yin thinks my eyes don't pop out as much. Am I still radioactive?"

"No, that's finished. I'll write you a prescription for more thyroid pills."

———◇———

Mike fingered his head wound as he drove to his appointment.

Miss Lu greeted him. "Good morning, Mr. Cagle, Dr. Chow will see you soon. Just take a seat."

Mike lowered himself into a side chair just as Ah Yeng walked into the reception room, trailed by Teow Seng, who said, "No, no, I told you that there is no need for an operation. Yes, I'll remember. A week from tomorrow at eight."

Ah Yeng said, "Make sure … special dinner … bird nest from Niah. I know you like that." She noticed Mike seated against the wall, watching a Moorish idol swimming with no place to go in a bubbling marine aquarium. "Ah, new English patient?"

Teow Seng said, "New patient, but he's American. Mrs. Tan, this is Mr. Cagle, from the US embassy." Mike stood and they shook hands.

"American—we owe much to America. Where would we be if America didn't bomb the Japanese? Are you enjoying our country, Mr. Cagle?"

"Yes, very much."

"And our food? It must be new for you. It's important to us—maybe too important—but it's part of our tradition. Ah, maybe if you are not busy, you might wish to join us for dinner at my house—a week from tomorrow at eight. You will meet my sister, Su Yin, and a few of my friends, and they will be pleased to meet you—I am sure. Dr. Chow is coming. He can give you my address."

"Thanks for the invitation, Mrs. Tan. If there is no embassy business, I'll be happy to join you."

"Good. I hope you can make it. Oh, Dr. Chow, I almost forgot. Maimunah visited last week—still carrying on with the Barisan. She wants you to meet her in the village. There's a medical problem that she wants to discuss with you."

The name Maimunah reminded Mike of the attack on the embassy.

———◁◦▷———

Teow Seng inspected his handiwork. "A little inflammation, but the scalp is healing nicely. The clips can come out. We'll x-ray the finger to make sure that it's still holding together. You'll enjoy dinner next week, if you can make it. I don't usually socialize with my patients, but I make an exception for Mrs. Tan. By the way, I will spare you some confusion by telling you that she and her sister—the two Mrs. Tans—were both married to the same man at the same time. I know nothing of their particular circumstances, but it is not uncommon, even today, for a Chinese man to have more than one wife. She's a wonderful cook—Mandarin style. She ran a successful restaurant in Singapore for a few years after the war. I'm talking about the big war, more than twenty years ago. You probably weren't even born then."

Mike saw the sadness in Teow Seng's face and said, "I was born in the middle of the war. I was about five years old when it ended. I know about the occupation of Singapore. You must still have nightmares about it."

"At least I lived to talk about it. My family was killed in the first days, during what's called the Sook Ching massacre—aimless slaughter." Teow Seng blinked back the rising tears.

Mike said, "That's hard to move past. I had my own taste of the war. My dad was a marine—killed on Guadalcanal. All I have of him is what was sent back by one of his buddies out there—a sword and a wallet from a Jap that he killed."

Teow Seng said, "Another sad story. Is your mother still alive?"

"Yes, alive and remarried to my father's marine pal, Thaddeus Gorton. I never knew my father, so my stepfather became a real father to me. He told me about my dad's heroic actions that earned him the Medal of Honor."

Teow Seng listened gravely. "At least you have that. I have nothing. On another subject, you might like to come with me to visit Maimunah's village for the weekend. She wants to ask me about a medical problem. I'll also do some doctoring. Every Malay village has a native doctor, called a bomoh, who does some palliative treatment with herbs and incantations. I try to be careful not to step on his toes during my visits. He greets me when I arrive, but he is glad to see me go."

Chapter 22
Bewitched

They crossed the causeway and stopped for lunch at a food stall in the forest. Teow Seng greeted the Malay proprietor, who ladled bowls of chili crab from a huge iron kettle resting on a bed of smoldering coconut husks.

Teow Seng said, "This is the national dish of Singapore. There are more than fifty species of edible crab in the local waters, and the cook dumps in any he can collect in the tide pools." They sat on a log, shaded by a mango tree festooned with white pigeon orchids, and consumed the house specialty with a bottle of Tiger. Stringy, iridescent jungle fowl pecked at the ground around them.

After their meal, a sampan operator ferried them to the kampong.

Mike asked, "Where do we spend the night?"

"Let's just walk through the center of the village. Something will turn up," said Dr. Chow.

The village seemed deserted when they walked in, but soon they were surrounded by children and dogs. A lean, grizzled Malay approached with a wide smile. "Hello, Dr. Chow. We are happy to see you," he said and offered a handshake, grasping his own right wrist with his left hand in the Malay gesture of polite deference toward friend and stranger alike.

"Hello, Penghulu. I am pleased to see you looking well," said Dr. Chow in his fluent Malay. "I'd like you to meet my friend, Mike Cagle, of the American embassy in Singapore. Mike, this is Dain Mohammad, penghulu of this village."

"Welcome to my village, Mr. Cagle. The first thing is to give you a place to stay for as long as you wish. Come to my home."

They followed the penghulu to the house occupied by his first wife, Zaharah, and dropped their bags next to sleeping mats.

Teow Seng said, "If you visit the outhouse at night, watch out for snakes. Take a flashlight, and walk slowly. The little banded krait is common around here. The only danger is if you step on one. It's venomous but so shy that the Malays think it's harmless. Now, let's go out to Yussef's shop for a cold drink."

They walked to an attap shelter serving as a food shop, and Dr. Chow greeted several of the men by name. "Greetings, Yussef, how is business? Hello, Saleh—good to see you looking well. Ah, there is Maimunah."

Maimunah moved from table to table, serving iced drinks and bottles of beer. She approached, and Dr. Chow took her hand. "Hello, Maimunah. I'm happy to see you again. Meet my American friend, Mike Cagle. He works at the American embassy."

Maimunah said in careful English, "How do you do, Mr. Cagle."

Mike was momentarily speechless before the beautiful form wrapped in a batik sarong. He said, "Hi. Please call me Mike."

She said, "Okay, Mike. I am Maimunah."

Mike and Dr. Chow ate some of the fruit that Maimunah brought to their table—rambutans, mangosteens, and sections of the malodorous durian. They sipped orange-colored Sinalco, a sweet beverage with an undefinable flavor. Maimunah brought a platter of glutinous pastries, brightly layered in blue, white, and red. "Malay cakes," she explained, "made with ground coconut and agar." Mike's eyes followed her as she moved with easy familiarity among the patrons.

Mike's interest did not escape Teow Seng, who said, "Look, but don't touch." He nodded in the direction of a Malay who sat quietly with a kris tucked into his waistband. "That's Saleh, her protector. Now it's time for some doctoring. I set up shop in a vacant old house near the beach, and patients probably are already waiting for me. You can explore the village or take a walk on the beach. By the way, to avoid an awkward explanation, I'll tell Maimunah that you broke your finger playing rugby."

"Thanks for thinking ahead. I'll hang around here for a while and stay out of the sun. See you later."

Mike remained under the attap, resting in a rotan armchair, eyes half shut but constantly aware of Maimunah's location, like a moth drawn to a pheromone. When they made brief eye contact, Mike was thrilled by her quick little smile. Teow Seng returned in an hour and joined Maimunah and Saleh in earnest conversation at a distant table.

Maimunah left the table and walked over to Mike. "I saw you napping in the heat. The weather is cooler in the monsoon seasons." He felt the light touch of her fingers on his arm and then on Mei Lin's scratch tracks on his cheek. She said teasingly, "It looks like your girlfriend plays rough, or you have been attacked by a tiger."

Fully awake, Mike ignored the probing flippancy and spoke directly. "Maimunah, I'm happy that we met today, but I have seen you before—at the American embassy, with the rock throwers at what I was told was a socialist demonstration. You are very different here in the village. It may be none of my business, but I'm curious about who you really are."

Her expression darkened. "I am who I choose to be. You can see that I am not a Malay, but this is my refuge from a heartless world. You are an American, and your people are slaughtering people like me. Can you say why this is so? We cannot fight you with guns and bombs, but maybe the sound of broken glass at your embassy will be heard in Washington. Some of your young men had the strength to resist. They went to Canada to avoid killing people who meant them no harm."

"Dodging the draft is not my way. It was not my father's way either. He was killed fighting the Japanese—fighting for people like you, as I am fighting for people like you." Mike cringed inwardly as he thought, *I wish I hadn't said that.*

Maimunah ignored the remark and said, "Isn't it strange that political differences are settled by mass murder, with each side trying to pile up more corpses than the other?"

———◦———

Teow Seng invited Mike to accompany him later that evening on his medical visits. "Actually, one of the main reasons for my work here is to treat yaws in children. It's caused by a treponema spirochaete, and it's quite contagious. I try to catch all the children and check the lesions for secondary infections.

About all I can do is apply a topical antibiotic and bandage the lesions. The kids rip off the dressings as soon as I leave and pass the infection to one another. The Malays have been living with yaws forever. They think it's a normal part of life."

They returned to Zaharah's house to spend the night and saw that Maimunah was asleep on her mat next to theirs. "She was born here," explained Teow Seng. "The penghulu raised her as his own daughter."

They awoke to a blazing morning sun. Teow Seng said, "There's a well in a little alcove off the kitchen. If you want, Maimunah will give you a bathing sarong."

Mike visited the outhouse and returned to put on a batik sarong that Maimunah had left on his mat. He walked to the well, passing Zaharah in the kitchen. Maimunah greeted him with a smile. "Ready for your washup?" she asked.

"Uh, yes, I guess so. How do I go about it?"

"If you want water, drop the bucket down the well and haul it up. Oh, I understand. You are modest. Okay, I'll leave, and you can do your washup."

"Oh no, I mean, you don't have to …"

She left.

They went to the food shop and joined Saleh for a breakfast of toast and cafe au lait. A sudden monsoon downpour drove the villagers inside to avoid the *hantu hutan*, the spirits of the forest. Teow Seng, Mike, and Saleh went into Zaharah's house and found Maimunah asleep on her mat, using Mike's sweaty T-shirt as a pillow.

She opened her eyes and hastily but casually pushed the T-shirt off the mat. "Oh, hello. I was just planning to do some laundry, and I must have dozed off." The rain stopped, and quiet pressed down on the kampong.

It was time to leave. Mike held Maimunah's hand and whispered, "I hope we meet again—soon."

She looked into his eyes, and he looked away, flustered by her direct gaze. She lowered her eyes and replied softly, "Anything is possible. Dr. Chow told me that he and you were invited to Mrs. Tan's banquet. Saleh and I shall be there as well."

Mike said, "That's wonderful. We will see each other in a few days."

She said, "You can let go of my hand now."

Chapter 23
Ah Yeng's Banquet

Mike located the Tan villa on Tanglin Road. Two casuarina trees stood as sentinels on either side of the driveway. He drove through an open gateway into a small landscaped garden, with spotlights illuminating shrubs and small trees. A Malay houseboy greeted him. "Good evening, tuan. Follow me, please."

The guests were in the drawing room, sipping tea and picking at platters of satay. His throat tightened as he saw Maimunah sitting on an ornate silk pillow, with her legs drawn up under her. Her creamy cheongsam was slit high, exposing a satiny thigh.

Mike greeted the two gray-haired Mrs. Tans. Both were clad in ornate silk dresses, and both of their throats were adorned with necklaces of imperial jade beads.

"Thank you for asking me to dinner, Mrs. Tan," he said.

"Please call me Ah Yeng," said the older sister, "and my sister is Su Yin."

"Yes, I am Su Yin," said the younger sister. "How do you do, Mr. Cagle. Maimunah has told us about you." Maimunah looked at Su Yin with a slight frown.

Mike said, "Please call me Mike."

"Thank you, Mike," both sisters said in unison.

Ah Yeng introduced Mike to the other guests. "My cousin, Rosi Kow; Saleh bin Rafiq, one of my closest friends …"

Mike and Saleh nodded. "We meet again," said Saleh.

The introductions continued. "Our guest of honor, Mrs. Lee, the mother of our prime minister and a teacher of Chinese cooking styles. She taught me many of the finer points of the art. Mr. Tham Kai Han, another great Chinese chef. Mr. Tham is writing a Chinese cookbook. This happens to be my month for the banquet. I believe it's Mr. Tham's turn next month." There were nods and handshakes throughout the introductions.

After meeting the guests, Mike walked to Maimunah, who raised her hand from her pillow perch. "Hello, Mike. How nice to see you again."

Mike took her hand awkwardly, running his thumb lightly over the knuckle connecting her middle finger to the rest of her hand. It stirred him as a deeply erotic contact. "Delighted to meet you. I mean, happy to see you again." He felt the flush rise to his cheeks as a faint smile flickered at the corners of her mouth.

He was rescued by a maid entering the room with a tray of glasses. "Would you care for an aperitif, Mike?" offered the older sister. "A pahit, perhaps?" Noting Mike's quizzical expression, she explained, "A pahit is merely gin and bitters with a squirt of lime. The English are quite fond of it. I am not much of a gin drinker, but why don't you try it—if you drink spirits."

Mike took a pahit from the tray.

They sipped and soon were engaged in polite conversation. Mike described his life in America and how it differed from life in Asia.

"Are there many Chinese people in America?" asked Ah Yeng. "We know about the railroad workers, but that was long ago. How about now?"

Mike said, "I live in Massachusetts. There are many Chinese restaurants in the city of Boston, in a section called Chinatown." He paused, wondering if Chinatown were an acceptable term.

Sensing his discomfort, Maimunah giggled and said, "Oh, we have an Old Chinatown in Singapore, don't we, aunties? It has many restaurants, just as in Mike's Boston."

The older sister said, "Where is Dr. Chow? I thought you would arrive together."

Just then, Teow Seng followed the houseboy into the drawing room. "Good evening. Sorry I'm late, but I stopped to help a young woman who was knocked off her bicycle by a trishaw."

The others in the room commiserated, and then it was time for dinner. The guests hunted for their place cards and complimented Ah Yeng on the dishes displayed on the large teak turntable.

The meal was memorable, as promised by Teow Seng. Chinese women discussed food constantly, and the Tans regaled Mike with descriptions of how each dish was prepared. The first of ten courses was shark fin soup, which required an hour of concentrated effort by one of the kitchen girls to pick the minute spindles of muscle tissue from between the cartilaginous fin rays of the shark. The fin tissue was stewed briefly and combined with crab roe and flaked crab meat. Then the mixture was added to chicken stock, thickened slightly with corn starch, and flavored with special spices. At the last moment, a generous cupful of tiny boiled quail eggs was added to the pot. Black vinegar was provided separately for those who enjoyed that condiment. The soup was spectacular.

The shark fin was followed by another labor-intensive dish—the delicate bird's nest soup. The kitchen workers boiled the dried nests to soften them, so that feathers and bits of down and twigs could be removed. The nests were created by cave swifts, which extruded a mucinoid salivary secretion that hardened in air, producing small, saucer-shaped nests cemented to the walls of the cave. The caves were leased by collector families, who seemed to have hereditary rights to the business. Excellent birds' nests for the demanding chefs of Singapore were gathered in the Niah caves in Sarawak. The soup was subtly aromatic with an exquisite flavor. Although the nests were quite expensive, street hawkers in Singapore offered a sweet, refreshing bird's nest drink in coconut water at low cost.

Mike accepted a second egg roll from Ah Yeng.

Teow Seng watched him eat and said, "Do you like that?"

"Oh yes, very much," said Mike. "It's a special kind of egg roll, isn't it?"

"I would say so," said Teow Seng. "Do you know what the outer covering is?"

"No, but it's delicious," said Mike.

"Pig omentum," said Teow Seng. "It rolls up nicely and holds the stuff inside very well during the deep frying."

Mike saw that Ah Yeng was careful to offer Saleh platters of pork-free delicacies.

The banquet went on for hours, washed down with Chinese beer and wine. Each dish was a masterpiece, and Mike was dazzled by the play of flavors and textures. For dessert, there was gula melaka poured over sweet bean curd. Teow Seng explained to Mike that gula melaka was liquid palm sugar, collected by licensed individuals, who climbed coconut palms and dipped the nectar from a depression at the junction of the uppermost fronds. Occasionally, the liquid fermented, producing *arrack*—raw spirits with a high alcohol content. After several collectors fell from the trees in drunken stupors, strict laws were passed banning collection by unlicensed people.

The meal came to an end with a heaping platter of fresh lichees and pineapple wedges and slices of fluffy sponge cake.

The Tan sisters looked at Mike expectantly, and he said, "It was a remarkable meal. I'll remember it forever."

They returned to the drawing room for after-dinner socializing, warmed by tiny glasses of cognac. Soon, Teow Seng glanced at his watch and said, "Well, I think I had better head home. I have a long day in the clinic, starting at eight in the morning." The other guests took that as a signal to leave. Maimunah remained in the drawing room.

Mike started to get up, but Ah Yeng said, "Mike, why don't you stay for a while. We don't have that many visitors, and we enjoy your company—especially since you like our cooking so much. Maimunah is staying with us, so you won't be stuck with two old ladies."

Su Yin echoed her older sister. "Please stay-lah. We are happy to have you in our home."

Mike remained seated and complimented the sisters on their hospitality and on their beautiful home and furnishings.

"Would you like to see the rest of the house?" asked Ah Yeng. "The bedrooms are upstairs. Maimunah has her own room for whenever she comes down from Kuala Lumpur."

They went downstairs to the kitchen, where three Malay maids were having their own meal of leftovers. The dirty dishes and glassware were stacked on a long counter next to the sink.

"Come out here, Mike," said Ah Yeng, opening the rear door. Mike stepped through the door into a greenhouse filled with orchids clinging to bark slabs, hanging from the ceiling and growing on bamboo stakes in terra cotta pots. The flowers were illuminated by ultraviolet grow-lights. There were a dozen varieties of cymbidium; a profusion of small, white pigeon orchids; and many wild and hybrid cattleyas of all colors and sizes.

"This is my favorite room in the house-lah," said Ah Yeng.

"I can see why," said Mike. "They're gorgeous. Those are pigeon orchids, aren't they?" He pointed to the great white clusters.

"Yes," said Ah Yeng. "We belong to the Singapore Orchid Society. It's a popular hobby here. You might have seen the orchid greenhouses all over the island. We are fanatical about orchid culture. You would find it most interesting to visit the Mandai Orchid Gardens. Singapore is an exporter of orchids to many countries. People in the UK are famous gardeners, and most of our plants are sent there. However, there is a problem that I am almost too embarrassed to mention."

"Really? What's that?" asked Mike.

Ah Yeng explained, "Some people are so obsessed with collecting and raising orchids that they will sneak into private greenhouses and steal plants. It's a serious crime in Singapore."

Mike noticed several wire cages covered with muslin hoods among the orchids. The occupants of the cages, disturbed by the visitors, set up an assortment of squawks and chirps, signifying that they were awake when they would prefer to be asleep. Su Yin raised the hoods and cooed at the birds, who cocked their heads at her and became still.

"Su Yin has a way with those birds," said Ah Yeng. "She prefers to spend time with them while I tend to the orchids. It's pleasant when we are out here together, taking care of our little hobbies."

Mike admired two white cockatiels in separate cages and the tiny multicolored loriquets, abundant in the mountainous Malay forests. One of the cockatiels started a guttural vocalization. Su Yin smiled shyly and said, "I taught him a few words in Mandarin."

Ah Yeng laughed and said, "To go with my cooking."

Su Yin looked alarmed and said, "You are planning to cook the birds?"

"No, little sister, the parrot speaks Mandarin, and I cook Mandarin. That's all. Never mind."

Maimunah moved among the orchids with a small pruning scissors, carefully clipping dead fronds. Ah Yeng picked up another pair of shears, clipped off a purple-throated Cattleya, and handed it to Mike.

"Here, Mike, this orchid would look so nice in Maimunah's hair, no? It will make her even more beautiful."

Mike accepted the flower and went to Maimunah's side and said, "May I?"

"Yes," she whispered. Mike carefully slipped the stem under her hair above her right ear.

"Thank you," she murmured and squeezed his arm slightly.

"Well," said Ah Yeng, "I think it's time for us to go upstairs. Come, Su Yin. Time for bed. You young people can stay as long as you like. Good-night."

"Good-night," said Mike.

"Good-night," said Maimunah.

The women climbed the staircase, and Mike and Maimunah went to the drawing room and sat together on the damask settee.

One of the maids knocked on the wall of the drawing room.

"Yes? What is it?" said Maimunah.

"Sorry to disturb. Dishes all washed-lah. Something else?"

"No, Fatima, go-lah," said Maimunah.

Mike took her hand and moved closer on the settee. She sat quietly and said, "Mike, there is no rush. For now, you can kiss me good-night, and I will call you at the embassy in a day or two."

Mike drew her close and pressed his lips to hers in a lingering kiss. Her lips parted, and their tongues touched gently as he inhaled her breath.

He drove home, with Maimunah filling his thoughts. In his distraction, he found himself on the right side of the road, narrowly avoiding a collision with a "honey wagon." The truck's horn and the driver's furious expression broke Mike's reverie, and he forced himself to focus on the road rather than Maimunah's lovely face and supple body.

The next morning, at an early breakfast, Maimunah and her aunties reviewed the dinner of the previous evening. "I think you like Mike a lot," said Ah Yeng.

Chapter 24
Konfrontasi

Caruso and Cagle joined Ambassador Duncan in his office. The ambassador spoke. "Gentlemen, as you know, during this state of konfrontasi, which we call confrontation, there is no diplomatic exchange between Singapore and Indonesia. It's the local cold war that's starting to heat up in Sarawak. The Indian High Commissioner has agreed to represent Singapore if negotiations become necessary. Ralph, what have you picked up from your back-alley connection with the marine police?"

"Well, sir, they've been holding the crew of the dope canoe from the Riaus. They were blocked from dealing with the Indonesian authorities, so they turned Kalam's body over to me. I made arrangements with our embassy in Jakarta to return Kalam to his family on Pulau Batam. I also softened their grief with a comfortable cash payment from the Benevolent Fund, as you suggested. While I was there, I was approached by one of Sukarno's lackeys to see if they could retrieve the other canoers—the live ones. He proposed a trade. They are still holding the dope dealers' boat that the Indonesian Coast Guard grabbed on Batam. It turned out that the boat was registered in Sumatra, to a fisherman named Saleh bin Rafiq, at an address in the Malay settlement here in Singapore, but Saleh's primary residence is in his home village on the east coast of Johore. The Indonesians wanted to swap the boat for the canoe crew. That was a job for the Singapore authorities. They approved the swap, with the Indian High Commissioner as the mediator. The trade-off was made yesterday out on the Singapore Straits at the buoy marking the border between us and them. Now, here's where you come into the picture, Mike. Kalam told me that Saleh made several dope deliveries to Chu San, and I know that you visited Saleh's village with Dr. Chow. You don't have to know how I know. The marine police agreed to hold off on picking up Saleh because we might use him to get to the source. I want you to track Saleh back to the head of the outfit. On a more personal note, tread lightly with Maimunah."

Mike slammed a fist on the table. "What the hell has she got to do with this?"

"Probably nothing, but she's a political troublemaker, hooked up with the Barisan and who knows what other extreme elements. I'm sure she's a fascinating playmate, but be careful when you get to the pillow talk. There are communists under every rock in this part of the world. We kill all we can find in 'Nam, and we're buddies with other commie-killers, wherever we find 'em. You may know of the massacres in Indonesia … whole villages wiped out if there is the slightest suspicion of procommunism. We don't necessarily encourage that, but we don't discourage it either. So watch your step. If word seeps out of the embassy that you're a flyboy up in 'Nam, you might have a target on your back."

Mike was surprised to hear the same words that he heard at the Board of Inquiry not so long ago.

The ambassador said, "You're on your own, gentlemen, but keep me in the loop. Try not to embarrass the embassy. Oh, there's one more thing. The prime minister will be leaving next week for a ten-day visit to the USA. While he's away, the deputy PM will be the acting PM."

Mike said, "If they're so touchy about the Vietnam War, what's his reason for visiting the Great Satan?"

"Politicians have personal reasons that do not always coincide with their public statements. In the PM's case, he's going on an official visit to meet the people of America. I recommended him for a visiting fellowship at the Harvard Business School next year."

Mike said, "He might be angling for a Harvard honorary degree."

The ambassador laughed. "You said that, Mike, not I. Let me finish what I have to say. During the PM's absence, the deputy PM has arranged a state dinner at the Istana. I received an invitation from his office but sent my regrets. As you know, my wife is not well. Ralph should stay out of view, and Wendell is in uniform. That leaves you, Mike, if you would care to represent the embassy. You may take your young lady, if you wish. The guest list includes the Indian High Commissioner and his wife. He's tangled up in activities that involve us in some way, so it might be a good idea to get to know him."

The meeting ended, and Mike returned to his office. He trotted the last few steps as he heard the ringing of his desk phone. He picked it up. "Mike Cagle's office."

"Hello, Mr. Cagle. This is Edith Loh at the reception desk. A Miss Maimunah Mohammad is on the line. Do you wish to speak to her?"

"Yes, thank you, Edith."

"Hello, Mike. This is Maimunah."

"Hello, Maimunah. I'm glad to hear your voice. I didn't know if I would ever hear it again."

"Don't be silly. I'm calling to invite you to the prime minister's speech tonight at the university. I like to keep tabs on what the boss man has in mind for the little people. Are you interested?"

"Absolutely. If the speech is boring, I'll be excited just sitting next to you."

"Down, boy. I'll meet you at the entrance to Lecture Hall 1 at the Bukit Timah campus off Cluny Road. Do you know where that is?"

"I'll find it."

"Okay. The speech is scheduled to start at eight; be there at seven forty-five."

"I'll be there."

Chapter 25
The PM's Speech

Mike walked through the gathering crowd and saw Maimunah standing near the entrance, smartly dressed in a hip-hugging white linen skirt and pale-blue silk blouse. She carried a brown leather shoulder bag. Mike felt a shiver of jealousy as the students eyed her from head to toe in what he thought of as retinal rape.

"Over here, Mike," she called, and a smile brightened her face. He moved rapidly to her side, and she offered her cheek for a neutral kiss. They picked up flyers announcing the PM's address on "Academic Freedom and Social Responsibility." Lecture Hall 1 was jammed, except for the press rows, which were vacant. They seated themselves in the third press row to await the PM's entrance.

Maimunah explained the background of the speech. "The trouble started last October, when the university students were granted a parade permit to demonstrate for autonomy, academic freedom, and abolition of the 'suitability certificate,' which gave the state arbitrary control of university admissions. The prime minister had agreed to debate these matters as the climax of the day of student antigovernment demonstrations, which included carrying a coffin representing the death of academic freedom. The PM withdrew from the debate, blaming the students' clumsy handling of certain protocol aspects of the confrontation. He was irritated further because the University of Singapore students had covertly invited the students of Nanyang University to join them in the protest. The PM objected to this because the Nanyang students were in the 'Chinese language stream' and had ample experience in mass demonstrations and pressure tactics, trained by socialist rabble-rousers." She smiled broadly, adding, "People like me."

The PM arrived in a cream-colored Jaguar sedan, surrounded by his security force, but he walked into the hall alone, dressed in English-style gray slacks and a short-sleeved blue shirt a bit overly generous in cut. He was an interesting-looking man, with bulbous orbital ridges, almost no eyebrows, and smooth eye pouches. He hitched his shoulders constantly as he spoke, either to emphasize his statements or as an involuntary tic.

He was angry. He started by warning the students that their deportment during the program would be duly noted by him and his colleagues and would be taken into account in deciding the fate of the University of Singapore. He made it clear that their appearance in the audience on the university campus was a privilege bestowed by him personally.

He informed them that he made the university, and he would decide its future direction. He spoke passionately, eloquently, at times irrationally, and always imprudently. He attacked the current vice chancellor of the university as a weak, vain man who attended international meetings of university leaders and deluded himself into thinking that he was the equal of the heads of Oxford and Cambridge. He traced the shortcomings of the University of Singapore to the nonlocal administrative and academic personalities who dominated much of the faculty. He accused European department heads of teaching out of the context of Singapore. He said, "Who is Sir Francis Drake to our students? What is the meaning of 'daffodils in springtime' to students who never will see a daffodil?"

He extended his attack to the non-European expatriates who came from an underdeveloped land, seeking a better life, but brought with them an "existentialist philosophy of universality" that drained the students' vitality and resolve. These staff members he identified as Indians, and he referred to them as "birds of passage."

The prime minister verbally assaulted the students themselves, accusing them of being spineless, gutless, and mediocre, craving the security of a position in government service and generally lacking in resources. He expressed pity for them and pointed out that their plight derived from their education in the English-speaking stream, with its pallid pseudo-Western values.

By contrast, he pointed to the Chinese middle schools, with their academic discipline and the inculcation of cultural and spiritual values that engendered verve and vitality. Unfortunately for Singapore, the middle schools also were the spawning grounds for communism. He declared his resolve to crush the sources of communist indoctrination in the Chinese-stream schools, while preserving the strength of the Chinese cultural heritage. He hoped that admission of the Chinese-language students into the National University of Singapore, currently in the planning stage, would bring in some new energy, but he hoped that extremism would not flow in through the same gate. He made it clear that he intended to co-opt the Chinese-speaking students and neutralize their antiauthoritarian tendencies.

The speech was loaded with first-person statements that made it clear that he considered himself to be an absolute monarch with total extra-parliamentary authority. Harkening back to the October demonstration, he railed, "You want academic freedom? I will give you all the freedom you need if you can prove your worth. If you don't measure up, I will consider reducing this university to an administrative-training institute and sending the most promising students abroad for their education. We know how many digits are required for efficient operation of the civil service and how many digits for the private sector"—he described the citizens of Singapore repeatedly as "digits" who had to be manipulated to produce the greatest social benefit.

He also pointed out that he had four units of riot police specially trained in quelling without hurting, but they also were trained to hurt without noise, should that be required by circumstances. He said that he would not hesitate to use force if he deemed it necessary.

After the talk, during the question-and-answer period, the PM side-stepped three questions from student leaders, instead restating his general theme of the timid, deculturized university student.

They filed out, and Maimunah said, "Well, what do you think?"

"Tough guy. Singapore will be what the PM wants it to be. What now? Somewhere for a nightcap? The Goodwood Park's not too far."

She said, "Okay. I haven't been there for a while. I'm driving an old Panhard."

Mike said, "Let's take my car."

—◇—

Mike ordered gin slings at the Goodwood lounge, and they looked out over the scattering of Asian faces among the Europeans.

Maimunah said, "Before the war, there wouldn't have been many locals in this crowd. Now, the social order has been changed, but everyone eventually finds someone to hate. I don't think we were born that way, but it's a lesson that's easy to learn." They sipped the pink liquid.

Mike asked, "Is it easy to learn more about you?"

Maimunah laughed and said, "You will learn sooner or later. I will begin by telling you that I am a teacher in Kuala Lumpur. I was born twenty-four years ago in the Malay village and became an anak beli. That's the Malay term that translates to 'bought child'—a non-Malay baby adopted by a Malay family and raised in the Malay culture. I was adopted by Dain and Zaharah, and I think of them as my parents. I was educated in the kampong school for the first few years. I learned along with the Malay children. I read the Koran and memorized some verses, and I was even given a small prayer rug, but there was nothing much beyond that. They allowed me to seek my own way, with or without Islam, as I pleased. The Malays are gentle people, especially with the children, who never are punished for anything. They come and go as they please. They don't even have to attend school if they don't want to. The parents just smile and pamper them. It's a wonderful life for a child, but they tend to grow up ignorant, and the adult males can fall into a state of lassitude that is best described by the Malay term *tidak apu*— that can be translated as 'no matter.' In my classroom, I encourage them to open their minds to the world beyond the kampong. I don't know how much my efforts are appreciated by the political authorities. The prime minister of Malaysia, Abdul Rahman, has made public statements criticizing the Chinese and threatening their positions in Malaysian society."

Mike said, "You had the same early education as the Malay children. How do you explain your state of mind?"

"My education was broadened in Switzerland. My classmates and I were a bunch of spoiled brats, teasing those dull Swiss boys shamelessly. My roommate, Valerie, was one of the wildest—she guzzled gin until she couldn't see straight. I think by now she must be a total alcoholic, just like her mother. I met her mom a few times and never saw her sober. And her father—a starchy old fogy who thought that Hitler might have been good for England. I will also tell you that I recently learned about my mother.

For many years, I thought of her only as my auntie, but Saleh told me that she is my real mother. He won't speak of my father, so he must know who he is—or was. He also told me that my mother needs medical attention for a serious drug problem. Ah Yeng urged Dr. Chow to meet me in the village, and he brought you with him. I asked him to treat my mother at her estate in Kelantan, and he agreed to help her as soon as he could get away from the clinic for a few days."

Mike listened and said, "Singapore medicine is very good, and the general hospital is one of the best in this part of the world. Why doesn't she go there?"

"She's reluctant to travel to Singapore, although she once lived here with her parents—my grandparents. I know nothing about them. Now you know more about me than I know about you. What's your story?"

Mike said, "You are twenty-four, and I am twenty-six. You never knew your father, and I don't remember much about my father."

"Why is that?"

"He left us to join the marines and was killed on Guadalcanal. Care for another sling?"

"I'll pass."

"How about my place for a nightcap?"

"We can do that."

Chapter 26
The Skyscraper

Mike pulled into his parking space in the Skyscraper garage and escorted Maimunah up to his sparsely furnished flat. He turned on the air conditioner.

"Well, here it is. What do you think?"

Maimunah giggled and said, "It looks as though nobody lives here."

Mike said, "I suppose it could stand a woman's touch. Can I get you something? Tea or a cold drink? How about a gunner? I don't have much to eat here. We could go to the market just a couple of blocks away."

Maimunah tossed her bag onto the divan. She looked at him with a slightly mocking smile and said, "Are you hungry for food, Mike? Your shirt is drenched. Why don't you take a nice cool shower, and then we'll see."

"Good idea," said Mike. He went to the bedroom, undressed, and put on a terry robe. He walked to the bathroom, taped a polythene sandwich bag over his left hand, and stepped into the shower stall.

As he shampooed his hair, the shower curtains parted, and a naked Maimunah stepped in and said, "Would you like some company?" He gazed at the lithe, tawny body. Her glistening, black hair, with Ah Yeng's orchid tucked over an ear, streamed down her back to the swell of her buttocks. He folded her in his arms. She pressed her pelvis against his and said, "Please hand me the soap, darling."

Mike asked solicitously, "Is there a concern for pregnancy? What I mean is, shall I put on a—"

"Condom? No, my dear, that won't be necessary. You haven't been here long enough to learn about our family planning programs in Singapore. The

175

prudish Chinese housewives have learned to take these things in stride. I am properly equipped, so have no fear. You know, someday we might dispense with the protection and have us a cute little baby. Do you think your family would like that?" she asked teasingly.

"I am sure they would," said Mike. "I know I would."

They spent the afternoon in bed, delighting in their discoveries. Then they lay together placidly, calm after the tempest. Night fell, slamming down as it did near the equator, depriving that part of the world of the softness of evening.

Maimunah lay cradled in Mike's left arm, her head on his chest. She turned to kiss him with little love nips. "I think now we might dress and go out for a light meal," she said. "Before we go, I must call the sisters and tell them that I will be with you tonight."

They repeated their shower together, dressed, and walked to the market. They passed through the crowd, holding hands and attracting cold stares from many of the older Chinese.

"Ignore them," said Maimunah. "They're still locked in the old ways."

They went to Mike's favorite stall and ordered sticks of pork satay, a platter of roast goose, and a bottle of Tiger that they shared in paper cups. They sat together on a wooden bench and ate, surrounded by Chinese women in black trousers and flip-flops, cigarette-smoking men in singlets and shorts, and Malays in colorful sarongs.

They returned to the flat and watched the late news on a small television set that Mike had purchased from an ad tacked on the lobby bulletin board. Mike said, "There's no mention of the PM's speech. How can that be?"

Maimunah said, "We're accustomed to that. You saw that the press rows in the lecture hall were vacant. The reporters choose not to waste their time taking notes on an event that never will see the light of day. Let's think of us. I can stay with you for a few days, if you would like that."

"Of course, but why just for a few days?"

"The long vac ends soon, and I must return to my teaching in Kuala Lumpur. I'm also going to visit my mother. Saleh insists on coming with me. He thinks I still need his protection from the evils of the world."

"I know how you feel about Saleh, but how much do you know about his activities?"

"He's a fisherman and has helped me for as long as I can remember. Why do you ask?"

"Just curious."

<hr />

The next day, Maimunah went back to pack a valise and told Ah Yeng and Su Yin about her day with Mike.

Ah Yeng said, "I think he is falling under your spell."

"I know nothing about spells, but I wish to tell you that I will stay with him at his flat, if he would welcome my company."

"How could he not?" said Ah Yeng. "The young man is not made of stone. You know that we want the best for you. Su Yin and I have been through much heartache in the war. I don't know how we managed. We never could have survived without your mother's help."

Maimunah was surprised at Ah Yeng's remark. "My mother? You knew that auntie Li Lian was my mother? You never told me. Please don't cry," she said, as both sisters began sobbing. "Calm yourselves. Saleh told me about her, and I hope to persuade Dr. Chow to help her with her drug problem."

"I will tell you what we have kept from you for so many years," said Ah Yeng. "With all that has happened in the past, we both have become changed people. Our old-fashioned ideas kept us in a terrible life with Mr. Tan, our husband. You knew that we were married to the same man, not? He was cruel and had a man's appetites, but he was very rich, and we wanted for nothing, so we put aside normal feelings and stayed. Isn't that so, Su Yin?" Her sister murmured her assent.

"What can you tell me about my mother?" asked Maimunah.

"Your mother was a jungle fighter, and she saved us from the Japanese. We owe her everything. She was such a brave woman and so strong."

Su Yin echoed her older sister. "So brave and strong and so beautiful."

"Yes," agreed Ah Yeng, "and so beautiful."

Maimunah said softly, "I am twenty-four years old and never knew where I belonged. I love my Malay family. They have been kind to me all my life, but I am different. Why did my mother abandon me?"

"Be patient," said Ah Yeng. "She pledged us to silence. Now, about you and Mike. We have lost much of our traditional thinking. The idea of a Chinese woman taking up with a European man is unthinkable to most of our generation. Su Yin can have her own thoughts on the matter."

"I think as you think, my sister," interjected Su Yin.

"Before the war, there would have been no question. The young woman would have been rejected by her family and friends, and she would have had a lonely life with her Caucasian lover or husband. Now, however, I feel another way. We saw so much misery and destruction of the human spirit that I think people should find happiness in any way they can. Life is too short to have overly strict rules of conduct. If you want Mike, why not?" She laughed a tight little laugh. "I had thought that Dr. Chow might be a good match for you. He would be a good provider, and he has a modern outlook. Whatever you decide, we will always love you and support you."

The telephone rang, and Su Yin answered it in the foyer. She returned in a moment and said, "Maimunah, Mike is on the phone."

Maimunah returned shortly and said, "Mike will pick me up in a few minutes. Here is his address and telephone number, if you need me for anything."

◄○►

Mike drove to the Tans' house and rang the doorbell. Maimunah opened the door and brushed his lips with a friendly kiss. He followed her into the parlor and greeted the sisters, who were sitting together on one of the settees with their hands folded in their laps.

"Hello, Mike. Will you stay for a while and have some tea?" said Ah Yeng.

Mike glanced at Maimunah and saw the slight nod of her head. "Yes, of course. Thank you very much. No sugar, please, and just a bit of milk."

They sat quietly for a few minutes, sipping tea, and nibbling almond cookies. Maimunah said, "Time to leave, Mike." She kissed the sisters.

Ah Yeng said, "Wait—I have something for you." She hurried out to the greenhouse and returned with several cymbidium sprays. "These will cheer up the flat. Oh, there is one more thing; I'll be right back." She ran up the stairs and came down carrying a batik handbag. She handed the bag to Maimunah and said, "This belonged to your mother. She left it with the penghulu at the kampong many years ago. It is all that is left of your mother's early life. Saleh told me to give it to you when I thought it was the right time."

"What's in it?" asked Maimunah.

"I don't know. I never looked inside," said Ah Yeng. "You can find out for yourself."

Maimunah took the bag and said, "Thank you. We must go now. Good-bye, aunties." They closed the door behind them, climbed into the Consul, and returned to the Skyscraper.

In the bedroom, Maimunah said, "My mother's bag. I think I'll have a look." She took the bag into the living room and dumped its contents onto the coffee table. Cosmetics, perfume vials, a few loose cigarettes, silk slippers, a silk kerchief, tarnished coins, paper money, a small notebook, two pencil stubs, jade earrings, a pearl choker, some folded papers, two nondescript sealed packets, and several ticket stubs with Japanese characters all fell into a jumbled pile.

With a hand to her forehead, she said, "I am feeling dizzy. Mike, I love you. Neither of us was responsible for the past. Can we go to bed now?"

They lay in each other's arms, with the ceiling fan moving the humid air over their moist bodies. Their intimacy deepened, but there was an undercurrent of sadness with each passing day.

To Mike, she was a doe in the forest who might dash off if startled. He wanted her in his life and wondered if that meant that he was in love.

On Sunday, they joined families strolling through the manicured grounds of the Istana. Maimunah pointed to a curly-haired boy squatting at the edge of a lotus pond, poking at a patch of sensitive mimosas. An American woman's voice said, "Come, Chris, it's time for lunch at the club." A little girl, holding her mother's hand, said, "Hurry up, Chrissy. Stop bothering those plants."

Maimunah said, "Mike, if we had a little boy, would you have the patience to wait while he touched every plant to make it collapse?"

In the afternoon, they went to high tea at Raffles and sat at a lawn table against a backdrop of traveller's palms. Mike took her hand and said, "I'm not ready to let you go yet, but I know you have to get back to your classroom. Before you go, I would like to invite you to a fancy dinner at the Istana. We'll be guests of the deputy prime minister. Can you make it next Friday?"

Maimunah brightened and said, "Of course. We have a week to get to know each other. Then we can celebrate with the deputy PM."

"It's a date. After I clear up a few things at the embassy, I'll drive up and stay with you for a while in Kuala Lumpur."

Chapter 27
The Deputy PM's Dinner

The guests milled about, searching for their place cards and sipping aperitifs. After a few minutes of casual socializing, they settled into their seats at the great round table, anticipating a luxurious ten-course banquet.

Acting Prime Minister Tam stood at the head of the table and introduced the guests. "Most of us know each other, but please raise your hands for the benefit of our newcomers. Minister of Education, Dr. and Mrs. Ong An Bao; Minister of Health, Dr. and Mrs. Leonard Tham; Dean of the Medical Faculty, Dr. and Mrs. Lim Bok An; Visiting Professor at the Medical Faculty, Dr. and Mrs. Philip Thayer from the United States; Indian High Commissioner, Raja Surendra Singh Alirajpur and his lovely wife, Mina; and the representative of the American embassy, Mr. Michael Cagle and his companion, Miss Maimunah Mohammad. Now, let us enjoy this wonderful feast, and be prepared to favor us with brief after-dinner comments on anything that you might consider appropriate for the occasion."

Raja Surendra was in his early forties, with a neatly trimmed black mustache on a handsome, slightly puffy face. He oozed his worldly charm on Maimunah, who sat to his right. "Do you realize that your friend Michael and I are the most fortunate men in Singapore?"

Maimunah edged away from the soft pressure of his upper arm and said, "When did you decide that, Raja? You have known him for only five minutes."

"I knew it the moment I saw you on his arm. We are with the two most beautiful women on this island."

She tilted her head slightly toward Mike, trying to pick up his conversation with Mina.

Mike said, "You must have a busy social life as the rani. How often do you attend dinners like this?"

Mina was a young woman of flawless beauty, dressed in a luxurious silk sari. She suppressed the jingling of gold bangles by casually tossing a cashmere scarf over her arm. The guests' eyes drifted continuously in her direction. Her soft voice scarcely rose above the background conversation. "Please, my name is Mina. I don't think about my social life. I do what is expected of me."

Mike recognized a certain reluctance to communicate and offered what he thought would be a welcome suggestion. "I can understand the demands of someone in your position. I am sure Maimunah also would like to get to know you. If I exchanged seats with her, she would be able to enjoy your companionship at the table, and I would enjoy talking to your husband."

Mina raised her head slightly and murmured, "That will be fine."

Mike whispered to Maimunah. She nodded and turned to the raja. "A pleasure meeting you, and now I should like to spend some time with your lovely wife."

The raja offered a courtly bow and said, "We can continue our conversation later."

Mike rose, and they exchanged seats. He was relieved that Maimunah had not had time to express her contempt for hereditary authority.

Mina greeted Maimunah, and Mike picked up fragments of their conversation amid the clacking of chopsticks.

Maimunah: "A wonderful banquet …"

Mina: "The jingling attracts attention."

Maimunah: "Do you wear them all day?"

Mina: "I don't know if they actually belong to me."

Maimunah: "But he's an important man here."

Mina: "I'm just his toy."

Maimunah: "Any special work?"

Mina: "My only job is to keep myself clean for his pleasure."

Maimunah: "But I plan to leave soon."

Mina: "Please stay, if you possibly can. I'm so lonely."

The diners picked the platters clean, and it was time for the after-dinner speakers.

The minister of health reminded the small audience of how Singapore had solved the perplexing problem of providing medical services to the entire population. "Our three-prong approach thus far has done a good job. Any Singaporean can find covered care at General Hospital. The well-to-do may wish to open their wallets on the private side, and catastrophic conditions for the indigent are financed by the national treasury. This may become a model for the rest of the world." He sat to scattered applause.

Next to rise was the minister of education. "Friends and colleagues …" He stopped as a police sergeant, with a truncheon secured under his right arm, strode directly to Dr. Tam and whispered for a few seconds. Both glanced discreetly in Maimunah's direction.

The policeman walked to Maimunah and said, "Miss Mohammad, I must take you into custody for disturbing the peace. Please come quietly." He grasped Maimunah's upper arm and started to lift her.

Mike stood instantly, driving the heavy teak dining chair to the floor. He grabbed the sergeant's shirt. "Get your hands off her, you little prick!"

The sergeant released Maimunah and gripped Mike's wrist. "Control yourself, sir. This lady broke the law."

Mike did not resist and allowed his anger to subside. "Sorry, Officer, what's the charge?"

"Disturbing the peace and damaging public property. We have her on film, managing a street demonstration and destroying windows at the American embassy."

"That's US territory. Has the embassy filed charges?"

The sergeant thought for a moment. "As the host nation, we are taking action as a courtesy to your people."

Mike showed his credentials and said, "As the embassy representative, I request that all charges be dismissed."

The sergeant walked to the deputy prime minister and spoke quietly. Dr. Tam listened intently and nodded. The sergeant left the hall.

Raja Surendra smiled broadly and said, "Quick thinking, Mike. That was a close one. You're a budding diplomat. Now that the battle is over, I wish to invite you and Maimunah to our residence to continue our evening in more peaceful surroundings."

Mike said, "If Maimunah isn't too tired—"

Mina cut him off. "She is fine. Come with us. We must spend more time together." She took Maimunah's hand.

Maimunah sensed a touch of desperation in the rani. "That will be lovely. Mike and I will be happy to spend the rest of the evening with you."

The raja said, "I'm sure you will enjoy seeing our home. It's called India House, at 2 Peirce Drive. My government bought it as a convenience for diplomatic representatives in Singapore. Just follow me. I'm driving a white Mercedes."

◦

Mike and Maimunah discussed the evening as they followed the raja, whose driving bordered on the reckless. Mike commented on Mina, "She's a real beauty but seems a bit vacant. What did you talk about in the ladies room?"

Maimunah said, "I spoke little. She spoke much. I wouldn't describe her as vacant. Uneducated, perhaps, and sensitive to what she sees as a predicament rather than a position of privilege. She's twenty-three, and they have been married for four years. They met when the raja judged a regional beauty contest and selected her as the winner—and his bed companion. He has a taste for virgins. She thinks she will be discarded after the next beauty contest."

The Consul followed the Mercedes to India House, where turbaned syces took charge of the cars. The raja escorted them into the foyer, which was carpeted with several tiger skins, complete with claws and heads. Mike and Maimunah avoided stepping on the skins. They entered the lavish living room, paved with more tiger skins. A surprising feature was a rosewood coffee table holding a large round jigsaw puzzle, with no design except for the center logo of a monocled rabbit. The outer circular rim was complete, but the rest of the puzzle lay in a jumble of solid red pieces.

The raja explained, "That's a most challenging puzzle, with nothing but the Playboy rabbit in the middle. I gave it to Mina to keep her mind occupied during the day." He spoke without irony and ignored Mina's forlorn expression.

A servant padded in, bearing a large tray holding a bottle of champagne and four glasses. A second servant followed him, carrying a bowl of golden caviar and a platter of toast points. The raja poured the wine, and the rani served the precious eggs.

In an expansive mood, the raja led his guests on a tour of the tiger skins. "I shot every one. I took that big boy in the foyer with a Lancaster howdah pistol. Let me show you that gun." He unlocked a cabinet and produced the weapon, stroking it gently along both barrels. "Powerful gun and accurate at short range, especially with the carbine stock. Do you hunt, Mike?"

"Never anything covered with fur and running on four legs."

Maimunah knelt and caressed one of the pelts. "Did you have to kill so many of these beautiful creatures?"

The raja pursed his lips into what he intended to be a sympathetic expression and said, "Yes, they are beautiful, and I understand your feelings about taking their lives. But you might try to understand that certain things are expected of me as the cultural leader of my small principality. Tiger hunting has always been a right of passage for young men of privilege. I take it as a ceremonial obligation, and my subjects take it as a great honor to accompany me on the hunt. Our elephants are pampered beasts, and the chief mahout is a figure of prominence in our society."

Mike said, "Thanks for your hospitality, but it's time for us to go. Maimunah is leaving for Kuala Lumpur early in the morning to start the school term."

Mina took Maimunah's hand and said, "Oh, so soon? When will we see you again? Here is my card. You must promise to call when you are back in town."

<hr />

They drove back to the Skyscraper and entered the lift. Maimunah kissed Mike as they rose to the tenth floor. She giggled and said, "I can still taste the beluga on your lips."

Mike said, "That was an expensive nightcap with the great tiger hunter."

"He's going to break her heart. Poor little thing."

Chapter 28
The Lims

Caruso said, "If you go to Kuala Lumpur, don't forget your job in Singapore. Try to find out if she knows about Saleh's dope runs to the Riaus. If he shows up, you might even be able to track him back to the source."

Mike said, "She's clean, but her mother's a junkie. I'll call you at the embassy if anything turns up."

"Watch your step. Dr. Fong reported Chu San's wound to the cops, and they've been looking for him. Your doctor friend, Chow Teow Seng, kept your name out of it. You can thank him for that."

———◦———

Maimunah drove up the west coast, occasionally glancing out at the cluttered shipping lanes of the Straits of Malacca. She passed the paddy fields of Kuala Langat, avoiding a half-ton water buffalo guided by a small boy perched on its haunches. Four hours later, she turned onto Sultan Street in Chinatown and arrived at her tiny cottage, sandwiched between a hardware store and a greengrocer. Across the unpaved road, two pigs wallowed in the mud, and a dozen chickens scratched optimistically at the stubbly ground.

She entered the little house and was satisfied that her furnishings were undisturbed. The walls were decorated with stone rubbings from Angkor Wat and a prized example of Chinese calligraphy. A kitchen shelf held several pieces of Selangor pewter.

Early Monday morning, Maimunah reported to the district school for the first day of the new term. She went to the faculty conference room for the customary orientation session and was confronted by the headmaster, *guru besar* Omar.

"*Selamat pagi*, Maimunah. We are surprised to see you today. Did you not receive the communication from the minister of education?"

"*Sama sama, Inche* Omar. What is this about? Where is Miss Ling? Where is Mrs. Tyler?" Maimunah saw that all the teachers in the room were Malays.

Guru Omar said, "The prime minister wishes to strengthen the Malay presence in all the professions. We now are required to replace non-Malay teachers with Malays who are sufficiently qualified. We also are required to speak *Bahasa Melayu* in our classrooms. I'm very sorry. You are an outstanding teacher, and I asked that you be retained, but the ministry is unwilling to grant a waiver. Your desk will be taken over by Karimah binti Ismail. You might take some satisfaction in knowing that Karimah was your own teaching assistant, and, through her, your spirit will be carried on in this school."

Maimunah smiled at Karimah, who looked away in embarrassment. "It's quite all right, Karimah. The PM made it clear that this would happen. I'm sure you will do well. Teach the children to think for themselves. *Selamat jalan* to all of you." She left the room and drove to the central post office to pick up her mail.

She returned to her cottage and set the mail aside while she made a pot of tea. Relaxing in the living room, she read the letter from the education ministry, informing her of her superannuation, along with a cash settlement. She tried to dismiss bitter feelings and thought, *Nothing to hold me here now. It's time to visit my mother.* With her mother in her thoughts, she brought out Li Lian's batik bag and fingered through its contents. She removed a few things randomly and placed them on the lamp table. Then she visited the greengrocer next door and purchased a half *kati* of mangosteens. She knew that the fruit was considered "cooling" in traditional Chinese medicine, capable of easing the temperament. Whether that idea was correct or not was of no concern to her. What she knew was that eating a perfectly ripened, delicious mangosteen gave her a sense of comfort that other foods did not provide.

She left the shop and saw a Chinese couple standing in front of her cottage. The man was about sixty, with a bandaged right arm in a sling. The woman was in her late forties and wore blue cotton trousers and a simple tan blouse. She had a poor complexion and straggly hair streaked with gray. Maimunah approached the couple.

The man smiled and said, "May I speak to you? I believe your name is Maimunah, is it not?"

Maimunah nodded and said, "Do I know you?"

The man said, "You do not know me, but I know of you. My name is Lim Chu San, and this is Mrs. Lim."

"Please call me Mei Lin," said the woman, extending her hand.

Maimunah shook her hand and then turned to Mr. Lim and said, "Why have you come to see me? And how did you find me?"

Chu San said, "My business associate, Saleh bin Rafiq, gave us your address. We have come from Singapore. There are matters that we would like to discuss with you."

Maimunah welcomed the visitors. "Would you like to come in and have some tea?"

"Thank you. We will stay for just a short while. Did you receive my letter? I wrote to invite you to a meeting of a few people who plan to participate in the political process, now that independence is upon us."

They entered the cottage, and Maimunah put water on the stove. She brought out a platter of biscuits. Mei Lin offered to help, but Maimunah said, "Thank you; that won't be necessary. Tea is simple enough, even for one unaccustomed to the kitchen."

Mr. Lim said, "We took the liberty of coming to see you because you did not respond to my letter, and the meeting is soon. I'll come right to the point, Maimunah. May I call you Maimunah?"

"Yes, of course."

"And please call me Chu San. We know of your activities with the Barisan in Singapore, and we heard of your excellent work at the school here in Kuala Lumpur. You have democratic ideas, and you are young and a woman. You are what we hope is to become the modern Malaysian. For that reason, we believe that you should represent your youthful contemporaries in helping to shape the new government and ensure that the country is not left to the corrupt old reactionaries, who are blind to the needs of the people

With your approval, we are prepared to back you for the city council in your district up here. And then, if all goes well, in a few years, the national parliament, starting with the House of Representatives. Confrontation is on its way out, and we should form a working partnership with Indonesia. There also is the possibility that the Singapore PM can be undermined, but unfortunately, the Barisan is a weak, ineffectual body down there, given mainly to throwing rocks at the US embassy. Pardon me; I know you have had a leading role in that activity, but it is not a serious effort. Attacking the United States is like a flea trying to consume a water buffalo. Are you interested?"

Maimunah thought for a moment and said, "This is so sudden. I never have been involved in elective politics. All I ever wanted to do is teach, but that has been taken from me by the government. I must think about this. Thank you for your confidence in me, but I really have done nothing to earn it."

The man said, "Will you at least come to the meeting and meet the rest of our group? There will be time for you to come to a decision about the council."

Mei Lin looked around the room idly as they waited for her answer. Suddenly, she stood up and pointed to the stack of ticket stubs resting on the bamboo lamp table. "Where did you get those slips?"

Maimunah was surprised by Mei Lin's unexpected question. "Why do you want to know?"

"Where did you get them?" she repeated. "Do you know what they are?"

Maimunah composed herself. "No, I don't know what they are. They belonged to my mother. They seem to be ticket stubs."

Mei Lin picked up the stubs and riffled through them. She seemed to be reading the handwritten characters. "Yes, these belonged to your mother." Her voice softened. She looked at Chu San, and he shrugged slightly.

"What are they?" asked Maimunah, somewhat perplexed.

Mei Lin lowered her eyes and said, "Saleh told us about you and your mother. I suppose you have a right to know. You are a grown woman now. I knew your mother. We shared a hard life together during the Japanese occupation. We were forced to become 'comfort women,' living in a military brothel as whores for the Japanese army. These tickets were purchased by the Japs for admission to the brothel. They gave a stub to the girl in return

190

for her favors. The girls could cash them in for Japanese occupation money, which could be used to buy little luxuries." She held out the handful of cardboard stubs. "These never were cashed in. I also knew your father. He was a Japanese officer who treated your mother badly. His name was—"

Maimunah suddenly screeched. "Stop! Do not mention his name. I never wish to hear it."

Mei Lin continued. "I understand, and I will finish the story. When she became pregnant with you, she had to escape from the place where we were kept, or she would have been killed. I helped her escape. I loved her and took my life in my hands to help her. She was so innocent. Sixteen years old at the time. Her full name was Goh Li Lian. Did you know that? She joined our jungle brigade and helped rid the country of the accursed Japs. She was a brave woman."

"Yes, she was," confirmed Chu San, "and she told us about you and how she cried at the thought of your growing up without a mother. You have a Malay name, Maimunah. She told us about leaving you in the kampong, where you were brought up in the Malay culture. She did what she thought was best. Then she left us, and we lost track of her for several years. We knew that she acquired a rubber estate, and we reconnected in some of her business activities."

Maimunah contained herself with difficulty. After twenty-four years, the reason for her abandonment by her mother became clear. Maimunah looked thoughtfully at Mei Lin and said, "As I told you, I never had an interest in politics. Wouldn't it be better if you ran for the council yourself? You seem so self-assured and experienced in political affairs."

Mei Lin said, "There are things in my past that might be held against me. Let's just leave it at that. You are a fresh young face, and that is an advantage in a new society."

"Can we look forward to seeing you at the meeting tomorrow?" asked Chu San.

Maimunah said, "I'll think about it, but I'm not promising anything. That's the best that I can do."

The Lims departed. As they walked away, Mei Lin said, "Do you think she can be elected in this district?"

"Perhaps, but we have much work to do. She will be a minority candidate. If she runs and wins, I believe that we can control her, provided that she is suitably indoctrinated. That will be your job, my dear. You already have made inroads with the story of her mother."

———<o>———

"Cagle, here. Yes, Edith, I'll speak to her."

"Hello, Mike. This is Maimunah. Something has happened that you should know about."

"Hi, sweetheart. What's going on?"

"I've been kicked out of my school by the government. There's nothing to hold me here in KL, so I'm leaving to be with my mother. Dr. Chow and Saleh are coming with me. Maybe you can find time for a visit."

"Of course. I'll drive up as soon as I hear from you. How do I get there?"

"That was the Tans' home long ago. Ah Yeng can give you the directions."

Chapter 29
The Reunion

"**R**ight there, next to the Panhard." Teow Seng eased his Mercedes into the narrow space pointed out by Saleh.

Maimunah waved a greeting from her doorstep and invited them into her living room. "I'm happy that you both are able to come with me."

Saleh said, "Maimunah, I want to talk to you about your mother. She is still a young woman and can lead a long and happy life but not if she is possessed by opium and heroin. It is just a matter of time until she swings from a rope for drug possession. She refuses to seek medical help herself, so we must visit her, unannounced."

"Saleh is right," said Teow Seng. "I hope we can help her. I have seen many opium addicts brought to the clinic by their families. Most are hopelessly deteriorated in mind and body and have given up all life's goals, except for the opium pipe. No effective treatment is available in Singapore. From what Saleh has told me, I fear that your mother is at that stage. I hope that you can give her the desire to try to conquer the addiction. I have arranged a brief leave of absence from the hospital, so we can leave immediately."

Saleh reached into an inner pocket of his jacket. "Here are three plane tickets. The flight from Kuala Lumpur to Kota Bharu leaves in two hours. When we arrive, we will be met by Li Lian's estate manager, a man named Wu Feng. He is loyal to her and was overjoyed when I called to tell him of our plans. We will leave Dr. Chow's car in the parking lot at the airport."

Maimunah packed hurriedly. They drove to the airport, and boarded Malaysian Airlines for the one-hour flight to Kota Bharu. The plane was half empty. A few Chinese tin miners smoked continuously and argued about tin futures on the London exchange. Maimunah's anxiety increased as the plane landed and taxied to the terminal, where Wu Feng waited in a Volkswagen bus. Maimunah never had ventured up to the wild highland country, and she was fascinated by the unfamiliar sights. They passed forests of teak and great stands of gracefully arching rotan. Wu Feng avoided a dead gibbon, either a traffic casualty or victim of a fall from the high canopy. They soon left the paved road and continued upward on a graveled forest road that became a muddy trail. The VW bus lumbered onward, with Wu Feng skillfully manipulating the manual shift to negotiate the sudden slopes and sharp curves.

In about an hour, the bus burst through a leafy overhang into a Malay village filled with dogs and children and glossy jungle fowl. Wu Feng slowed the bus and hailed a man, who waved from the doorway of a stilt house.

"That's Penghulu Ibrahim," said Wu Feng, turning to Maimunah and Teow Seng. The bus continued through the kampong and out to a dirt road that plunged back into the forest. Wu Feng maneuvered the bus around rocks and potholes for three miles, until they came upon a stand of old rubber trees with scarred tapping panels. "We never got around to replacing those rubber trees with oil palm," he explained. "Now that rubber prices have increased, we might start producing again," he said hopefully, addressing his comment to Maimunah, "now that you might be the new towkay."

Maimunah looked out in wonder at her mother's estate. They passed Dr. Sunteram's old house, currently occupied by Wu Feng and a village woman, who cooked, cleaned, and warmed his bed. The burned-out heroin factory and the old rubber warehouse were still in disrepair. The bus rolled to a stop in front of the villa.

"We are here," said Saleh. "I must prepare you for your meeting with your mother. She might not resemble the auntie Li Lian that you remember, but, in time, she might be restored to her former self."

Maimunah turned to Teow Seng and asked, "Is there some treatment that can help my mother?"

Teow Seng said, "Nothing can be guaranteed, of course, but I will have a better idea after I examine her, if she will allow it. Heroin addiction is not easily treated, but at least we can improve her nutrition. That always is necessary. If she can be built up physically, there is a drug that has been helpful in weaning addicts from heroin."

"Does that mean that they are cured of the addiction?" asked Maimunah.

Teow Seng explained, "No, I'm afraid not. We are merely substituting one drug for another. The new drug is methadone, a synthetic opiate with effects like those of heroin. It was synthesized by I. G. Farben about thirty years ago for use as a painkiller. Later, it was found that it could replace heroin in treating addicts."

Maimunah persisted, asking, "If methadone replaces heroin and acts like heroin, what's the point? Why not just keep the addict on heroin? What is being accomplished?"

"That's the usual question, Maimunah. The problem for the addict is that heroin is banned all over the world. England tried giving heroin to addicts, under medical supervision, but that practice was abandoned because of the public outcry. In America, there is a huge methadone maintenance program. The result is that the heroin addict becomes a methadone addict, but without many of the bad effects of heroin."

"Can we get this methadone?" asked Maimunah.

"I brought some with me," said Teow Seng. "Methadone maintenance is illegal in Singapore, but low-dose tablets for pain control are carried in the pharmacy. I brought enough for about three months. I must be careful to protect my medical license, so we must keep this confidential."

Maimunah listened appreciatively and, on a sudden impulse, threw her arms around Teow Seng and kissed him firmly. "Thank you, Dr. Chow. You have given me hope. Now, let us go in and see her. Come, Saleh."

The cook and maids were hovering in the entry, wringing their hands and wearing worried expressions.

Saleh said, "This is her daughter, Maimunah, and this is Dr. Chow. They have come to help. How is she?"

The cook said, "Not good. She eats nothing. All she wants is the opium pipe and the other drug. We can do nothing for her. Wu Feng is the only one who can talk to her. He brings her needles. He takes care of the household accounts. Okay, go in there and see her. It is shocking, not?"

They opened the door to the salon. Heavy opium vapors wafted out in the draft created by the opening of the door. They stepped into the room and peered into the gloom. As their eyes adjusted to the darkness, they could see Li Lian, lying on her side, clad in a dingy silk robe, holding the stem of the opium pipe as she drew the vapors deeply into her lungs. Her eyes were closed, and she seemed oblivious to the visitors.

Even in the darkened room, they could see Li Lian's emaciated state. Her hair was gray and uncombed. Her smooth ivory complexion had been replaced by a lined, sallow mask. A Tamil housemaid crouched next to her. As the visitors watched, the maid plucked an opium pellet from a porcelain bowl, heated it over charcoal embers in a bronze incense burner, and dropped it into Li Lian's pipe.

Saleh stepped forward and said, "Li Lian, it's Saleh."

She remained motionless with her eyes closed

"Li Lian, it's Saleh," he repeated.

Her lips moved, and she croaked, "I heard you. Go away. What do you want?"

Maimunah was aghast at the scene, but she knelt beside the recumbent figure and said, "Mother, it's Maimunah. I want to help you."

Li Lian opened her eyes and looked at her daughter's face. "Maimunah? How did you enjoy Switzerland?"

"Mother, I enjoyed it very much. Thank you for all your help. But I returned from Europe eight years ago and went to the National University of Singapore. Try to remember."

"Oh yes, you are a teacher now. You called me 'Mother.' Why is that?" Then she turned her head and noticed Saleh. "I see. He told you. Saleh, you promised. You broke your word."

Saleh said, "Yes, that is so. But I could no longer stand by while you destroyed yourself. I had nowhere else to turn. So I brought your daughter back to you. Do you remember the day that we saw her off to Europe? Look at her now. She is a grown woman, and she loves you."

Li Lian's eyes filled with tears as she gazed at her daughter. Then she noticed Teow Seng. "Who is that man? Why is he here?"

Maimunah said, "He is Dr. Chow, Mother, and he is here to help you get well."

"Dr. Chow?" she asked quizzically. "Are you the Dr. Chow who takes care of my friend Mrs. Tan Ah Yeng?"

Teow Seng said, "Yes, indeed. I have been her doctor for several years."

"How has she been feeling?" asked Li Lian. "I must visit her one of these days."

"She is doing quite well," said Teow Seng, "as long as she continues to take her medicine."

"She is fortunate to have a medicine that works for her," said Li Lian. "I am afraid that you would be wasting your time with me, Doctor. My life is here in this room." She beckoned to the maid to clear the side table of the opium apparatus. "And bring tea for my guests." The maid left the room, and the visitors seated themselves and took turns encouraging Li Lian to agree to treatment for her addiction. Li Lian slumped back on the sofa, closed her eyes again, and said, "I can't think. I haven't thought for months. Please … I am exhausted. Have the maid take me up to my bedroom. Perhaps I can sleep. You are all welcome to stay here. Maimunah, come to my room. Stay by me while I rest."

"Of course, Mother," said Maimunah.

The maid helped Li Lian up the stairs. The visitors watched sadly as the feeble Li Lian made her way laboriously, one step at a time. Teow Seng watched with clinical detachment.

Maimunah addressed Teow Seng. "She can barely walk. Can anything be done for her?"

Teow Seng said, "She is obviously wasted, so we must persuade her to eat. She has ulcerated injection sites on her arms and legs. The maid said that Wu Feng brought needles. I suppose he is her supplier. Once she is on methadone maintenance, she should feel better about herself."

"You said that the methadone has the same actions as heroin, and you will be substituting one addiction for another," said Maimunah. "How will that cure her?"

"Oh, I didn't say that it was a cure. I was careful to say that it is a maintenance program."

"For how long?"

"For the rest of her life, as long as I can provide the drug."

Maimunah looked worried and said, "Is that possible?"

Teow Seng said, "We can worry about that later."

Saleh said, "I will prepare sleeping quarters for us. I am familiar with this house."

They went up to Li Lian's room, and Saleh took over the domestic arrangements. He went out to check the electrical generators and the fuel supply. He assigned one of the Malay field hands to clean out the well house, and he assembled a crew to collect weeds and brush from the courtyard in front of the villa. When he passed the spot where he killed Kun Hua, he paused and scrutinized the gravel path for telltale signs. He asked the cook to make up a shopping list, which he delivered to Wu Feng, who was serving as the major domo of the household. Wu Feng left in a VW bus to buy provisions at the nearest Chinese market, thirty miles away.

Three days later, Li Lian sat out on the veranda with Maimunah and Saleh, while a maid served lamb curry with rice and mango chutney. Saleh picked indifferently at his lunch plate, flipping rice from his chopsticks for the benefit of a few mynah birds that had taken up residence in the bougainvilleas around the garden walls. A pair of large mountain pigeons swooped in to share the feast but were driven off by the smaller, aggressive mynahs.

Li Lian touched Saleh on the arm and said, "What is it? You are unusually quiet this afternoon. Are you not satisfied with the food?"

"Oh no, the food is good. I am not very hungry."

Li Lian persisted in her questioning. "What worries you?"

"We have reason to be concerned about our old business."

"Why now?" asked Li Lian. "The boat is gone, and we are no longer involved."

"That may be so," said Saleh, "but it has come back to haunt us. You know that the Indonesians took our boat. They found that the boat was registered to me in Sumatra, and they reported that to the Singapore authorities. I have been warned to stay undercover."

Li Lian said, "I am sorry for that. We needed the boat for our business, and I did not want my name to appear anywhere. Please forgive me for putting you in such danger. Who gave you the warning?"

"We have a helpful person in the American embassy. We are not the only ones in trouble. Chu San and Mei Lin also warned me about Mike Cagle."

It now was Maimunah's turn to react with surprise. "What about Mike? What has he got to do with all this?"

"Your boyfriend is not just a low-level embassy employee. He is carrying on his own war against our old business, and he shot Chu San last week."

"I must go." Maimunah left her seat and hurried away.

Li Lian said, "Who is this Mike Cagle?"

Saleh said, "He is Maimunah's friend."

"What kind of a person is he? Will my daughter be hurt by this man?"

"I believe they love each other. Mike has many good qualities. He can't be held responsible for the wicked actions of his country."

"Oh," said Li Lian, "you are making an individual exception. That is not the way your mind was shaped by the party."

"Perhaps, but I am glad that our business is finished."

"Yes, our small part of the business may be finished, but it goes on greater than ever. What we know for sure is that the triads still control much of the production and distribution of heroin. They are blood enemies of the communists. Maybe the two groups will destroy each other eventually. The triads have connections with the Corsican Mafia, and much of the Southeast Asian heroin makes its way to the American and European markets. We all have heard stories of addiction among the American forces in Vietnam. That is a problem that they must address in Washington sooner or later. I do not understand why it is allowed to continue. Then there is the yakuza. They are trying to cut into the business of the other groups. They also see the corruption of the American forces as a measure of retribution for Japan's defeat and the atomic bombs, not that they are particularly inspired by patriotism. I am relieved to be rid of the vile business."

"How do you know these things, Li Lian? You have been laid low by your ... ah ... illness for such a long time. We have newspapers like the *Straits Times* and the *Eastern Sun*, but they are mouthpieces for the government. They are not very daring in their journalism. Where do you get your information?"

Li Lian slyly smiled. "I have a very good loyal source. My trusted Wu Feng is a sponge for facts and rumors that he absorbs on his trips to Penang and elsewhere for marketing the rubber and palm oil. He tells me everything and leaves it to me to interpret—to extract kernels of truth from the chaff. Yes, Wu Feng has been important in my life for many years—along with you, of course," she added, as she saw the slight clouding of Saleh's expression.

"He has been a most dependable ally," said Saleh. "He has often told me of his love for you. I think he would like to enlist my support if you would be receptive to his courtship. He never would overstep in his relationship with you, but you must know how he has suffered in silence."

"Yes, I know of his feelings. After all, I am a woman, and I am not blind to his attentions."

"And those attentions included keeping you well supplied with the opiates."

"He understood my cravings, and he could not stand my pain."

"Did you never wonder how he happened to have such a large supply of opium and heroin?"

"Where he obtained it was of no concern to me. I assumed that Virinder had turned over his remaining supply before he returned to India."

"The truth is that he has been supplied by a refinery in the mountains. They pour tons of heroin a year into the life-blood of humanity. They drain off a few units for Wu Feng, for old time's sake. He pays market price for your drugs. Now that Dr. Chow is here, I hope that is a thing of the past."

"That is information that Wu Feng did not share with me," said Li Lian. "How did he happen to make contact with that refinery?"

"You were not the only opium processor up here. We thought we were, but I knew of other factories in the forest—on the Kra Isthmus and in the jungles of Thailand. All operated with no fear of discovery because of the wide-scale corruption of the police and the politicians. You must remember how much gold you threw at the locals. How many rajas and police chiefs did you have on your list? They were at your parties and dinners in this house and were happy to receive your hospitality, as well as your payoffs."

"So you have your own secrets that you did not share with me."

"There was no reason. We were doing fine. Did you know about the Japanese timber merchant? He came here in the years before the war and obtained timber concessions. I met him when I worked for Mr. Tan. He was a member of the Japanese secret police. A man named Kosaka. He set up the opium business for Mr. Tan and also did a lot of clear-cutting with Thai labor. He took out the timber but also created open fields for growing the poppy. You weren't the only one who tried that. I know these mountains from my wartime activities, and I know where these fields and factories are located. They are still in operation—on a grander scale than ever. Beyond the reach of the law. They rule through greed and fear."

"Preying on human weakness," said Li Lian. "Just as we did, not so long ago."

"*Benar,*" said Saleh, "but it has cost us as well."

"You refer to my illness?"

"Yes, and to Wu Feng's finger," said Saleh, somewhat cryptically.

"What do you mean?" asked Li Lian, obviously surprised.

"Have you not noticed his shortened little finger?" asked Saleh.

"Yes, but I understood that it was an accident with a tapping blade. Of course I remember. He was quite ill. The infection and fever almost cost him his life. Work on the estate slowed down without his supervision while he recovered. What are you trying to tell me?"

"It was not an accident. When your drugs were exhausted, he went into the forest to find another source. He found the Japanese heroin factory. Their guards seized him and brought him to the big bosses. They were amused by him and finally agreed to provide him with drugs to keep you going. They knew all about you and me and your estate. They sent him on his way, minus the end joint of his little finger, as a warning to keep his mouth shut."

Li Lian listened carefully and said with a trace of irritation, "I am surprised that you did not share that information with me before. Oh well, no matter now. We are finished with the drugs. It is much better that we have rid ourselves of the constant fear of discovery. My mind is at rest. Now if I can see my lovely daughter into a happy, secure future, I can die in peace."

"Please, Li Lian, don't speak of dying. You are still a young woman. Only forty-one. Do you still celebrate your birthdays?"

"I try to forget. It brings back unbearable memories of my loving family. Memories that I have hidden away for a quarter of a century. Horrible memories. Ohhh …" Her piercing wail startled Saleh. Her body stiffened, and she gripped the ends of the upholstered armrests of her chair, staring vacantly at the trees surrounding the villa, as images filled her mind.

Saleh looked at her with deep concern and said, "I understand. We all have burdens. Some are heavier than others. But in some ways, we have been most fortunate, have we not? We have shared memories as well. The one that I cherish most is when Boon Hok and I were able to extract you from your torture in Singapore during the dark days, with our lovely Maimunah developing within you."

Li Lian's expression softened, and she turned to Saleh and said, "Yes, the lost years, but now, time for recovery. Look there." She pointed to the orderly rows of rubber trees, their dark-green oval leaves glistening in the afternoon sunlight.

Maimunah and Teow Seng came strolling through the grove in easy conversation. They walked through the iron gate into the courtyard and joined Li Lian and Saleh on the veranda.

Maimunah pushed strands of hair away from Li Lian's cheeks. "Hello, Mama. Did you leave us any lunch?" Then she called through the screen door, "Fatiah, some iced tea for the doctor and me, if you please. And for Mama and Saleh as well."

"Thank you," said Li Lian. "So how does the new oil palm acreage look? The crop should be ready by the end of the year."

"Very good. Don't you agree, Teow Seng?"

Dr. Chow took off his spectacles and wiped them. "Oh, you know I am no expert in these matters, but the trees look fine to me. When you replant the estate with oil palm, I hope you leave a small stand of rubber trees as a sentimental reminder of the past."

"I will do that for you, Dr. Chow," said Li Lian, "if you agree to stay with us here on the estate. You are needed here, you know."

"That may be, but I am needed in Singapore also. Many patients still depend on me."

"You can practice medicine here as well. I am not the only one who requires your services. We can build a clinic for you. Design it yourself. There must be some attractions here." Li Lian unconsciously glanced at Maimunah.

Maimunah spoke up. "We have talked of my ideas for an elementary school and his ideas about public health and eradicating contagious diseases. We think alike on many of these subjects. Perhaps he can be persuaded to remain here." She turned to Teow Seng. "Is it possible?"

"Who can say what is possible?" Dr. Chow answered. "I must have some time in Singapore."

Chapter 30
Valerie

The days moved slowly, and Mike sensed the fading of Maimunah's image. He forced himself to retrieve memories of the curve of her hip as she lay on her side in his bed and the swelling of her nipples against his tongue.

Caruso interrupted his reverie. "We can't keep you here much longer. Time to wrap up the operation."

"Okay, Ralph, I've been waiting to hear from her, but I've waited long enough."

At the embassy the next day, his telephone rang. He picked it up. "Hello?"

"Hello. Is this Mike Cagle?" asked an English-accented woman's voice.

"Yes, who is this?"

"My name is Valerie Barlow," said the voice. "I was Maimunah's roommate at school in Switzerland. She and I have kept up a correspondence, and she mentioned you in one of her letters. You and she are good friends, aren't you?"

"Yes, we are very good friends, and she has mentioned you to me also. I'm glad to finally have the chance to talk to you."

"And so am I," she said. "The reason for this call is that my parents have decided to leave England and settle in New Zealand. They feel that they will be more comfortable in the social climate of New Zealand. I agreed to join them there, at least until I figure out what to do with my life, and decided to stop off in Singapore to look up Maimunah. I am here now, staying at the Adelphi Hotel. The last letter from her had a return address in Kuala

Lumpur. I found her phone number in the KL directory and called her several times, but there was no answer. Do you know where she is?"

"She is not in Kuala Lumpur right now, but I will tell her that you called."

"Thank you, Mike. I am planning to go to Bangkok for a few days for a brief tour of Thailand and then on to Aukland. If she shows up, will you tell her that I am anxious to get together with her? She can leave a message at the Adelphi. It's been nice meeting you, if only on the telephone. Well, good-bye, Mike."

Chapter 31
Please Come

"Mike, I miss you. I need you. Please come." Maimunah's voice was sad and tearful. "Ah Yeng can give you directions."

"I'm on my way, sweetheart. How's your mother?"

"She's improving. Dr. Chow is treating her for the terrible heroin addiction."

Mike hung up the telephone and went to Caruso's office. "Ralph, I think we can finish our job here. I'm going up to Li Lian's estate. She may be the answer to our problem, and I hope you'll agree to handle her gently."

"Fair enough. I decided that some time ago, but I gave you enough time to figure it out for yourself. How do you want to proceed?"

"I'll call you when I get there, and we can work something out. She's protected by the locals, so we don't want to start a war." Mike returned to his office and dialed. Ah Yeng answered. "Ah Yeng, this is Mike Cagle. How are you and your sister?"

"Oh, very well, Mike. And you?"

"I'm fine, but I must talk to you. May I come over?"

Ah Yeng spoke hesitantly. "Can you tell me what you wish to discuss? Is it not something that we can talk about on the telephone?"

"I would prefer to see you at your home."

"I don't know, Mike, I have many things to do."

"Please, Ah Yeng. It's very important. It is about your friends."

"Which friends? I have many friends."

"I don't know all your friends. You know which friends I mean. I must speak to you about Li Lian and Maimunah."

"Oh, Mike, please try to forget Maimunah. I call her on the telephone. She is following her sense of duty. Her mother's suffering may never end, but Maimunah hopes to relieve it as much as possible, and Dr. Chow is a very good man. He can help Li Lian."

"What I wish to see you about concerns all of them, including Saleh. I will be at your house in fifteen minutes to explain."

"Very well, Mike. I will be here waiting for you."

———◄○►———

They sat in the Tans' drawing room, sipping tea as the houseboy silently padded away.

"I will speak candidly, Ah Yeng, so you will appreciate the seriousness of this matter."

"Mike, you are making me afraid. Not for myself, but for the others. What is this about?" Ah Yeng listened attentively as Mike explained the purpose of his visit.

"Government people have information that points to Saleh and Li Lian as possible drug traders. They made their suspicions known to me and asked if I would assist them in tracing the source of the drugs that enter Singapore illegally."

"And you think that Li Lian and Saleh are connected to this?"

"I didn't say that. Others are wondering if there might be such a connection."

"I can assure you that there is no such connection. Tell those others that they would be wasting their time with Li Lian and Saleh. Tell them to look for the real culprits, who probably are right under their noses."

"I can tell them that, but it would only be a guess. They know that drug dealing is widespread, but they do have the names of our friends and intend to track them down for questioning. It would be better if I located them before the others find them."

"What would you do if you found those others? How could you help?"

"I'm not sure, but I want to visit the estate in Kelantan and help in any way possible. Maimunah needs me as well. She told me that you can tell me how to get there." As Mike spoke, he sensed another presence in the room. He turned and saw a ghostly Su Yin standing in the doorway, her hair hanging loosely around her shoulders. She wore a white robe over a nightgown.

Ah Yeng said gently, "Hello, little sister. I am happy that you have roused yourself. Mike is paying us a social visit." Then, as though speaking on a sudden impulse, she said, "I am going away with him for a while. You will be quite comfortable here without me. The servants will take good care of you, and I will be back before you ever miss me. Now, why don't you go back to your room, or go visit the birds in the greenhouse? I am sure they will be glad to see you again."

Su Yin laboriously climbed the stairs.

Ah Yeng said, "She has been in failing health for some time. Her mind has been unable to support the weight of the past. She speaks now of joining our dear cousin, Rosi, in the cemetery. She leaves the house only to bring offerings to Rosi's grave. Alas, what does it matter? We all will be there soon enough."

Mike felt a surge of sympathy for Su Yin, but he was uncomfortable with Ah Yeng's fatalistic pronouncement. He said, "You told Su Yin that you were going with me."

"Yes, it would be better to clear the air. Then we all can rest well."

"Will you call them to announce our arrival?"

Ah Yeng suddenly gave in to a crying fit that left her speechless for several long moments. She tried to apologize through her racking sobs and managed to say, "Yes, I will call and tell them to expect us. It will be strange to visit my old home. I am surprised that I can still function, but I must continue for the sake of my sister. If anything happens to me, I hate to think of how she will end up. In a mental hospital, I suppose."

Chapter 32
Dengue

Mike drove back to his flat and flopped on his bed, drenched in perspiration. He sat up to take a shower and was seized with an excruciating headache that caused him to cry out. He fell back onto the sodden bedsheets, gasping with the pain of his aching head and muscles. He felt his flushed face, and the skin was rough to the touch. A rash extended from face and neck onto his chest. As his misery increased, he realized that he required medical attention. Teow Seng was unavailable, so he decided to call Dr. Chih, a private physician who occasionally dropped in for lunch at the Alumni Center.

Chih was a tall, self-confident extrovert. He towered over his colleagues, in personality as well as physical stature. He smoked long, thin cigars, and his Panama hat and white linen suit gave him the jaunty appearance of a successful tin miner. His outfit was embellished with a diamond pinky ring and gold-banded Rolex. He drove a large air-conditioned Pontiac equipped with a tape deck. The rear seat featured a pull-out bar and a five-inch television set. Dr. Chih was a physician on the "private side," as distinct from most of the doctors in Singapore, who were government-salaried on the "public side." Dr. Chih was viewed somewhat derisively by the public-service doctors, who felt that they pursued a higher calling. Dr. Chih seemed not to mind at all, as he conducted his private practice and accumulated generous fees. He also happened to be an excellent doctor and expected to be well paid for his services.

Mike called Dr. Chih's office and left a message with his nurse to return the call. Two hours later, Dr. Chih called and greeted Mike. He said, "Sorry

I missed you, Mike, but I was out on the course at the Island Club. Shot an eighty-four. Not bad, wouldn't you say? How can I help you?"

Mike described his symptoms and asked Dr. Chih if he would be kind enough to make a house visit.

Dr. Chih said, "I will visit if you insist, but the diagnosis is unmistakable. Mike, you have dengue fever, a nasty little viral disorder, carried by mosquitoes. The intense muscle pain is called myalgia, and that explains its other name—breakbone fever. There is no particular treatment for dengue, except for time. It is self-limiting and will be all over in four or five days. Drink fluids and take it easy." He chuckled. "I guess I don't have to tell you that. You won't be able to do much of anything anyway. You'll just be flat on your back. Now that I have told you that, if you still want me to visit for some hand-holding, I will be glad to do so. By the way, have you been traveling up-country? There is plenty of dengue in the villages. You can't neglect the mosquito repellent. If you've noticed, there are no mosquitoes in Singapore. Trucks are out spraying DDT everywhere. If you develop chills, call me right away. We also have to worry about malaria."

Mike was relieved to hear Dr. Chih's diagnosis. "I've heard about dengue, and I can sweat it out on my own. Thanks very much."

Dr. Chih said, "Fine, Mike, but if there is any doubt in your mind, call my office. Good-bye."

"Good-bye." He sagged back on the bed and allowed himself to groan softly. He called the embassy and told Edith Loh that he had dengue fever and would be out of commission for a while.

The disease ran its course, and he prepared to drive to Kelantan.

Chapter 33
Another Reunion

Mike drove the Consul into the Tans' driveway at dawn. Ah Yeng was waiting on the terrace, dressed in loose-fitting cotton shantung trousers, a jacket, and a wide straw hat. He loaded her valise into the trunk next to his, and they drove north along the mountainous spine of Malaysia. She told Mike that she had called her old estate earlier, and they would be expected the following day. They stopped at an inn for the night. In the morning, they had a light breakfast and continued on to the estate, with Ah Yeng showing the way into the mountains and through the forest. As they drove through the plantation, the field workers stared at them with curiosity.

They drove up to the villa and saw the entire household assembled to greet them. Li Lian and Saleh walked to the car, followed by Maimunah and Teow Seng. Wu Feng lingered on the veranda, standing next to a pretty young Thai woman in a batik sarong. The domestic staff peeked from windows on the upper and lower floors.

Ah Yeng climbed out of the car, blubbering, and fell into the arms of Li Lian, who patted her comfortingly on the back. Mike ran to Maimunah, and they kissed passionately.

She whispered, "My darling, I love you. Never leave me."

Teow Seng stood with slumped shoulders and downcast eyes.

Li Lian extended both hands to Mike and said, "It's a pleasure to meet you at last. I have heard a great deal about you from Maimunah. Come; let us go inside and relax. You can stay with us for as long as you like. You may

not have the luxuries of Singapore, but you can be quite comfortable here."
She ordered a servant to carry the valises upstairs to the guest rooms.

As they walked from the courtyard gate to the veranda, a distance of
about two hundred feet, Mike looked around in wonder. He took in the
expanse of the villa and its several additions, some of them with crumbling
masonry and shuttered windows. The main house was typical of British
colonial architecture, although not as splendid as the great mansions of the
wealthy European planters. Wings were added as apparent afterthoughts,
some extending through and beyond the walls of the courtyard. The entire
structure was covered in stucco that showed many structural cracks, and
the red-tiled roof supported shaggy patches of moss, with ferns and small
saplings growing out from the spaces between the tiles. A double door on
the second story opened onto a wooden balcony with peeling white paint
above the veranda. Several ornate balusters were missing from the balcony
railing. Pomegranate trees lined the inner surface of the courtyard wall,
with scarlet fruit studding the ground below. A profusion of red splashes
decorated the wall, the product of the congregation of small birds pecking
energetically at the ripe fruit.

Ah Yeng walked with Mike and softly said, "My husband made this our
Istana. We had a very large family in those days." She peered at the wall next
to the front gate, focusing on some depressions near the gateposts. "Look,
Mike. The bullet holes are still here."

Mike went to her side and saw the conical pits in the stuccoed surface
of the cinder block wall. Amateurish repairs had been made, replacing some
of the shattered blocks with irregular granite rocks held in place with terra
cotta mud. "Did bullets do this?"

"Yes, machine-gun bullets. Fired by Li Lian and her guerrillas when
they rescued us from the Japanese. You have not heard that part of our
story, have you?"

Mike whistled in surprise. "Whew, sometimes I forget what you have
been through. I have a lot to learn."

Teow Seng shouted, "Come on, you two! The meal is almost ready."

Mike and Ah Yeng walked to the veranda and accepted glasses of cold
coconut milk from a tray proffered by one of the maids. They were escorted
to separate bathrooms. After showering and dressing in fresh clothing, they
joined the others in the dining room.

Ah Yeng ran her fingers over the polished surface of the heavy teak table and, addressing no one in particular, said, "I remember when my husband had this table built. It seated twenty comfortably. Oh, the happy gatherings we had in those days." She turned to Li Lian. "What happened to the rest of the chairs?"

"We had no need for so many. Wu Feng took two or three. Didn't you, Wu Feng?"

"Yes," said Wu Feng, who now dined regularly, along with his Thai mistress, in the main residence. "We have Virinder's old furniture, but Thani would like to replace it eventually. I don't care, but you know women. They like pretty things." Thani sat demurely, understanding none of the conversation, which, in deference to Mike, was conducted in English.

Teow Seng spoke to Ah Yeng. "How is your sister getting along? The last time I saw her, she seemed burdened by the weight of past memories. How is she now?"

"Alas, Dr. Chow, I am sad to tell you that her mind has snapped. I can't imagine what is in store for her. She never was a very strong woman, but now I fear that she cannot function on her own. I shall do the best I can, of course, but her recovery may not be possible. Perhaps there is some sort of medicine that could help her. Is there something that you could do for her?"

"It saddens me to hear that," said Teow Seng. "I plan to visit Singapore to reassign my patients, and I will look in on her, if you wish. Is she in good hands now?"

"Oh yes, the servants are quite dependable. They have known Su Yin for many years and will take good care of her."

As the meal progressed, Li Lian gradually turned the conversation to another theme. "Mike, this might be a good time to clear the air. There is no need for secrecy now. Saleh and I understand your interest in our old business. Wu Feng and Ah Yeng know of the business that was carried out by Mr. Tan before he was killed during the war, and I have followed in his footsteps. You must understand; it was necessary because of the postwar decline in rubber prices. Otherwise, I could not have continued to support the estate workers. They remained here, working the rubber, but we lost much money on that operation, and they depended on me for their very existence. It would not have been possible without the other business. Of course, it took its toll on me, and I have my daughter and Dr. Chow to thank for pulling me back from the abyss." Maimunah and Teow Seng sat silently with lowered eyes. They had not heard Li Lian speak this way before.

Li Lian then said, "Mike, if you have some questions about our present activities, you might wish to raise them now. Please be candid."

"Very well," said Mike. "To come directly to the point, Saleh has been identified as a drug-runner by the Indonesian authorities, and they have made that known to the Singapore police. You, Li Lian, are known as an addict. The police discovered that by prying into Dr. Chow's medical records. They have concluded that you might be behind the smuggling of heroin into Singapore." Saleh and Li Lian glanced at each other, shaking their heads slightly as though denying the possibility of such a thought.

Mike continued. "It's a serious problem for American soldiers on leave from Vietnam. I was dragged into this situation to see if I might be willing to help shed some light on who might be responsible for the illicit drug dealing. How or why I became involved is not important. I agreed to help, and the people who recruited me want me to try to trace the pipeline. Saleh warned me that I could be in danger if I pursued this search. I hope he did not mean that the danger might lie in this house."

Maimunah broke in, saying, "Of course not, Mike. How could you even think such a thing?" Then she said, "Isn't that right, Mama?"

Li Lian smiled tenderly at her daughter and said, "Certainly, darling. I admit that there might be reason to think that we were still in that business, but that is over and done with." Then to Mike, she said, "We are not involved in this trade. Tell your friends that they can look elsewhere."

"Where can they look? They told me that if I come up with nothing, they will track you down as their only suspects. That could create problems."

Saleh looked at Li Lian and said, "May I speak?" When she nodded, he spoke to Mike. "We are out of it and have no intention of getting back in. We would not be allowed, even if we wished to return to the business."

Mike interrupted. "Not allowed? By whom?"

"By those who control the trade now. They probably are the ones your friends should be hunting down, but they will need an army to clear them out."

"Do you know who they are," asked Mike, "and where they are located?"

Wu Feng looked away and squirmed uncomfortably in his chair.

Saleh said, "They are everywhere in Southeast Asia—Burma, Thailand,

Malaysia. The jungles are filled with poppy fields and heroin factories. Any one of them could be the supplier to Singapore. Stay clear of them, Mike. Those men are ruthless murderers."

Saleh's comments brought the discussion to an end. The diners left the table and walked outside for a stroll in the gardens. Wu Feng bid the others good-night and guided Thani through the main gate and onto the path to their house.

Mike watched Wu Feng leave, wondering if there were a reason for his hasty departure. He caught up with Teow Seng and Maimunah and said, "Did any of this surprise you?"

"I shut out the possibilities," said Teow Seng. He laughed derisively and said, "I accepted the myth of the confidentiality of the doctor/patient relationship, but I should have known better. I am under no illusions that my treatment of Li Lian will be taken in stride by the Singapore authorities. They can make it hot for me, if they wish. I helped myself to a load of methadone from the hospital pharmacy. Well, I will keep it up as long as she needs me. She is making wonderful progress, don't you think?"

"Yes, indeed," said Mike. "I can see where Maimunah gets her beauty."

The monotonous *chonk! chonk! chonk!* of the nightjars could be heard from the garden wall. A servant ran past the drawing room and out the front door to shoo them away.

"Annoying birds," muttered Li Lian, and she left for her bedroom.

<hr />

In the morning, the houseguests gathered for a convivial breakfast on the veranda. Wu Feng and Thani sat inconspicuously, a bit apart from the others, uttering nothing more than polite salutations. Wu Feng lifted his cup of tea, and Mike saw that the first joint of his little finger was missing. Serious knife cuts were a common occupational hazard among rubber tappers. Wu Feng quickly put the teacup on the side table when he saw Mike looking his way. When the morning meal came to an end, Wu Feng left hastily, followed by Thani, trailing good-days to all.

Suddenly, Mike arose and trotted after them. "Wait up, Wu Feng. I'd like a word with you. Can you spare a minute?"

Wu Feng turned and said, "I must go and check the tank trucks. We are sending out the oil tomorrow." Then he told Thani to go to their house without him.

"Just one or two questions. Maybe you can clear up something for me. It's important."

"No, no, I don't think I can help you. I must go." He walked briskly out to the main oil storage tank, where the drivers lounged about, waiting for the field hands to complete filling the tank trucks.

Mike returned to the veranda and sat next to Saleh. "Saleh, I believe you are no longer responsible for drug smuggling, but I want to find out who is. Can you help me? Where are the heroin factories located? If I have some evidence of their existence, I can pass that along to others, and maybe that will lift the suspicion from you and Li Lian. Where are the poppy fields, and who is running the operation?"

Saleh slouched in the cane chair, rubbing the side of his jaw with a thumb and musing silently. Then he said, "Well, Mike, I don't know how or why you are involved in this business. Those who run the drug trade now will never be stopped. Not by you and not by your government. The drugs are everywhere. Poppies grow like weeds in this land, and thousands of tons of opium leap out of the ground year after year. We even grew it here a few years ago but no more. There are many heroin factories in these forests. No attempt is made by the local governments to put an end to the business. All profit from it. The closest source of opium is about fifty kilometers from where we sit. Deep in the forest, and there is a small village there to house the workers. None ever leave. Woe to those who try and also to those who try to discover the location."

"If that is the case," said Mike, "how do you know about it?"

"I have explored these highlands for many years, going back to the time of the Japanese. I know one of the men who started the drug business here. He was working for the Japanese government before the war, and he is still at it, privately. He is much older now and very powerful. I think he might be the supplier of heroin to the American military in Singapore. Stay away from him, Mike."

"I will, but can you tell me where he is? I would like to tell certain people about him so they will leave you alone. Will you show me on a map? I have to take something back to Singapore."

"You are much too persistent. It can bring harm to you. I saw you staring at Wu Feng's finger."

216

"Oh, that. Yes, what happened? An accident with a tapping knife?"

"You are almost right, except that it was not an accident."

"What do you mean?" asked Mike.

"It was a warning. Let's leave it at that," said Saleh.

◄◦►

In the evening, as the sun was setting, Mike went out to walk through the rows of rubber trees. The field workers had departed, and the bright green foliage was cool and inviting. He wandered for twenty minutes, marveling at the silent vastness of the plantation. A half mile from the villa, he entered the oil palm acreage and found Wu Feng slashing at a tree with a parang.

Mike walked up to him, smiling, and said, "Good evening, Wu Feng. Are you trying to kill that tree?"

Wu Feng stepped away from the tree, which was overgrown with staghorn ferns. "Oh, hello, Mr. Cagle …"

"Please call me Mike."

"Yes, Mike, I am trying to rid this old tree of the ferns that are choking the life out of it. I told the workers three days ago to rid the old trees of the ferns. They haven't done it yet. They will hear from me tomorrow."

Mike said "Why remove them? They don't harm the tree."

Wu Feng laughed and said, "That's right; they do not harm the tree, but they grow over the nuts, and that interferes with the yield of oil. Well, these are some of the oldest trees here, and I think we will uproot them after the next harvest."

Mike said, "There is something else, and I think you can help me."

Wu Feng slashed at a fern and said, "I told you this morning that I had nothing to say. It would be better if you gave up whatever you are trying to do. You are chasing trouble. I heard what you said last night at dinner. Give up the search and return to Singapore." Wu Feng caught himself and added, "I am sorry, Mike, if I sounded rude. Stay as long as you like. Have a nice rest. We have horses you can ride and a mountain stream. You can even catch fish. It's better than Cameron Highlands for a relaxing time in the cool country."

Mike stood with folded arms and said, "I am close to something, and I don't intend to leave until I discover where the heroin comes from. If I give

217

up, the people I know could make life difficult for Li Lian and Saleh. Have you considered that?"

Wu Feng hesitated and then said, "You could be badly hurt or even killed in this foolish hunt. Think of how that would make Li Lian feel. I can tell that she is very fond of you."

"And I am fond of her and Saleh and the others. I will take my chances. All I want is to verify that the poppy fields and heroin factory still exist. Then I can pass the information on to the people in Singapore. A view from a distance will be sufficient. Would that be possible?"

"Very well. I see that you are determined to carry through with this foolishness. You saw us topping off our tank trucks today. Early tomorrow morning, we are sending out our weekly convoy of five trucks with six thousand imperial gallons of palm oil per truck. That is thirty thousand gallons of oil. Do you see that smokestack over there about a mile beyond the rubber trees? That is the oil-processing plant." He said proudly, "It earns more money for the estate than we ever realized from the rubber. The trucks go out on our road that was constructed by the Japanese during the war, when they occupied this estate. We improved it over the years. The road runs for about forty kilometers down to a state highway. About halfway down, there is another road that goes into the forest. We never go in there. It extends about fifteen kilometers up into the mountains. At the end of that road is a thousand hectares of poppies and a heroin factory run by a Japanese gang. The field workers are Thai, for the most part. There may be a scattering of Malays, but there are no Chinese. There is an airstrip for sending out the heroin. Their road is used mainly for supply trucks. If we run across one of those trucks, we take no notice."

Mike listened carefully and said, "How do you know all this—about the road and the poppy fields? Have you seen it yourself?"

"Yes," said Wu Feng. "I have seen everything, since the time of the Japanese. They even forced me to work for them when they stole this estate from Mr. Tan. I was here when Li Lian and her friends attacked this villa and wiped out the Japanese soldiers who lived here. Ah, what a night that was. When the smoke cleared, I joined Li Lian's brigade until the war ended." He halted in his personal narrative but added. "Yes, I have been all the way up to the poppy fields. This is what I got for my trouble." His eyes blazed as he held up his hand and displayed the shortened little finger. "The price of doing business with those demons." He set his mouth firmly, and it was apparent that he would go no further in his account.

"Are you willing to take me there?" asked Mike.

Wu Feng said, "There is a reason for my telling you as much as I told you. If you will be ready when the sun comes up, we can follow the tank trucks in your car. I will drive. I will take you to a high place overlooking a great plateau where the poppies are grown. We dare go no closer, but you can see the fields from that distance. Then we must get out quickly. We should be back to the estate before dark. I want you to agree to keep this between us."

"I agree," said Mike.

Chapter 34
The End of the Road

At dawn, the rubber tappers already were hard at work, when the truck engines started with an earth-shattering roar. Mike was in the passenger seat of his Consul as Wu Feng eased the car behind the convoy. Mike looked back at the villa and glimpsed Saleh standing on the veranda.

The line of vehicles moved onto the laterite road out of the estate and maintained moderate speed for several kilometers. When they came to a long downhill grade, the oil-heavy tankers downshifted and continued slowly for fifteen minutes, like a file of fat black caterpillars on a tree branch. When they passed the road leading to the poppy fields, the last truck in the convoy blasted his air horn. Wu Feng gave an answering "beep" and turned the Consul onto the road into the forest.

The tree canopy enclosed them, and they drove uneventfully through the green tunnel for several more kilometers, climbing a steep grade and recovering the altitude they had previously given up on the way down from the estate.

"We are climbing another mountain," said Wu Feng. "This road appears on no map, and it cannot be seen from the air."

"Are you sure that we will not be discovered?" asked Mike.

"That should not be a problem. Their trucks venture out for supplies only once a week. They are very well organized up there. This is not their day to travel. I try to work around them with our oil shipments."

Without warning, Wu Feng turned the steering wheel abruptly and guided the car onto a narrow trail.

"Hey!" shouted Mike, gripping the armrest to steady himself as they jounced over the forest litter. "Where are you going?"

The car stalled about a hundred feet into the jumble of vegetation. Wu Feng laughed and said, "Don't worry. This trail is used only by elephants and aborigines—and now, by us. We are where we want to be. This is the end of the road." He reached into the backseat for a small canvas bag and his parang and forced the door open against the bushes that pressed against the side of the car. He eased himself out of the door and said, "Let's go. Follow me."

Mike pushed himself out of the car and looked dolefully at the heavy paint scratches on the passenger side, with metal gleaming through in several spots. "I suppose your side is all scratched up as well," he said to Wu Feng.

"Don't worry about it," said Wu Feng. "Paint jobs are cheap in Singapore. Come; we have a long hike through the forest. Here—can you use this?" He drew a handgun from his canvas bag and handed it to Mike. "For snakes." He clicked the safety off and on and said, "Keep it on safety until you have to use it."

Mike carefully accepted the gun and tucked it into his belt, next to his own Special.

Wu Feng led the way, slashing at overhanging branches and vines, with Mike following closely. After an hour of laborious plodding uphill along the lonely trail, they came to a clearing being reclaimed by the forest. Wu Feng beckoned to Mike. At the far edge of the clearing, the cloudless sky could be seen between tree trunks. They were on a high ridge, with the forest growth descending gradually away from them toward a broad plateau, bounded by distant mountains.

"There are your poppies," said Wu Feng, handing Mike binoculars that he'd taken from his bag.

Mike adjusted the focus, and the expanse of varicolored blossoms spread before him like a crazy quilt. A village lay next to a mountain stream, and a huge chateau, complete with towers and an inner courtyard, overlooked what appeared to be a gray factory building. An airstrip with a hangar at one end was cut through the poppies. Field workers swarmed through the flowers like an army of ants. He took a tiny spy camera from his pocket and snapped a few pictures.

"Seen enough?" asked Wu Feng.

Mike nodded and said, "I'm ready to leave."

The leisurely downhill walk back to the car was a welcome relief from the lung-busting earlier ascent to the ridge. They entered the Consul, and Wu Feng backed it carefully onto the road. He drove down toward the laterite estate road, with Mike speaking animatedly of the vast poppy farm hidden in the mountains.

They negotiated a steep curve about a kilometer from the estate road and suddenly came face-to-face with a canvas-covered military truck of a type used for transport of men and supplies. The truck was stationary in the center of the road, and two men in green coveralls were examining tire tracks on the road bed. They each carried a shotgun. A third man stood nearby, moving the barrel of a submachine gun back and forth, as though he were playing a water hose on the jungle vegetation.

Wu Feng slammed on the brakes, saying, "They shouldn't be here today."

Mike swiftly transferred the guns from his belt to the glove compartment and locked it with a tiny key. "Oh shit, what happens now?"

"Sit still," hissed Wu Feng.

The men with the shotguns ran to the car, one on each side. They pounded on the doors and motioned to the occupants to get out. Wu Feng told Mike to get out quickly. The man with the machine gun strode to Wu Feng, speaking harshly. Wu Feng answered.

In a flash, the machine gunner smashed Wu Feng on the side of the face with the gun butt. Wu Feng slipped to his knees, bleeding from his gashed cheek. Mike moved to help him to his feet, but the other two pinned him against the car with their shotguns. The machine gunner shouted orders to his comrades, and one of them got into the Consul, started it, and pulled it to the side of the road. They swiftly and roughly tied the prisoners' hands behind them, blindfolded them, and heaved them into the rear of the truck, where they lay among cartons and burlap sacks filled with food supplies. The machine gunner climbed in and sat on a bulging sack, with his gun leveled at them.

Mike felt the truck lurch forward as it started up the hill. Wu Feng lay on his side, groaning and semiconscious. Mike clumsily tried to right himself and struggled to a sitting position. His guard thrust the gun barrel into his chest and shoved him backward.

Mike was gripped by a helpless feeling. He was under absolute control. He was floating with no time reference, as in a dream, bouncing in the rear of the truck, with crates and cartons banging painfully against his head, legs, and back.

The truck reached its destination and stopped. The guard climbed out over the tailgate and stood with his weapon slung over his shoulder. The other two men got out of the cab and let down the tailgate. They climbed into the rear of the truck and shoved Mike and Wu Feng sprawling to the ground, still blindfolded. The truckers hoisted them to their feet and poked them ahead with gun barrels for about fifty yards. The two captives were kicked to their feet several times when they stumbled and fell. They were prodded up two wooden steps and into a building permeated with the odor of vinegar. Rough hands guided them through a doorway and into a quiet room. Their blindfolds were ripped off, and they faced a smiling, gray-haired Japanese man, sitting at a small wooden table, idly spinning a bone-handled skinning knife. He peered over his spectacles at the two helpless captives and said in English, "Welcome, my friends. I am honored by your presence. We have very few visitors up here." The smile vanished, and his face hardened. He impaled Wu Feng with his stare and said, "You! I thought I had seen the last of you. You left with your life, and now you are bringing it back to this place. Explain."

Wu Feng, terrified and with blood still oozing from his cheek, could scarcely speak. Finally, he was able to say, "I meant no harm. I merely wanted to show my friend the beauty of these mountains. Please forgive me, Mr. Kosaka."

Mike was startled to hear Wu Feng address the Japanese by name. Mr. Kosaka then looked at Mike and said, almost gently, "And do you find these mountains beautiful"—then he added facetiously—"sir?"

"Y-yes. Yes, sir, I do," stammered Mike.

Again, the baleful glare. "What is your name? And what is your business here?"

"Uh … Mike Cagle, sir."

"You are English? American?"

"American."

Kosaka repeated angrily, "And your business here?"

"Just visiting. I was visiting a friend here, before I return to my country."

Encouraged by his ability to control his sense of panic, Mike added, "These ropes are very tight. Would you be good enough to have them removed?"

The smile returned to Kosaka's face. "Ah yes, of course. How thoughtless of me." Barking an order, he gestured with a twirling motion of his index finger to a glowering guard, who still cradled a shotgun in the crook of his arm. The guard stepped behind Mike and cut the rope binding his wrists. He did the same for Wu Feng. Still smiling, Kosaka said, "Now, does that feel better?"

"Much," said Mike and Wu Feng in unison, as both men rubbed their wrists to restore circulation.

"I want you to understand that I am not a cruel man," said Kosaka, "but there are certain conditions that must be respected. The most important is that you must take no note of our existence. We have shared these beautiful mountains with the Tan estate for many years without incident. You can attest to that, Wu Feng, can you not?"

"Quite true," said Wu Feng.

"You have received a warning that you must honor the rules, or coexistence will no longer be possible, have you not?" said Kosaka, pointing at Wu Feng's finger with the missing terminal joint.

Wu Feng nodded with downcast eyes.

As Kosaka raised his hand to point, Mike saw that he too was missing the end joint of his little finger. He turned to look at the guards and saw that they also were shy a finger joint.

"A second warning will be issued … *now!*" Kosaka screamed. Two of the guards seized Mike and bent him over the table. The third guard grabbed Mike's wrist in an iron grip and forced his fingers flat on the table. In a lightning motion, Kosaka slashed down on Mike's little finger with the skinning knife, severing the terminal joint.

Mike's felt only a sudden pressure but no pain. He was thankful that the nerves had not yet regenerated from Dr. Fong's handiwork. One of the guards tied a cotton cord tourniquet around the base of the shortened finger. Then he poured something over the cut end and bound it in surgical gauze and adhesive tape. One of the other guards busied himself with mopping Mike's blood from the table."

Kosaka's face contorted into a twisted smirk. "Ah, the American takes it without a flinch. No further warnings will be issued. If the rules are broken again, Li Lian will suffer. Her fate is in your hands. I have told the guards to drive you down to your car and free you. I am a generous man." He left the room.

His orders were carried out, and in less than an hour, Wu Feng and Mike were seated in the Consul, driving back to the villa. Wu Feng commiserated and apologized profusely, declaring himself responsible for the outrage inflicted upon Mike. Mike did his best to reassure Wu Feng that he, Mike, through his insistence on being taken to the heroin source, was at fault.

Wu Feng suffered his own damage in silence. The swelling on his cheek blurred his vision on one side, and he turned his head slightly to favor the intact eye.

They arrived at the villa as the sun disappeared. Li Lian and the others were seated on the veranda with evening libations. Maimunah looked at them with dismay. She saw Mike's hand covered with the bloody bandage and Wu Feng's bruised and bloody face. In a shocked voice, she said, "What happened to you? Who did this to you?"

Teow Seng went to the injured men, and his doctoring instincts took over. He told Maimunah to take both of them into the kitchen, while he went to fetch his supplies. When he returned, he found Maimunah gently washing Wu Feng's face. Mike was sitting at the table, carefully peeling the bandage from his pinkie. Teow Seng laid out a few instruments, a bottle of alcohol, a dark brown antibacterial solution, swabs, gauze bandages, and tape. Assessing the situation, he went first to Wu Feng. He lightly touched the swollen cheek and said, "Blunt trauma. There is crushing damage to the zygomatic arch. We will need X-rays to see how bad it is, but at present, there is no treatment but time." He expertly cleansed and disinfected the wound and covered it with gauze and tape.

Teow Seng told Maimunah to accompany Wu Feng and Thani to their house and see to it that he was put to bed. Maimunah returned to stand by as Teow Seng went to work on Mike.

"How can I explain this to Dr. Fong? Let's have a look." To preclude pain as the blood returned to the finger, Teow Seng numbed the hand with procaine and removed the tourniquet. He went to work, cleaning, suturing the skin to cover the exposed bone, and disinfecting. He applied an antibiotic powder to the wound and wrapped it in surgical gauze. He finished the treatment with a penicillin injection and a tetanus shot. When he was done, he said, "Feeling better?"

Mike nodded. "Nice job."

Maimunah took Mike's intact hand and led him up to his bedroom. She undressed him and put him to bed. Then she removed her own clothing and lay next to him. "I love you, my darling. You must never leave me."

"That thought never entered my mind." Mike kissed her hair, her ear, her neck, her breast.

Maimunah pushed him gently back onto the pillow. "Relax, my love. Don't move. I'll do it all."

———◦———

The next morning, Mike called the embassy. "Morning, Ralph. Are you in the mood for a punch-up?"

"Anytime. What's the deal?"

"There's a big-time poppy farm up here. We need to take it out. Agent Orange should do the trick. I'm checked out on Hueys. Can you locate one down there?"

"I'll see what I can do. I can fly a Huey, if I can find a Huey. The Brits used Agent Orange against the Malayan communists not too long ago, so there might be a few barrels lying around. Give me twenty-four hours. Call me tomorrow. How goes it with your lady?"

"Can't help lovin' that gal. Call you tomorrow."

"Fair enough. By the way, I turned the case of kilo blocks over to the cops in Singapore. They have a dragnet out for the Lims."

———◦———

Mike called Ralph the next day. "Hello again. Any luck?"

"All we need. There's a Huey gunship out at Seletar. Almost ready for the scrap heap, but they maintain it to give the RAF chopper pilots their flying hours. I wheedled it away from the CO by promising to take good care of it. It has one rocket pod and a fifty-caliber machine gun in working order. It's also equipped with the tank and spray for Agent Orange. They used it up-country a couple of years ago to starve out the commie jungle brigades. When the RAF abandons the base at the end of the year, they have to dispose of forty drums of Agent Orange that's stored in their warehouse.

I took a couple of hundred gallons off their hands. I'll refuel at Ipoh, and you'll see me sometime tomorrow."

"A genius at work. Are the armaments armed?"

"Oh yeah, it took a little expediting, but the ambassador is good at that."

"The ambassador's in on this?"

"Forget I said that, Mike."

"Okay. You can beam in on the magnetic bug that you planted under the Consul when I wasn't looking."

"I knew that would come in handy. *Ciao.*"

A day later, they all gathered on the veranda for four o'clock tiffin. Mike and Wu Feng sat together in the camaraderie of wounded warriors. Li Lian was stunned to hear of the mammoth poppy plantation a morning's drive from her estate. She looked accusingly at Saleh, who turned his head away and remained silent. Ah Yeng flitted about, pouring tea, running to the kitchen, and returning with platters of dumplings, crumpets, and fresh fruit. When she left the kitchen, the cooks and maids grumbled about the unwelcome visitor trying to take over their jobs.

They all were sipping tea when the silence was disturbed by an unfamiliar sound. With great beating of blades, a helicopter circled the villa and landed in an open field.

Li Lian sat transfixed with horror as she witnessed the stately descent of the helicopter. She choked out, "They're back."

Mike patted Li Lian's shoulder. "Don't worry; they're our guys."

The doors of the helicopter slid back, and two men leaped to the ground. They cradled submachine guns as they raced in a crouch toward the villa. They burst through the gate with their guns leveled at the veranda, and one of them shouted, "Don't get up, folks. We're just dropping in for tea." His companion wore the uniform of an RAF flight officer.

The people on the veranda sat frozen in their seats. Mike jumped up and shouted, "Caruso, you crazy bastard. Who're you gonna rub out with those tommy guns?"

Caruso lowered his gun barrel and grinned broadly. "Hello, Mike. How ya doin'? This coulda been the wrong address. You never know."

Mike reassured the breakfast group. "It's all right, everybody. I know this guy. He's here for a little payback." To Caruso, he said, "Glad you made it, and who's your friend?"

"Mike, this is Squadron Leader Darrol Stanton. The RAF wants their bird back in one piece, and Darrol is here to make sure that happens."

Caruso walked to the Consul and reached far under the rear bumper. "I can use this again," he said, slipping the magnetic bug into a pocket of his flight jacket.

Li Lian said with surprise, "Is he a friend of yours?"

"Only the best," said Mike. "It's a long story, but I think you are entitled to a full explanation. Don't you agree, Ralph?"

Li Lian's thoughts flashed back to an earlier time when she was a principle in a similar helicopter action, but she quickly regained her sangfroid. "Mike, why don't you invite your friends to put down their guns and join us?" Then she addressed the newcomers. "May I offer you gentlemen some refreshment?" Without waiting for a response, she told a maid to set two more places and bring fresh food for the guests.

A servant brought out extra chairs, but Caruso remained standing and armed. He said, "This is not a social visit. Mike, am I correct in assuming that the Malay gentleman is named Saleh ... and that is Li Lian?" He jabbed the gun barrel in the direction of Li Lian.

"You are correct in that assumption," said Li Lian, "and is there an explanation for your arriving this way ... and for your lack of courtesy?"

"It appears that everyone is asking for explanations," said Caruso. "Well, who wants to go first? Any volunteers?" He relaxed and said, "Okay, I guess I do owe you an explanation. Do they know why you came here, Mike?"

"They do now," said Mike. "We're wasting our time with them. They're not involved."

"I know that," said Caruso. "If they were still active, I probably would have been picked off by now by a sharpshooter from an upstairs window."

"Involved in what?" asked Li Lian.

"Your old trade," said Caruso. "We know about your drug business. If you've given it up, fine. It's none of our affair. The local authorities can go after you, if they feel like it." He looked at Mike and Wu Feng and said, "Looks like you two have been in a brawl. Who won?"

"Nothing like that," said Mike. "It's quite a story. We're lucky to be alive. I came up here to find out about the drug running. I'm satisfied that Saleh and Li Lian have retired. But then we tangled with the other guys."

"So I see," said Caruso. "What happened?"

Mike held up his bandaged hand and said, "They kept a piece of me. Those Japs play rough."

"Japanese?" Caruso raised his eyebrows. "Looks like they took the same joint that Chu San's triad guy chopped at Bugis Street. What else can you tell me about them?"

"Nothing much, except that they have a huge drug operation in the mountains. We saw their poppy plantation and heroin factory. They caught us and messed us up, and the ones who did it also were missing pinkie joints."

Caruso reacted to that information. "Jesus, you're lucky they let you go. They sound like the yakuza. They self-mutilate by chopping off a finger as a sign of loyalty to the gang, and they chop off other people's fingers as punishment for being too nosey. That is, if they're in a good mood. Otherwise, they hack folks to death as another option. They're untouchable. They control much of the drug traffic around the world. They are into heroin, all right, all the way to San Francisco, and amphetamines big time in Tokyo. Some of the top Japanese politicians are in their hip pocket. A few members of the Diet are said to be missing a finger. Hell, we even used the yakuza after the war as cold warriors to drop the dime on high-level Japanese with communist sympathies. What a world."

"What can we do about this lot?" asked Mike.

"If the yakuza are behind the drug running into Singapore, they're too big for us to stop, but at least we can wipe out whoever gave you a hard time. Now, we'd like a spot of tea."

Chapter 35
Air Raid

Caruso sat at the controls and turned to Squadron Leader Stanton. "Darrol, do you want to drive the bird?"

"No, I'm just supercargo on this run. When you get it out of your system, I'll bring it home to roost."

"Okay, we're on our way."

The Huey rose majestically and headed in the direction indicated by Wu Feng's index finger. Mike sat at the machine-gun port, arranging the ammunition belt in orderly layers. Caruso looked over the controls for the rocket launcher and the defoliant spray.

In a half hour, Wu Feng touched Caruso's arm and said, "Just over that ridge."

Caruso nodded and guided the Huey up and over the forested ridge. The valley floor lay below, covered in a blanket of jungle white. The Huey descended, and Caruso activated the spray, crisscrossing the vast acreage almost at blossom level. Workers ran for cover in wooden sheds. Several men, armed with rifles, emerged from the large factory building. An occasional *ping* sounded within the Huey, as a rifle bullet found its mark but bounced harmlessly off the armor plate.

Mike shouted, "My finger's in that building, Ralph. Time for a cremation."

Caruso nodded and triggered the launcher. The factory building exploded in flames, fed by the vats of solvent used to extract the opiate. The flames spread to a detached garage, and three trucks were added to the conflagration.

"Now for the plane."

Caruso guided the Huey to the airstrip, and Mike blasted away at the lone airplane tethered in front of the hangar. The machine-gun bullets tore through the sitting duck, and it became a fireball.

Mike said, "That just about does it. Let's go home."

—◦—

Kosaka stood in the carnage, quivering with rage. He ordered several armed men into a surviving truck and took the wheel himself. He sped over the ridge to Li Lian's estate, muttering, "They all die."

—◦—

Caruso brought the Huey down gently. The four passengers emerged and walked to the veranda, where Li Lian, Maimunah, Saleh, Ah Yeng; and Teow Seng waited anxiously. Caruso said, "I'm afraid it's not over yet."

Wu Feng said, "Mr. Kosaka will seek vengeance. We must be prepared."

Ah Yeng shrieked, "Kosaka, did you say? That beast is still here?"

A maid came out on the veranda and walked to Li Lian. "Madam, Penghulu Ibrahim is on the telephone. He wishes to speak to you."

Li Lian went to the phone. She returned and informed the group, "Ibrahim told me that a truckload of men just sped through the village, heading in our direction. He said that the truck was driven by an older Japanese man. What shall we do?"

Mike ran to the Consul and removed both guns from the glove compartment. He checked the clips and handed the Walther to Wu Feng. He pocketed his Special.

Caruso and Stanton already had their machine guns ready. Mike herded his friends into the villa.

Teow Seng said, "I can handle a gun. Li Lian, you must have guns here. Get one for me."

Li Lian already was armed with the Beretta that Chu San gave her many years ago. She'd kept it cleaned and loaded ever since that time, even through her years of drug use. She said, "I will use this myself."

Saleh threw back his shoulders and stood as a Malay warrior, with kris in hand. He said, "I fight my own way."

Mike looked at him with respect and thought, *It's good that he's on our side.*

The little army crouched behind the stone wall, guarding the villa, and waited for the adversary. Caruso said, "Let's avoid a massacre, if we can. I will take out the driver as soon as they show up. He's the boss. If the others want to fight, we'll have to finish them as well. Here they come."

The truck roared through the stand of oil palm and approached the villa. As it arrived at the main gate, Caruso stood and leveled the machine gun at the driver. He squeezed the trigger—and the gun jammed. A rifleman standing in the truck bed fired, and Caruso reeled back and fell. Two shots came from behind the stone wall, and the truck veered off the road and crashed into a tree. Kosaka tumbled out and sprawled on the laterite, with a Special slug in the head and a Beretta slug in the chest. Mike and Li Lian stood side by side, holding smoking guns. The man who shot Caruso also flew out of the truck as it struck the tree. Saleh was on him in an instant, knee on his chest and kris at his throat.

Mike shouted, "Don't kill him!"

Stanton leveled his machine gun at the men still in the truck and shouted, "Raise a gun, and I'll spray the lot of you. Wu Feng, gather up the artillery."

Maimunah knelt next to Caruso, holding his head gently in her lap. He muttered, "No wonder the marines dumped the tommy gun. I shoulda had a BAR."

Teow Seng rushed up and assessed the damage. "Looks like the bullet bounced off a rib. Let's get you inside. Maimunah can help me patch you up."

Suddenly, Ah Yeng raced from the villa, waving a large butcher knife. She ran up to the lifeless Kosaka and spat in his face. She screamed, "You vicious monster! Where are my children? I will cut off your head and feed it to the pigs!"

Mike ran to her and wrapped her in his arms. "It's all over now. Try to let it go."

She cried hysterically as he led her up to the veranda and eased her into a wicker rocking chair.

Wu Feng and Saleh took charge of the six riflemen, who were Thais from a village on the Kra Isthmus. Li Lian decided that it would be wise to take them on to work the oil palm. That way, they could be kept from spreading the story of their little war. They were grateful to have their lives spared and pledged loyalty to their benefactress.

Kosaka's body presented a problem, but that was resolved by Stanton. "We can fly him off the northern tip of Sumatra, and Wu Feng can shove him into the Andaman Sea. I'll bring the chopper back and pick up anyone who wants a ride to Singapore."

———◇———

That night, Mike held Maimunah close. He loved her deeply and was entranced by her kind nature and generous spirit. She felt protected in his arms. "Mike, you must never leave me. I must have you in my life forever. I want you to be my husband. Please marry me. We can have a good life— here, if you are willing, or anywhere else that you wish. I belong to you."

"My darling, I love you and want you, but it's time for the rest of my story. I never lied to you, but I kept certain information to myself."

Maimunah was alarmed to hear this. "What information?"

"I'm not just an ordinary embassy employee. I'm an officer in the American air force. Officially, I'm Captain Michael Cagle, a fighter pilot in the Vietnam War. I was assigned to the American embassy in Singapore to try to disrupt the drug traffic to our soldiers on leave. The job we just did on Kosaka's operation brings me to the end of my stay here. Soon, I'll be shipped back to my outfit—and out of your life."

Maimunah's tears were in full flow. "I don't care. I love you, and you say you love me. Why can't we be together? I don't want you out of my life."

"I don't know what I'll be facing when I'm back in combat. We live day to day, and it's not easy on the nerves. I couldn't stand the thought of saddling you with the worries of an army wife."

"But I want to be saddled. I want to give you everything a woman can give to a man."

They were filled with sadness and joy throughout the night, and they made love hungrily, as though it were for the last time.

Chapter 36
Hello, Vietnam

The thumping beat of the Huey brought them out to the veranda. Stanton and Wu Feng dismounted and joined their friends.

Li Lian said, "Join us for lunch?"

Stanton said, "Thanks. What's on the menu?"

Lunch was served, and the conversation was awkward, avoiding any mention of the Andaman Sea.

Stanton took a deep drag on his Parliament and said, "Time to be on our way. Whoever wants a ride should pack and be ready to go in an hour."

An hour later, Mike, Ah Yeng, and Caruso climbed into the Huey, and they headed south.

Teow Seng remained at the estate to continue Li Lian's treatment.

Maimunah remained to bond with her mother. "You don't have to hide your secrets, Mama. Mei Lin found me. She told me about the horrible life she shared with you. I know that my father was a Japanese soldier. Now, I would like to know his name."

"Oh, my darling, I have tried to blot out the memories. He was Hideo Hoda. I escaped from Singapore, and he is gone forever. Whatever might be left of him is in you."

"And what can you tell me about your family? That is more important to me."

"More memories to haunt me. Japanese soldiers killed my young brother, Ronald. Your uncle Ronnie will be fourteen years old forever. They also drove my parents out of our home. I can't bear to wonder about their fate.

Now tell me about Mike. I see strength of character in that young man—a man of action. He also is very handsome. What is there between you?"

"I love him dearly, Mama. I want to share his life."

—◇—

Mike and Caruso joined Ambassador Duncan in his office.

"Well, gentlemen, you carried out your assignment, and I commend you privately. Publicly? That's a different story. How's the rib, Ralph?"

"I know it's there, but it's not keeping me awake at night."

"Good. This is supposed to be a debriefing, but I don't have to know all the details. Just tell me enough to keep me from sounding stupid, if or when I'm asked about your miniwar."

The conference was over in twenty minutes.

"Ralph, I know you're itching for more variety in your secret life, but we're going to keep you here for a while to keep an eye on our soldiers on R&R. Mike, you did more than we might have expected, and it's time to rejoin your outfit."

Mike and Ralph went up to their offices on the second floor.

Ralph said, "What we did was just a temporary fix. Others will rush in to fill the hole we made. There will still be thousands of junkies going home when this fucking war is over. We are inflicting a drug culture on the good old U-S-of-A. By the way, I solved another mystery. Do you remember how the guys at Serenity House ducked away when I showed up? That was because of an inside informer. A couple of nights ago, I came back to my office for something or other, and I found Edith Loh going through my desk. She turned out to be a communist mole."

Mike chuckled. "That explains our new receptionist. Sounds like you still have some work to do around here. I'll drop you a line from 'Nam. We can become pen pals."

—◇—

Mike returned to Cam Ranh Bay and resumed his old routine of flying air cover on bombing missions up north, with orders to avoid engaging the enemy in aerial combat. That made no sense to him, and he saw the war as a pointless, anticommunist panic attack. He viewed the military leadership as feckless and incompetent, led by a pompous general with MacArthur delusions.

He wrote to Maimunah, and his life centered on mail call for her daily letters. She never left his mind, and he lay in his bunk at night, holding her tenderly in his arms until he fell asleep.

———◄○►———

Two months after Mike left Singapore, Wendell Frost went to Caruso's office.

"Morning, Wen. What's happening today?"

"Nothing yet, Ralph. Have you heard of an English woman named Valerie Barlow?"

"No. What about her?"

"I'm afraid she has come to a bad end. She called Mike a couple of months ago. The receptionist picked her up on our phone log."

"What do you mean? What bad end?"

"Read this clipping from the *Malayan Star*."

It was a short piece:

> Miss Valerie Barlow, a British subject traveling in Malaysia, was executed by hanging under the provisions of the Dangerous Drugs Act of 1952. Miss Barlow was detained in Penang with a kilo block of heroin in her luggage. With that much dangerous drug in her possession, she was tried and convicted as a trafficker in narcotics. A representative of Amnesty International protested the mandatory death sentence required under the drug laws. Miss Barlow's parents flew from their home in New Zealand to claim the body.

When Caruso was done reading, Frost said, "There's no telling when one of our guys might meet the same fate."

Caruso said, "Jesus, they're really doing what they said they'd do. Can I have the clipping? I want to tack it up on the bulletin board at Serenity House. I'll write to Mike about this. I don't know how he knew her, but he might want the information."

When Caruso answered the phone, Ambassador Duncan said, "Ralph, will you come to my office, please?"

Ralph entered and was alarmed at the ambassador's grave countenance.

"Have a seat. This morning, I received the casualty report from 'Nam. Our dear friend Mike Cagle was lost in aerial combat. I just called Colonel Sloan, CO of Mike's fighter wing, to follow up on the bare report. It seems that he was flying air cover, and his bomber group came under MiG attack. Mike broke off to engage three MiGs. He shot down two, but the third nailed him with a heat-seeking missile. One of the bomber pilots saw him eject over Hanoi. I'm terribly sorry to bring you this sad news."

Janine Gorton opened the letter from Cam Ranh Bay.

> Dear Mrs. Gorton,
>
> I regret to inform you that your son Captain Michael Cagle was lost in aerial combat on November 15, 1967. He was seen to eject from his aircraft after it was struck by a missile. His parachute opened, but he was lost to view. If he landed safely, he might have been taken prisoner of war. Until we hear otherwise, we declare him to be missing in action. I urge you to keep your hopes high. He is a strong, resourceful young man, and you can be proud of his service to our country. As a courtesy, we will forward his personal belongings to you to keep until he is able to return, God willing, to claim them himself.
>
> My kindest regards to you and your family,
> Col. Raymond Sloan

Janine Gorton sat at her kitchen table in Standish, Massachusetts, weeping over the package delivered from Mike's air base. A pile of tear-soaked tissues lay on the floor next to her. Her mind turned to her husband's package long ago from Guadalcanal. Now she held her son's from Vietnam.

Under Mike's uniforms, she found a stack of envelopes secured with a rubber band. She spread them on the table and arranged them sequentially. All were in the same hand; all were postmarked from Kota Bharu; and all were opened, except for the last. She held the last envelope tenderly, pressed between her palms in a prayerful gesture. Almost as though she were violating a confidence, she slipped a thin blade under the flap and slowly and carefully slit the envelope. She removed the sheet of violet onion-skin paper and read.

My dearest, darling Mike,

Your last letter filled me with indescribable joy. I carry it with me constantly and read it over and over and over. Mama is delighted that you want the wedding to take place at the villa. She is happy to have you as a son-in-law, and I hope your mother will like her new daughter-in-law. I imagine that Ralph will be your best man. You could have asked Teow Seng, but he has returned to Singapore. He left a large jar of tablets, so we can treat Mama for many months. He assured me that he will fly back if we need him for a medical emergency. He also confessed that he agreed to come to the estate to treat Mama because of his love for me. He hoped that I might eventually return his love. I assured him that I did love him but not in the way he had in mind. He is overcome with guilt at what he sees as an unforgivable betrayal of you, his best friend. Perhaps you could write to him and offer some consolation. I hope he will be able to accept our friendship and come to our wedding. Finally, this bloody war must come to an end, and you can come to me. Please, my darling, take care of yourself, and know that I will love you until the day I die. I am your Maimunah forever.

The last envelope was postmarked three days after Mike's F-4 became scrap metal.

———◆———

She called her husband at his law office. "Thaddeus, please come home. Mike's things just arrived, and I can't stop crying."

"I'm leaving right now, darling. I love you."

———◇———

She held out the stack of letters. "Look, Thad. All from a woman named Maimunah. She loves our son very much, and they are planning a wedding. It will be nice to have a daughter-in-law, but ..." Janine's tears flowed.

Thaddeus said, "She probably doesn't know about Mike. She must be told. The postmarks are all from Kota Bharu, Malaysia. We must write, but we only have a first name and no address."

Janine said, "Her name is Maimunah Goh. I found it in her first letter. She explained to Mike that she has taken her mother's family name. I don't know what that's all about. She just signs 'Maimunah' to the others. I will send our letter to general delivery and hope that she gets it."

———◇———

A month later, Janine received a letter from Kota Bharu.

Dear Mr. and Mrs. Gorton,

I was devastated to receive your letter and learn that Mike was lost in the terrible war. I assumed that missing in action most likely meant that he was dead. Now I know otherwise, and I am ecstatically happy to learn that he is alive. Just yesterday, I received a letter from my darling that he is a POW in Hanoi. Some of the letter was blacked out by the censors, but all I care about is that he lives, and I love him more than life itself. He has written to you also. Perhaps you already have received his letter. Someday we shall meet. Until then, my love to you both.

From your future daughter-in-law,
Maimunah Goh

Chapter 37
The Hanoi Hilton

Mike regained consciousness, his body numb against the hard slab serving as a bed. He gingerly touched a wet lump on the side of his head and flinched. He looked at his bloodstained fingertips. His ribs ached. One eye remained half closed.

The man on the next slab looked over with a wry smile. "Wake up, buddy. Looks like they worked you over pretty good. How do you feel?"

Mike turned his head with difficulty, unable to dispel the throbbing pain. The neighbor's face was bruised. His right arm was suspended in midair, splinted, and wrapped from wrist to shoulder. "You're no bargain either. Where the fuck are we?"

"Welcome to the Hanoi Hilton. I beat you here by a month. Got the special rate. What brings you here?"

"F-4 nailed by a heat-seeker. Ejected into salt water—I'm pretty sure it was Halong Bay. Fractured a tibia on the outrigger of a fishing boat. The fishermen dragged me out of the water and unbuckled my parachute. They probably turned it into a sail. How about you?"

"Skyhawk took it in the ass by a SAM. I ejected into fresh water. At least it satisfied my thirst. From your looks, I figure you were questioned by that sadistic cocksucker we call the Weasel. Did you give him anything?"

"Name, rank, and serial number."

"Good. We're trying to keep it that way. Last week a couple of guys cracked and signed a statement attacking the warmongers in Washington. Don't know how long I can hold out." His face contorted. "Oh shit, the leg's killing me. Good luck, buddy."

The years passed. Mike hobbled about with a crutch fashioned from a tree branch. In deference to the International Red Cross, his captors allowed him to write bland letters to family and friends. His existence centered on return mail from Maimunah, Ralph, and his parents. His slab neighbor refused repatriation, telling his captors, "I'm not leaving this shit house unless we all go together."

In 1972, a guard ordered Mike to clean up and join a group of prisoners assigned to meet with an antiwar delegation calling themselves Women's Strike for Peace. The men were seated at a conference table. The door opened. Women filed in, clutching lists of prepared questions.

Mike sat with head bowed, indifferent to the program, until he heard a whispered, "Mike." He looked up directly into the eyes of Maimunah. He lurched to his feet—speechless. The years had been kind to her, fine-tuning her beautiful face and form. They faced each other, trying not to look like lovers.

She said, "My darling, I'm sorry to shock you like this, but I was afraid to say anything in my letters. I heard about this group and barged in on Ambassador Duncan. I begged him to pull strings for a visa. He was a great help in getting me this far. Ralph threatened to kill anyone who tried to stop me."

Mike searched for words. "I can never express how deeply I love you."

"Keep trying, sweetheart. I can wait."

"I must ask you—how is your mother? How is she dealing with her problem?"

"She is coping, with the help of Teow Seng. He visits when she needs him, always accompanied by his new wife." Maimunah giggled. "He gave up on me and married Dr. Fong. When they come to the estate, she never lets him out of her sight. He has been appointed minister of health. We are so proud of him. One of his goals is to establish a government-financed methadone maintenance program in Singapore. He has managed to install an experimental program for elderly opium users, but the parliament is reluctant to extend it to other opiates."

"Not surprised to hear that. They're a careful lot. I remember what the PM said about 'digits.' Does she have a social life?"

"To everyone's surprise, she married her lawyer, Roger Adams. He had been so tied into the drug trade that he was unable to return to a conventional law practice. They live comfortably in the villa, and he attends to the palm oil business. At least she has a caring companion. I think he might be gay but no matter."

"And Wu Feng?"

"He and Thani moved into the villa. They're filling one of the wings with little children. Wu Feng still manages the plantation. Saleh has moved into Ibrahim's village and still acts as my mother's protector. I never understood him completely. There are things in his past that are beyond me."

"What now?"

"I rented a little flat in Hanoi. I want to be near you until the war ends, and you are released. After that, who knows?"

"I know. When that day comes, we marry, and I take you home to meet my parents."

———◇———

The Paris Peace Accords brought about a ceasefire in January 1973. Mike was released a month later, and a military plane flew him to Hawaii after a stopover in Manila. Maimunah took an earlier commercial flight and was waiting for him at the Honolulu International Airport. They bought a tourist marriage package—a barefoot wedding on Waikiki Beach, followed by a honeymoon special at the Royal Hawaiian Hotel.

Mike said, "It's a slight improvement over the Hanoi Hilton."

———◇———

They entered the arrivals section at Logan International Airport. Mike located familiar figures in the waiting crowd. He threw his arms around his tearstained parents. "Mr. and Mrs. Gorton, I wish to present Mrs. Cagle." Tears, hugs, and laughter happened all the way to the parking lot. Thaddeus drove them to the family home in Standish, a seaside town on the north shore of Boston Harbor.

Mike and Maimunah moved into Mike's old bedroom, decorated with posters of Ted Williams and Chuckin' Charlie O'Rourke. A sword was suspended on hooks above the headboard.

Maimunah touched everything and said, "I never thought of you as a little kid. Where did you get that sword?"

"Oh, I guess you might call it spoils of war. My dad—my 'now' dad—sent it home from Guadalcanal. He saw my real dad kill the Japanese owner of the sword. My real dad was killed later. I never knew him. I have a wallet that belonged to the Japanese guy. His name was Hoda. There's a photo ID in the wallet." Mike saw Maimunah's stricken expression. "What's the matter, honey?"

"Do you still have the wallet? Can I see it?"

"Of course—if it's still where I left it." He opened a dresser drawer. "Here it is."

Maimunah took the wallet and leafed through its contents. She withdrew two items. "Look, Mike—this is the ID card with his photo. He is my father, Hideo Hoda. This other piece is an unused brothel ticket. I've seen the ticket stubs before—in my mother's carryall bag. Look at the back, written in pencil, 'Li Lian tonight.' Michael, my love, I must tell you that your daddy killed my daddy."

"How charming. Well, neither of us knew either of them, so they can stay strangers."

———◇———

In a few days, they rented a furnished apartment, and Mike introduced his wife to a simple amenity of New England life. "We can go out to the beach at low tide and dig a load of softshells. I haven't had a bucket of steamers for years."

———◇———

The phone rang, and a familiar voice said, "Hiya, Mike. How ya been?"

"Ralph, how the hell are you? And where are you?"

"Weekend at the Parker House. On my way to Washington to talk to the stuffed shirts at some committee hearing. They want to hear about the dope trade that they say doesn't exist. How's Maimunah? Can't wait to see her. You too, of course. Meet me tomorrow for dinner—Locke-Ober's at eight."

The next evening, Mike led Maimunah along Winter Place to the tired old restaurant that once excluded women from the main dining room. They entered and were greeted by the maître d'. "Follow me, please." He escorted them to a table.

Ralph Caruso, in full air force regalia, stood and extended his hand.

Mike took the hand. "A bird colonel. Ralph, you old sonnavabitch."

"Colonel Sonnavabitch to you, my boy. I was reclaimed by the air force."

Maimunah said, "Whoopee! We're all together again. Cagle and Caruso—sounds like a vaudeville act." She threw her arms around Ralph and kissed him on the lips. "How's the cracked rib?"

He said, "Until a minute ago, the highlight of my life was lying on the ground, bleeding, with my head in your lap. Now I have a new highlight. You can kiss me anytime. Mike, what are your plans for the future?"

"Still undecided. I mustered out as a major. Had enough of playing soldier. My dad would be happy if I went to law school. He's chairman of the board of selectman of our town, and the local folks want him to run for Congress. If he runs and wins, he would like me to take over his law practice. Don't know if there's much excitement in that."

Maimunah yanked on his tie. "You don't need any more excitement. Have you ever thought of settling down and leading a normal existence?"

"What would you do for fun? Let's order." Ralph gestured for the waiter.

They worked their way through three orders of Lobster Savannah and a decent bottle of Sancerre, and they talked and talked until closing time.

Mike and Maimunah walked Ralph back to the Parker House. As they embraced, Ralph said, "No good-byes. It ain't over."

—◦—

Later, in their little apartment in Standish, Mike said, "Ready for bed, baby?"

"Sounds like you're looking to start a family."

"We're not getting any younger. Let's try for twins."

—◦—

Li Lian and Roger Adams were sitting on the veranda, sipping evening pahits, when Wu Feng drove through the main gate.

"Evening, folks. Just back from Kota Bharu. Here's the mail." He handed Li Lian a few envelopes. "There's one there from Maimunah."

Li Lian turned to Roger. "My darling's monthly report on the progress of her pregnancy." She opened the letter and read.

> Dearest Mama,
>
> I'm happy to tell you that you have a grandson. We have named him after my uncle Ronald. Mike is fascinated by Ronnie's *Mongolian blue spot*. He says it proves that he is descended from Genghis Khan and will grow up to rule the world. I just hope he gets a decent education and a good job.
>
> On another note, I was astonished to learn from some war souvenirs that Mike's father killed a Japanese soldier on Guadalcanal, who turned out to be my father, Hideo Hoda. I don't know if I ever will tell Ronnie that one of his grandfathers killed his other grandfather. We send our love and best wishes to you and Roger. We haven't forgotten Saleh and Wu Feng. Our greetings to them as well.
>
> Your loving daughter,
> Maimunah

"Well, Roger, what do you think?"

"Too much of a coincidence, my dear. You never could put that in a book or movie. Nobody ever would believe it."

Li Lian raised her pahit. "I am the towkay, and that's the way it happened."

Glossary

stengah (Malay)—Whiskey and soda, half-and-half (from the Malay word *setengah*, meaning middle).

lah (Malay)—Enclitic employed by both Malay-speaking and English-speaking Singaporeans.

rotan (Malay)—Rattan.

godown (Malay)—Warehouse.

padang (Malay)—Large playing field.

dhobi ghat (Urdu)—Riparian laundering site.

kelong (Malay)—Fish trap topped with thatched hut.

penghulu (Malay)—Headman of a Malay village.

trepang (Malay)—Sea cucumber.

kampong (Malay)—Malay village.

brok (Malay)—Coconut-collecting macaque.

kupu-kupu (Malay)—Butterfly.

anak beli (Malay)—Bought child.

attap (Malay)—Palm leaves used for roofing.

lintah (Malay)—Leech.

orang asli (Malay)—Original people; aborigines of the Malay forest.

harimau (Malay)—Tiger.

gajah tunggal (Malay)—Rogue elephant.

Syonan Ryokan (Japanese)—Raffles Hotel (renamed by the Japanese).

chandu (Chinese)—Opium.

gula Melaka (Malay)—Palm sugar.

towkay (Chinese)—Business owner, esp. Malayan Chinese.

dadah (Malay)—Drugs.

pahit (Malay)—Gin and bitters.

China White—Highest quality number-four heroin.

bomoh (Malay)—Native herb doctor in kampong.

ah ku (Chinese)—Chinese prostitute.

Barisan Sosialis (Malay)—Socialist opposition party in Singapore.

gu ba (Malay)—Beef.

Bahasa Indonesia (Indonesian)—Indonesian language.

mengerti (Malay)—Understand.

Pulau Bukum (Malay)—Bukum Island.

makan (Malay)—Eat.

kai tai (Malay)—Female or transgender hustlers/prostitutes.

hantu hutan (Malay)—Forest spirit.

guru besar (Malay)—Headmaster.

selamat pagi (Malay)—Good morning.

sama sama (Malay)—The same to you.

inche (Malay)—Mister.

Bahasa Melayu (Malay)—Malayan language.

selamat jalan (Malay)—Good-bye or safe journey.

kati (Malay)—Weight equivalent to one and a half pounds.

benar (Malay)—True.

Mongolian blue spot—Blue patch, resembling a bruise, appearing at the base of the spine in Asian babies of both sexes. The spots disappear gradually.

Printed in the United States
By Bookmasters